To Joanne ~

A brief history wrapped around a love story.

Enjoy the read!!

Best,

John Wemlinger

Readers are encouraged to go to www.MissionPointPress.
com to contact the author or to find information on how
to buy this book in bulk at a discounted rate.

Published by Mission Point Press
2554 Chandler Rd.
Traverse City, MI 49696
(231) 421-9513
www.MissionPointPress.com

Cover illustration by Tajín Robles

ISBN: 978-1-954786-23-3
Library of Congress Control Number: 2021907788

Printed in the United States of America

JOHN WEMLINGER
THE CUT

To all the people of Onekama, Michigan...
past, present and future.

FOREWORD

Almost ten years ago, my wife, Diane, our two dogs, Mattie and Sydney, and I moved to Onekama (pronounced Oh-neck-ah-mah), Michigan. The magnificence of the area's natural beauty is surpassed only by the terrific friends we've made since our arrival. This place inspired me to begin writing in earnest.

Shortly after settling in, I heard of two different *force majeures* occurring in the early days of Manistee County's development. One of these forces of nature happened right in Onekama, the other in Manistee. One created a rather positive result; the other, a disaster. The former was a purely manmade event; something locals called "the cut." The latter was the Great Fire of 1871, which was a national tragedy involving a huge storm with high winds for a sustained period of time and is blamed for starting massive fires in Chicago, eastern Wisconsin and across the state of Michigan.

As is often the case, there are facts, rumors and legends that swirl around events like these. I had heard there were dozens of people and animals killed by the cut and the great fire in Manistee. It turns out that isn't exactly true, thankfully. To my amazement, the cut yielded no casualties, and there was only one human casualty of the fire. Research, it turns out, does separate facts from rumor and legend.

I was honored when asked by the OneKama OneFifty committee to write "a story about those times." Had I not been asked, I likely would never have known how serious the tensions between the farmers and the lumbermen were in 1870-1871. The two interests were feuding on a scale similar to the famous Hatfield and McCoy family feud. Likewise, I would not have known the struggles of a city to survive after it had burned to the ground.

The characters are, for the most part, entirely fictional as are their love affairs. What I've tried to remain true to, however, are the motives that pushed people to behave as they did in 1870-1871 in Manistee County, Michigan. It was important to me to get the setting right; to accurately depict life as it was in Manistee, the settlement of Portage, and on the farms around Portage Lake.

If you are among those of us who are lucky enough to live here, I hope this book will afford you an expanded knowledge of some of our local history. If, however, it's been a while since you've visited us, or perhaps you've never been to Onekama, then I hope you'll come and see us ... and while you are here, please enjoy the read!

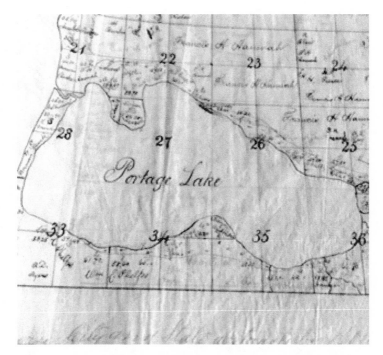

Photo courtesy of The Manistee County Historical Museum.

This is a plat map from circa 1870 depicting Portage Lake and various plots of farmland.

For orientation purposes, North is at the top of the map. The Price farm, a fictional place, was located between sectors 33 and 34.

Looking west of the marking for sector 33, the reader may observe the narrowest part of the isthmus separating Portage Lake from Lake Michigan. The width of the isthmus at this point in 1871 was a mere 30 rods or approximately 500 feet. It is here, in the southwest corner of Portage Lake that the farmers opened up the cut on the early morning of May 14, 1871.

In the northwest corner of Portage Lake between the markings for section 21 and 28, the reader may note Portage Creek, at the time, the only natural outlet between Portage Lake and Lake Michigan. The settlement of Portage was in this vicinity. The Porter & Company sawmill spanned this creek and used a water-driven wheel to operate the muley saw to cut logs. After the opening of the cut, Portage Creek eventually dried up and the waterwheel at the mill sat well above the ground, useless.

Photo is from Tackabbury County Atlas, circa 1873 courtesy of John Adams of Holland and Onekama, Michigan.

The distance between Manistee and Portage Lake, as the crow flies, is only 10-12 miles. Today that distance can be covered in 15-20 minutes. In 1870-1871, however, there were few developed roads, the entire distance between Manistee and Portage Lake was densely forested, and the horseless carriage, which had been invented in 1803, would have been of little use in the backwoods of Manistee County. The Ford Motor Car Company was still 32 years away from its founding in 1903.

First light, Sunday morning, May 14, 1871

The steamer *John A. Dix* was on a run between Traverse City and Manistee, Michigan. It had been late leaving Traverse City due to a delay in loading a mix of cargo and a few passengers. Though it was overcast and the night was moonless, the weather appeared to be calm, so to make up for lost time, the ship's captain made the decision to leave in the middle of the night. It was just after 1:00 a.m. when the *Dix* cleared the mouth of Grand Traverse Bay. The captain kept the speed down as he directed the helmsman to steer a course that would take them well west of the Manitou Islands and out into some of the deepest parts of Lake Michigan. He'd made this trip many times, but almost always in the light of day. He considered the passage around the Manitous to be the most dangerous part of this trip, and he did not want to be caught by the constantly shifting currents and shoals around these two islands whose reputation was one of a graveyard for ships whose masters failed to respect their treachery. Once they'd passed the Manitous, the captain directed the engine room to go to full speed, and before retiring to his cabin, he joined two of the six passengers on board in the dining room just outside the ship's galley for a small libation—an excellent port wine one of them had brought aboard.

It was just first light, and the trip had been, as it usually was, monotonous, until he was called on deck by the

1

first mate knocking frantically on his cabin door. "Captain... Captain, come quick. I...I don't know... I can't figure how we..."

Groggy from sleep, the captain sat up in his bunk. "I'll be right there. Let me..."

"No time, Captain. We're in a forest. Quick. I don't know what to do...I don't know how..."

"A forest. What in God's name?" the captain muttered as he scrambled down the passageway after the mate, still struggling to pull his pants on under his nightshirt. Fifteen or twenty feet ahead of the captain, the mate opened the main deck hatch, and as the captain stepped through, the green needles of a hemlock brushed his mutton-chop whiskers on the right side of his face as the ship slid past... *what the hell... What is this? A tree? How?* They were, in fact, in the middle of what appeared to be a forest of trees, some of which towered twenty-five to thirty feet above the water's surface. *Not possible!* There were hundreds of them, on all sides of his ship, a mix of evergreen and deciduous trees. Adrenaline erased the grogginess of his rude awakening and he began to try to reason with what he was seeing. *Trees! Huge trees! But we're moving. We're not run aground.* A minute later, the captain flung open the door of the wheelhouse and stepped in. The helmsman looked at him with a dazed and confused look. The captain pushed him out of the way and looked at the compass. The ship was on the correct south-by-southeast course.

The captain grabbed the handle on the Chadburn device that stood next to the ship's wheel and yanked it to the Full Stop position. Simultaneously, the Chadburn in the engine room clanged and moved to Full Stop. These mechanically operated Chadburns were the primary method of communicating a vessel's power requirements from the ship's bridge to the engine room. But just to confirm the immediacy of his need to stop the vessel, he screamed into the voice pipe, "Full stop, now!"

Buried deep in the bowels of the ship, the *Dix's* chief engineer couldn't see what was going on outside but shouted to a seaman to close the valve delivering the steam that drove the vessel's huge water wheel, located amidships. As its revolutions decreased, the vessel began to slow.

From his vantage point on the *Dix's* bridge, all the captain could do was watch and listen as the gunnel of his ship banged against the watery green giants that surrounded them as the vessel continued to slow. The trees didn't seem to be rooted. They listlessly tipped to either starboard or port as the ship's bow collided with them. As he watched them harmlessly slide by one side or the other, he became less concerned about a collision, focusing instead on the possibility one of the trees might foul the huge water wheel propelling the *Dix*. But he knew he couldn't just come to a complete stop in this... *What is this? A forest in the middle of Lake Michigan?* Thinking his ship had somehow maneuvered too close to the shore east of him, he spun the wheel to the right and watched the compass move slowly around to a westerly heading. As the ship continued to slow, the captain moved the Chadburn to All Ahead, Slow, and spoke into the voice pipe, this time more calmly, "Go to all ahead, slow, but be prepared to come to full stop if the helmsman directs."

"We've got to maneuver our way out of this," the captain muttered to his mate and the helmsman. In the wheelhouse they could feel the vessel slowly come back to life as the engine room's crew reapplied power to the wheel that propelled it. When he was underway on a due west course, the captain gave the ship's wheel back to the helmsman, "Maintain this course. I'm going to the bow. Keep an eye on me." He drew an index finger across his throat. "If I go like this, then direct the engine room to go to full stop immediately."

"Aye, aye, Captain."

Making their way to the ship's bow, the captain and the

first mate dodged the branches of huge trees as the *Dix* crept past them. They were underway again, but not out of danger. The first mate asked, "Will a westward course get us out of this?"

"Damned if I know," was the captain's reply. "All I know for sure is that deeper water is to the west. This forest, or whatever the hell it is, can't stretch all the way to Wisconsin."

The trees continued to part as the *Dix* moved slowly westward. Both men continued to watch and listen for some sign that their water wheel had been fouled by either a tree or the lake's bottom, but there was nothing. They kept looking behind them, toward the east, through their looking glasses. Now that the sun was up a bit higher, they could make out the beach and the sand dunes; the Lake Michigan shoreline lay behind them. Ahead of them, almost a hundred miles away, was Wisconsin. The captain scratched his head, looked at his first mate, and asked, "Where the hell did these trees come from? How did they get here?"

And then, as quickly as they sailed into them, they sailed out and found themselves once again in the open waters of Lake Michigan. Quickly, both men retreated to the ship's stern. Behind them, to the east, lay the floating forest. They tried to estimate its size, but the closest they could come was to say it covered acres of the lake's surface. "Where are we?" the captain asked.

"South of the Point Betsie Lighthouse. I saw her light about an hour ago. So, I'm guessing we're abreast of Portage Lake, just north of the Manistee River channel."

"And we're well offshore?" He was sure they were, but he wanted validation from his mate.

"Aye, Captain, we are for sure," the mate said as he pointed to the shoreline. "See for yourself. We're at least a mile, maybe a mile and a half offshore."

"Then how do ya explain these?" the captain asked as he pointed back to the vast expanse of trees, the tops of which towered above the surface. "My bet is those trees are like icebergs. What we're seeing above the surface is just a small part of the tree. Under the surface there's much more tree trunk, roots and dirt." Pointing, he said, "Look at that. Look at our wake through the trees. It's already almost disappeared. These trees certainly aren't anchored. No, they're floating."

"I cannot explain it, Captain. None of the crew has done anything wrong. Our speed and our course were true, just as it's been every time we've made this trip together, but we gotta get the word out to other vessels up and down the shore. We got lucky. The next ship might not fare so well. He gestured with his thumb over his shoulder in the direction of the trees, "Can you imagine what might happen if a schooner were to get caught up in that! The trees would foul their sails and all the rigging. A schooner couldn't get out of there like we just did."

Two hours later, the *John A. Dix* sailed up the Manistee River and docked. Longshoremen waiting to unload and then load the vessel kidded the first mate as he met with them before work began. "Hey, where'd ya get the greenery?" one asked him, pointing to the rather large branch of a hemlock lodged between the ship's gunnel and railing near the bow.

The *Dix* was one of the newer vessels plying the waters of Lake Michigan and considered to be a marvel of modern ship engineering. At one hundred seventy-five feet in length and twenty-eight feet at the beam, her crew took a lot of pride in her operation. She now sat safely at dock, her smokestack still belching black smoke as her boiler slowly cooled down. The first mate sneered at the offending longshoreman. "Not amusing. Not amusing at all. There's an entire forest floating just offshore a few miles north of here, somewhere around Portage by the best of my reckoning. We were lucky to get through it without fouling the wheel."

One of the longshoremen slapped another on the back and, loud enough for everyone to hear, exclaimed, "Well, if that don't beat all. Means there'll be plenty of work for us, boys. Looks like them lumbermen figured out how to grow forests overnight in Lake Michigan." Everyone laughed, except the first mate.

From the middle of May 1871 through the early winter of that year, vessels plying the waters between Point Betsie and Manistee lighthouses were warned of *dense debris floating from the shore to three miles offshore. The debris poses a threat to ship safety and human life. Mariners are warned to beware.*

All this was the result of a feud between lumbermen and farmers that had been going on for quite some time.

CHAPTER ONE

THE MEETING

A year earlier... Friday, June 3, 1870

Lydia Cockrum and Alvin Price's introduction was as funny as it was fortuitous. Lydia had just emerged from her Aunt Liliane's millinery shop, walking east on River Street in Manistee, Michigan. River Street is almost always windy. Lydia knew that. She'd grown up here. She'd walked down this street a thousand times. Lined with two- sand three-story buildings on each side for ten to twelve blocks, these buildings provided the perfect venturi, compressing the strong gusts of wind that blew in from the west off Lake Michigan, less than a half mile away and actually accelerating the gusts by five or ten miles per hour. The wind caught the basket Lydia had over her arm, tipping it sufficiently so most of its contents spilled onto the sidewalk in front of her. Fabric samples, packets of needles, spools of thread, and a few thimbles were suddenly scurrying along the ground as if they were trying to flee from her. She issued a very unladylike expletive under her breath and then bent forward, scrambling to collect what she could before the wind scattered everything into the street and beyond. The spilled items were important to her. Any one of the fabric samples was a possibility for the outer shell of a winter coat she and her mother were planning on making over the summer. Most importantly, the coat needed to be warm, but it should also be fashionable. Lydia would need it as she would be among the first women to be making their way this fall around the campus of The Agricultural College of the State of Michigan, located downstate in East Lansing.

At that moment, Alvin Price was walking west down River Street into the prevailing wind when fifteen to twenty feet in front of him, he saw the basket tip and the wind wreak its havoc. His instinctive reaction was to bend forward and start gathering the spilled contents. Neither of them realized the collision course they were on. Alvin was bareheaded, having left his usual straw farmer's hat in his wagon at the mercantile because he knew what the wind could do. There was a collective "Ow!" uttered from each of them at exactly the same time. When their noggins collided, it was with a force sufficient to set both of them back on their keesters. Stunned, Alvin suddenly found himself sitting on the sidewalk, his legs splayed out in front of him. When he looked up, he stared into the eyes of a beautiful young woman, sitting in exactly the same position across from him. He managed to stutter, "I...I'm so sorry. Are you...are you all right?"

Lydia wore a small hat, pinned at a jaunty angle on the side of her head, that had done nothing to blunt their collision. A loosely knit shawl of white lamb's wool was draped over her shoulders, its ends now dangling on the rather dirty sidewalk. Sitting there with her legs stretched out in front of her, she had never felt more unladylike. *This is the price you pay when you take the Lord's name in vain,* she thought, recalling the expletive she'd muttered as she realized where the wind was taking her things. With their shoes nearly touching, a diamond pattern formed between them that seemed to trap most of the basket's spilled contents. Her mind's eye conjured up a picture of what someone watching them would have just seen, and a smile began to cross her face. She looked up and into the bluest eyes she could ever recall seeing and noticed the man across from her was busy retrieving the items that lay between them. "Oh please, never mind those. Are you all right, sir?"

Embarrassed, Alvin merely nodded and repeated, "I'm so sorry. I should have been watching ... " Rather clumsily, he leaned toward her, stretched out his right hand filled with fabric samples he'd managed to recover and placed them in Lydia's basket.

"No, no really. The fault is mine. I know how windy it can be. I should have been more careful."

Alvin wanted to scramble to his feet and help her up, but scrambling to get up was something that didn't come easily to him. Alvin rolled heavily to his right side. As he supported his weight on his fully extended right arm, he pulled his legs up under him and stood. At six feet, two inches tall, he towered over her petite frame. As he turned to face her, he watched the expression on her face change from a smile to a frown as she noticed his disability. It had been seven years since it had happened. Alvin had become used to the reaction of others ... almost. Extending his right hand to her, she took it and he helped her to her feet. Facing her now, he pointed to his left side and said, "Lost my arm in the war."

Lydia stared back into his eyes, still struck by how blue they were. "I ... I'm sorry."

"It's all right," he said, smiling at her. "I've learned to live with it."

Her smile returned as she extended her hand, "I'm Lydia ... Lydia Cockrum."

"Alvin Price," he replied, shaking her hand.

For the briefest moment, awkwardness prevailed again. Both knew their unfortunate encounter was over, yet neither seemed ready to part ways. It was Lydia who asked, "Alvin, would you accompany me to the drug store across the street? I'd like to buy you a soda."

"You don't have to ... "

"I know, but I'd like to thank you, not just for helping me gather my things," she pointed to his missing arm, "but also for the sacrifice you made in the war. Would you allow me the privilege of doing that, please?"

Her smile was irresistible.

"Unless, of course, you have an appointment or something pressing that you must attend to," Lydia added.

He didn't know a lot of women close to his own age. He was a farmer. Trips like this one to Manistee didn't happen more than once or twice a month, and when they did, they had to be purposeful: supplies needed, bills paid, farm goods delivered, those kinds of things. And he was sure the few women he did know who were his age would never invite a total stranger to do anything with them. Alvin, however, managed to hide his surprise at her gutsiness. At this very moment in his twenty-six years of living, there could be nothing more pressing than stretching this encounter out. "No, Lydia, I've nothing else; it would be my pleasure." In a rather bold move of his own, he offered her his arm; she stepped to his right side and took it. Together they set out across the street to the drugstore and its newly constructed and wildly popular soda fountain.

CHAPTER TWO

SMALL TOWN

Fletcher's Drug Emporium was nearly empty when Lydia and Alvin entered. It was one-thirty in the afternoon, and the midday rush of patrons looking for a bite of lunch had come and gone. The two took up stools next to one another at the soda fountain. Alvin looked up and down the recently installed counter and took notice of the glasses, dishes, taps, silverware, cloth napkins, etc. that lined the shelves behind the counter's narrow workspace. Behind them were seven or eight tables, each covered in a crisp black and white checkered tablecloth. Food service in a pharmacy was an entirely new concept to him. Where Alvin was from, a pharmacy was a pharmacy, where powders were blended, elixirs were brewed to treat the infirmities of the local farmers, mill workers and their families. He said, "This is quite something. Do you come here often?"

Lydia nodded. "Oh yes. I was one of their first customers. You are going to like this, Alvin. You pick your flavor of ice cream. I like chocolate. They put it in one of those tall glasses," she pointed to them on one of the shelves, "and then they add this wonderful sparkling soda water to it. I don't know more than that except that the flavor is just wonderful." The clerk approached and asked what they would like.

Lydia asked, "What flavor ice cream would you like?"

"I'll go with your choice—chocolate."

"Two chocolate sodas, please." After the clerk nodded and stepped away, Lydia asked, "Are you from Manistee, Alvin?"

"I guess Portage would be the closest settlement. Do you know it?"

Lydia nodded.

Alvin continued, "My family has a farm on Portage Lake." He pointed to his missing left arm, "The work is a bit tougher. Can't throw a bale of hay the way I used to. Everything takes longer, but it still gets done. So, I count my blessings that my family has the farm and I was able to go back there after this happened," he said, again pointing to his missing arm. "A lot of men weren't that lucky," referring to the nearly half a million deaths on both sides in America's Civil War.

Lydia had been protected from that terrible conflict; first, by just the simple result of geography. While many Michiganders had fought in the Civil War, no battles had been fought on Michigan soil. And second, Lydia had enjoyed a rather privileged upbringing. So, it was natural her curiosity was aroused by this man with his war-related disability, and it gave way to a sudden insensibility. "You must have been quite young when you went off to ..." She cut herself off. As she heard herself utter it, she realized the inquiry was impertinent. *Who'd want to relive that?* She changed course, "Alvin, I'm sorry. Forget I said that ..."

He'd been facing the counter, but as he sensed her unease, he shifted around to face her. "I don't mind. I was sixteen when I enlisted." Then Alvin deftly shifted course, "How about you? Is Manistee home for you?"

Before she could answer, they were interrupted. From his vantage point at the pharmacy counter, Herb Fletcher, the store's owner, had watched the couple come in. "Hello, Lydia."

"Oh ... Hello, Mr. Fletcher," she replied, a hint of surprise in her voice as she hadn't seen him come up behind them. Looking first at Alvin and then back to Fletcher, she said, "I'd like you to meet Mr. Alvin Price."

"Pleased to make your acquaintance. I haven't seen you in here before, have I?"

"No, sir. I'm from Portage. Lydia and I just bumped into one another." They both chuckled at the inside joke, but the humor was short-lived.

With a superior edge to his voice, Fletcher replied, "Portage. Not much there. The mill and farms. Which are you? Lumberman or farmer?"

"My family owns a farm there."

Fletcher offered a dismissive, "Ummm," before turning his complete attention to Lydia. "Aleta and I will see you in church this Sunday?" He didn't wait for an answer, knowing Lydia and her parents were in church every Sunday as were the Fletchers. "By the way, Richard will soon be home for a month from his studies in Ann Arbor. I hope our families can get together."

Completely aware of the judgement Fletcher had already made of Alvin, it took everything inside of Lydia to control both her embarrassment and her temper. "Yes, see you in church," Lydia said, determined not to commit to visiting. She was glad he had to break away to assist a customer at the pharmacy counter. She gave a glance to Alvin while shaking her head, and said, "Mr. Fletcher owns this place. He's a friend of my father's."

Alvin gave her a serious look, and mocking Fletcher, said, "Ummm." Lydia giggled. He continued, "Well then, I might guess your father is more partial to lumbermen than farmers. Am I right?"

Shrugging her shoulders, Lydia began, "Lumber is king around here. My father's business relies on it. He's an engineer. We've lived in Manistee all my life, but he's traveled all over the country building railroads. Last year, some of the lumbermen started to discuss narrow-gauge railroads as a quicker, more efficient way to move more logs to the mills."

"Saw a lot of railroads while I was away at war. There aren't any up here yet, but it's only a matter of time."

"Father says it will be a while. He says it's because the forests north of Manistee and all across the northern tip of Michigan are so dense, they must be cut back before the railroads can be built. He guesses maybe they are ten years away, but he says when it happens, it will happen quickly, and there will be a lot of money to be made." She paused, and then said, "So, yes, my father is very partial to lumbermen."

Alvin didn't like the way big lumber was stripping the land around Manistee, and he was even angrier at the lumbermen for their disregard of the farmers around Portage Lake, where his family's homestead was located, but he had asked the question and appreciated her honesty. With a certain twinkle in his eye, he asked, "And what about you, Lydia? Where do you stand?"

She blushed, lowered her head and stared into her lap. The clerk placed a soda in front of each of them. Lydia thanked him and then said to Alvin, "Taste it and tell me what you think."

He could see he'd made her uncomfortable, so he didn't press her for an answer to his question. It was not his intention to either embarrass her or distress her in any way. He was smart enough to realize he was balanced on the razor's edge of propriety. He tasted his soda, turned to her and said, "This is delicious, Lydia."

That evening, after Lydia's father asked the blessing at their evening meal, he didn't waste any time getting to what was on his mind. "Lydia, Herb Fletcher came by to see me this afternoon. Says he saw you and some man ... a farmer ... sitting together at his soda fountain. Want to tell us what that is all about?"

Lydia glanced at her mother who nodded. The two of them had already carefully gone over how much she should tell her father and, equally important, what she should leave out. She recounted the strong gust of wind, the tipped basket, the scattered contents and how the two had managed to recover them. Laughing, she included the details of their collision. She told her father Alvin's name and that his family owned a farm near Portage Lake. She told him of his war injury and that she'd taken him to Fletcher's to buy him a soda for his help today and for his sacrifice in the war, knowing her father was a devout abolitionist and unionist.

Reilly Cockrum harrumphed, conveying to Lydia a double meaning; first, he accepted her story as a meaningless first-and-last encounter, and second, he was not pleased her companion this afternoon had been a farmer.

Irene Cockrum quickly changed the subject to some new flowers she'd planted that afternoon; the secret between Lydia and her as safe as if it were locked away in a bank vault. She firmly believed Reilly Cockrum did not need to know that Lydia and Alvin were going to meet in two weeks at the beach at the end of First Street in Manistee, a place where Herb Fletcher's prying eyes could not see them. She also knew full well that her daughter was already looking forward to her next encounter with this farmer, Alvin Price.

CHAPTER THREE

THE RIDE HOME

I t was late in the afternoon when Alvin left Lydia at Fletcher's Drug Emporium. He had two errands to run on River Street. His mother had asked him to pick up some sewing supplies. In the course of their conversation, Lydia had disclosed that her Aunt Liliane owned the town's only millinery shop. Laying his purchases on the counter, he asked, "Excuse me, ma'am, are you Liliane Burke?"

Somewhat surprised, she looked up at him, "Yes, I am."

"I just met your niece, Lydia. We bumped into each other on the sidewalk just down the street." He recounted the story of his and Lydia's meeting, and concluded with, "I'm Alvin ... Alvin Price."

Liliane giggled at the thought of her beautiful and quite proper niece sitting there on the sidewalk on River Street. "Well, Mr. Price ... "

He held up a hand, "Alvin, please, Mrs. Burke."

"Well then, if it's going to be Alvin, it has to be Liliane." She smiled, "I'm glad you both survived your collision. This street can be windy, especially if that wind is out of the west as it is most days." Alvin laid his money on the counter; she made change and packaged up his purchases. "Thanks for stopping in, Alvin. It was a pleasure meeting you."

As he stepped out of the shop, he was glad he'd mustered

up the courage to introduce himself. As he thought back on it, he could not recall even the slightest indication that she'd noticed his disability. Alvin had gotten used to the fleeting glance, perhaps a wince, and then a quick look away. Liliane Burke's nonchalance was a good thing, he thought. He was curious, however, about her last name— Burke, not Cockrum. He'd noticed she wasn't wearing a wedding ring.

After the millinery shop, he stopped at the tobacconist to pick up some pipe tobacco for his father.

By the time he returned to his wagon in front of the mercantile, he estimated it was five o'clock, give or take a few minutes. While he'd been away at war, he'd carried a timepiece, a gold pocket watch and chain. They had belonged to his grandfather and had been passed on to him by his father when he left to enlist. Time then was something that had been important to him, but at some point during the war, the watch had stopped working. After that, knowing the exact time became rather meaningless to him ... *It's early morning, midday, late afternoon.* But still, for the rest of the war, the watch never left his side. It became his beacon of hope, a constant reminder of his family and home. Once back home, he'd had it repaired. It now lay on the top of the chest in his room. He kept it wound, but seldom took it with him. He was home. He was alive. Time now only needed to be a generality: *early morning, midday, late afternoon* ... that was good enough.

Kip, Alvin's dog, sat on the wagon's seat and gave a single bark as Alvin approached. "Hey boy, thanks for keeping an eye on things." The black and white border collie barked once again and then lay down on the seat, as if his duty to guard the wagon was now complete with the return of his master. While Kip waited, Alvin went inside the mercantile to settle the bill for the supplies they'd loaded for him from the list he'd given them earlier in the day.

The climb onto the wagon's seat was a steep one even for a person with two hands; to do it with one hand had required Alvin to perfect his technique. He lifted his right foot up to a step that was about two feet off the ground. From there, he dipped slightly on his left leg and then pushed up with both legs while grabbing the side of the seat with his strong right hand, pulling himself up. Now, keeping his upward momentum, he swung his left leg another two feet or so over the side, into the wagon's bed. It was all well-practiced, even somewhat graceful, although mastering it had been difficult. Living with a disability like his was all about adapting, and even though he'd been without his left arm now for seven years, there were still occasions when he'd begin to do something only to discover he couldn't do it the way he'd been able to with both arms, both hands. He'd have to study it, analyze it, figure out how he'd have to adapt and then practice it, over and over again. How to board this wagon had been one such skill.

He sat down hard on the wagon's wooden seat padded by a piece of folded canvas. Before setting out, he looked at the clouds building in an ever-darkening western sky. He rubbed the dog's ears and said, "Looks like a storm's a-brewin', Kip. Let's see if we can get across the river before it starts." Two draft horses stood patiently in front of him. He took their four reins into his right hand, one rein laced between each of his fingers, another skill he'd managed to master over time. He whistled. Each horse's head bobbed in response. "Wake up, boys. Time to take us home." He slapped the reins gently across their backs, and the huge animals pulled the loaded wagon forward.

This time of year, the days were still lengthening. He was in no rush to get home, but as he continued to watch the sky, he knew he needed to make it across the bridge over the Manistee River and get a ways down the trail that led west, along the southwestern edge of Portage Lake before the impending storm hit. He had a particular spot in mind, really just a wide place in the trail rather than a campsite, and he hoped no other traveler heading in that direction would beat him to it. The place would be a good spot to take cover from the storm.

As they emerged from the congestion on River Street Alvin slapped the reins one more time to speed the horses' pace a bit. Once satisfied their gait was sufficient, he turned to his traveling companion and said, "She's quite something, Kip." The dog's eyes were riveted on him as if he could understand Alvin's every word; his tail thumped against the wagon seat. "She's beautiful—with a smile like nothing I've ever seen before. I'll see her again in a couple of weeks. We're going to have lunch together. Maybe you can come along." Then he added with a laugh, "But only if you behave yourself."

For nearly seven years now, this dog and Alvin had been nearly inseparable. Exactly how they'd come together defied explanation. He'd long ago stopped trying to figure it out. He was just thankful they'd found one another when they did.

The Battle of Gettysburg had raged for the first three days of July 1863. When it was over, the South had left their dead on the battlefield as they retreated; nearly 5,000 corpses. The North was little better, being slow, very slow, in recovering their dead; another 3,200 bodies. The massive task of burying them was undertaken by locals, disease control being as much of a motivator as mercy. There was no formal pattern to the burials. This would not come until November 1863, when Lincoln would say as he dedicated the new cemetery there, "We cannot dedicate, we cannot consecrate—we cannot hallow this ground." But for now, in these early, dreadfully hot days of summer, the dead were buried either right where they'd fallen, or moved to fence lines or along stone walls and buried there. Amazingly, most of the human remains were, at least temporarily, interred by July 10, 1863. What remained on the battlefield to rot in the hot summer sun were the carcasses of hundreds of dead horses and mules, and the stench from them hung over the area. In his nightmares, Alvin could to this day, seven years later, still smell that stench.

It was on the second of July, around midday, when a Confederate cannonball hit the ground some fifty feet in front of him. He'd actually seen it coming as it skidded off the ground, tore his left arm off and then exploded in a cloud of dirt and smoke some hundred feet behind him. After that he had no memory of what happened to him until he awoke in a crowded field hospital not far from the battlefield. His first vivid memory of the place was the stench of blood and death. To this day he cannot recall how long he'd been conscious, before realizing his left arm was missing and with that a deep despair began to beset him. It wasn't long after that when a nurse appeared over him, *like an angel,* he'd thought at the time. She told him he'd been unconscious for three days. He tried to sit up, but she put a hand on his good shoulder and told him to lie still. He needed to rest. There was still a good chance his wound could become infected. The best remedy against that was to lie still, keep calm, and let his body do all it could to fight it off. She was right. He was in that field hospital for fifteen days before he could even sit up. In that time, every time she would pass his cot she would offer words of encouragement. When he'd become ambulatory, he'd been discharged from the hospital, but told to come back every day for someone to take a look at his wound and change the dressing, if necessary. On August 30, 1863, he was discharged from the Union Army.

On the last day of August 1863, he could no longer abide the misery of Gettysburg, and with the assistance of a few other wounded survivors, he mounted a horse he'd bought using nearly all of his mustering-out money. He headed for Michigan and home, but he didn't get very far that first day. Fearing that he'd pass out and fall, further injuring himself, he stopped at a Pennsylvania farm only eight or nine miles from the battlefield. The farmer and his wife took him in, fed him, put him up in their barn, as there was no place in their small cabin, and cared for him for a couple of days. The food they offered him was the best he'd had in months. He was far enough away that only occasionally could he detect the stench of the battlefield when the wind was just right. He slept soundly. This brief respite was all he needed. On the morning of September 3, 1863, they fed him a hearty breakfast, and Alvin resumed his long journey home once again. But less than a quarter of a mile from the farm, he realized he was being followed by a dog. Thinking it was the farmer's dog, he led it back to the farm when it refused to be shooed in that direction. "He's intent on following me," Alvin told the farmer. "I would hate to repay your kindness by stealing your dog," he joked.

"Not ours," replied the farmer.

"Oh," Alvin replied. "Any idea who he might belong to?"

"Got neighbors on both sides of us. Know 'em pretty well. Never seen this dog before. Don't know where he might have come from. Seems like he's meant to be yours," the farmer said, smiling. Since then, one rarely saw Alvin without Kip nearby.

The storm held off until Alvin reached the wide spot in the trail he had remembered. This part of the trail was cut through a dense forest of hemlock. Some earlier traveler had created a space for the horses by removing some of the lower boughs of the hemlock. Alvin tied both securely to the trunks of a couple of trees, the branches over their heads providing some shelter from the rain which had just started to fall, lightly at first. He gave them sufficient tether to reach some grass that grew a short distance from the trees.

Kip had already taken cover under the wagon while Alvin removed the folded canvas from the wagon's seat along with several canvas bags from the cargo area. He tossed all of it under the wagon with the dog. Then he pulled out two long rolls of canvas from the wagon's bed. One he unrolled over the wagon's length, the other over its width. He weighted each end of the canvas with five or six large rocks he took from a nearby campfire ring some previous traveler had built. Several stronger gusts of wind came up, but the canvas covers remained in place. Satisfied they would be protected from the elements, he scrambled under the cargo area with Kip just as the rain began to fall harder.

Out of the elements now, Alvin spread the canvas he'd removed from the wagon's seat on the ground under the wagon and strung some netting to protect them against the mosquitoes and flies that were just beginning to populate the late-spring, early-summer nights.

All of this was well practiced. Since his return to the farm, Alvin had spent many nights just like this adjacent to the fields he'd worked during the day. He'd once calculated that over the course of one summer he'd saved himself the equivalent of an entire week just because he didn't have to travel back and forth from the farmhouse. But there was another reason he didn't mind, camping under his wagon with Kip. There was something about the solitude of nights like this that appealed to him.

This was difficult for him to understand, and as much as he tried, he wasn't able to make much sense of it. He loved his mother and father dearly. And then there was Jebediah, a fellow wounded veteran he'd met on his way home from Gettysburg, who lived on the Price farm with the three of them and was like a brother to him and like another son to Alvin's parents. Yet, he was never more content than when it was just Kip and him, alone, outside, night closing in, rain or shine.

Under the wagon, inside their canvas shell, Alvin could hear the wind and the rain picking up. Tomorrow morning that rainwater would collect in puddles on the canvas, and thoroughly soak every square inch of the closely-woven fabric, making it even heavier than it had been to roll out and harder for him to pack it all up.

The storm began to rage. A thunderous boom pinned Kip's ears back, flat against the side of his head, "It's okay, boy." Kip sidled just a bit closer. Alvin mixed some oats and a portion of pure maple syrup in a bowl. He reached for a bag of venison jerky, broke a few strips into smaller pieces, and added those to the bowl. He set the bowl on the ground in front of the dog who barked once, his ears now perked up, his tail wagging.

As the light faded, Alvin chewed some jerky, looked at Kip and said, "Glad I'm not home tonight." He didn't want to go home because he didn't want to go to a meeting—one his father wanted him to attend. As he thought about it, Alvin couldn't be sure if a feud was in the offing or if it had already arrived, but farmers, his father chief among them, were becoming more and more distressed by the lumbermen's non-compliance to an injunction against damming Portage Creek, the only natural outlet between Portage Lake and Lake Michigan. The lumbermen used water from the dam to power a water wheel, which in turn drove a muley saw, a huge contraption used to cut logs into lumber, shingles and the like. But it was the dam that created the bone of contention. It caused the water level of Portage Lake to rise dramatically; the high water then rendered hundreds of acres of farmland untillable. In the specific case of the Price Farm, it was his, his father's and Jeb's collective opinion they were losing fifteen acres of land from flooding caused by the dam. That meant they were losing almost fifteen percent of their available land, which limited the number of livestock the farm could support, the amount of food crops they could grow and—perhaps of greatest concern—cut down on the available land for the orchard they were hoping to expand. Alvin's father made no bones about it. "That damned dam costs us; first land, then money." The farmers' discontent with the lumbermen had become more and more vitriolic over the last two years.

Ten years ago, Alvin watched as the rhetoric rose to open war. He hadn't liked it then and he certainly didn't like it now. He was glad he would not be at this evening's meeting. He would hear enough about it from his father tomorrow when he returned home.

The thunder and lightning portion of the storm passed rather quickly, but the rains persisted. He was tired, and apparently, so was Kip, who settled in next to him. He reached down and rubbed the dog's ears. Alvin's thoughts turned to the young woman he'd met earlier. From the beautifully tailored outfit she wore, to her perfectly coiffed hair, her sparkling eyes, her easy way of talking to him, all of these things made him anxious to see her again. It had taken every ounce of his courage to ask her if he might be able to do that, and as much as it thrilled him, it was also something of a surprise to him when she had agreed. He lingered on these thoughts for a while and then said, "It's going to be a long two weeks, Kip." There was no perk of the ears, no thump of the tail. Kip was already fast asleep.

CHAPTER FOUR

IRENE COCKRUM

I rene Cockrum didn't like keeping things from her husband, but when Lydia came home earlier this afternoon and said she'd met a farmer and was planning on seeing him again, Irene had grown cautious. She knew both her daughter and her husband well. Lydia was smart, ambitious and could be precocious. Reilly, her husband, was loving, protective, and a bit too Victorian, especially when it came to who his daughter should or should not be seeing.

Outside, lightning flashed followed shortly by a loud bang of thunder which rattled the bedroom's windowpane. Irene lay in bed reading. Across the room, Reilly was changing into his nightshirt and said, "Herb Fletcher told me today Richard is due home soon for a month. I think we should plan on our families getting together. Maybe a week from Sunday, after church."

"I really don't think you should..."

Somewhat rudely, he didn't allow her to finish her thought. "I've already told Herb to plan on it. It will be fun and it will give Lydia and Richard a chance to become better acquainted."

Why is he so set on this? He knows she heads to college in September. There's no way she's going to fall hopelessly in love with Richard Fletcher, nor is he going to fall for her, Irene thought. She said, "He's eight years her senior. He's nearly completed medical school. Lydia's just eighteen. How can you ... ?"

Reilly turned toward her after pulling his nightshirt over his head and flashed a mischievous smile he knew she had trouble resisting. "Let me remind you, my dear, that you were a mere eighteen when we were wed."

"Her heart is set on going to college, Reilly. That may not be your plan for our daughter, but that is her plan. All your finagling with Herb Fletcher to match his son up with our daughter is doing is complicating all of our lives. I wish you'd just stop all of this ... this matchmaking."

"I am aware Lydia thinks she wants to go to college, and you know how I feel about that. I cannot understand how that school can waste precious admissions by giving them to women. There must be dozens of men waiting to attend. Neither can I understand why in the world Lydia is determined to study agriculture. Why does she need a college course of study to stick a seed in the ground and watch it grow? Look at me. I'm an engineer ... self-taught at that. If I didn't need college, why does she?"

Irene took a deep breath to calm herself so she wouldn't sound too harsh. But she wasn't going to just let him potentially ruin their daughter's life. "So, your plan is to just marry her off?"

"She could do far worse than Richard Fletcher ... soon to be Doctor Richard Fletcher, I might add."

Irene closed her book, extinguished the kerosene lamp on the table next to the bed and rolled onto her side facing away from him. When she could feel him settling into place, her back to him, she said, "Lydia is determined to go to college. I want her to have that opportunity, an opportunity I passed up when you came into my life." As she said that, she suddenly realized how harsh it sounded. She turned toward him, placed a hand along his cheek and looked into his eyes. "I'm sorry. That wasn't fair. I want you to know I have no regrets. The two of you are the light of my life, but times are changing, and I will not deny Lydia her chance to do something different with her life."

He put his arm over her and snuggled close. "Let's not go to sleep angry with one another. Let's just see where this thing with Richard Fletcher goes. Maybe the two will hit it off from the start."

"And if that is not the case?"

He kissed her softly on the cheek and said, "Well, let's just give it a chance."

She rolled away from him. He infuriated her at moments like this even though she'd spoken the truth when she told him she had no regrets. Together they'd prospered. He had made a good living designing railroads. Timing is often everything in life, and he'd gotten in on the ground floor of that industry. Now, especially after the work he'd done for the Union during the Civil War, he was a recognized expert. He was generous to a fault with both her and Lydia, a fact she could never deny—would never deny. But in all the years of their married life, Irene felt he'd never given her proper credit for her own intellect. This house had been built under her oversight while he was off building a railroad somewhere. She'd managed to cope with a builder who sought to take advantage of what he thought would be her inability to understand construction plans. She'd fought tooth and nail with that contractor to keep to the budget and won in nearly every instance of dispute. Reilly didn't know how much money they had in the bank; Irene managed their personal and his business accounts to the exact penny, freeing him up to concentrate on the engineering end of his business.

Even without having attended college, Irene Cockrum was a woman of letters. Socrates, Thucydides, Plato—all the classical thinkers' works appeared in the extensive library that lined the walls of their drawing room. But her tastes were not confined to the classics. Tonight, she'd been reading a short story from the collected works of

Edgar Allan Poe. She found his work extraordinarily dark, but was drawn to it because of what she considered to be his rather tragic life.

I could have gone to college, Reilly. I would have succeeded there, she thought as she heard the heavier breathing of his sleep behind her. *You will not deprive Lydia of that experience. I won't have her lying next to a man in twenty years and having the same regrets I now feel.*

CHAPTER FIVE

JOHN BARLEYCORN, THE UNINVITED GUEST

Early morning, Saturday, June 4, 1870

Alvin felt Kip get up from his spot next to him and heard him wriggle out from under the netting surrounding them. The same urge of nature that compelled Kip now compelled him as he pulled on his boots and followed his dog out from under the wagon and its protective tarps. First light was just appearing through the thick hemlocks and he could smell their aroma in the fresh-washed morning air. A light breeze ruffled the treetops towering fifty or sixty feet over his head, creating a shower of water drops. He hunched his shoulders against them. He was in no hurry; today would be a poor day to rush. The sky was cloudless now, but the rainfall had been steady for most of the night, and the trail ahead of them would be soaked. He estimated they were still twelve miles from the farm. With a dry trail, it might take them three to four hours to negotiate that distance. Today, however, the wagon's narrow steel-rimmed wooden wheels would sink into the rain-softened earth, making for a long pull home.

Checking on the horses, he found them none the worse for wear following last night's deluge. He fed Kip before beginning the arduous task of removing and rolling up the wet canvas that had sheltered them last night. He was sweating by the time his task was completed, so, by comparison, harnessing the horses was mere child's play.

As he sat on the wagon's seat, he could feel the warm, hemlock-filtered rays of the sun on his back. Grasping the reins in his right hand, he gently, almost imperceptibly, rolled the soft leather straps over their backs. The two giant horses, each approaching eighteen hands high and weighing nearly two thousand pounds apiece, were used to Alvin's gentle touch, and they reacted to it by pulling the wagon into motion. Kip, his belly full, with no work to be done for the next few hours, lay down on the seat next to him and quickly dozed off.

The sun had transited through noon and now shone in Alvin's eyes as he rounded the last westward-facing bend toward home. The trip had taken nearly twice as long as it normally did due to the muddy trail. In the distance he could see the family farmhouse, and he looked for some activity. Seeing none, he said to Kip, "Pa and Jeb must be in the field." The Price's eighty acres was a subsistence farm. The family took from it what they needed to live, day by day, season through season, year in and year out, with little to spare beyond their needs. Five years ago, they planted what they would optimistically refer to as "our cash crop": three hundred apple tree saplings. Alvin's father, Ben, Alvin and Jeb thought they'd never seen them bloom as beautifully as they had last month. Both hoped this year would be the first full crop of apples they could take to market in Manistee. They wanted to plant more fruit trees—peaches, pears, cherries—but they were running out of land; Portage Lake and its dam continued to flood them out of at least ten acres of good farmland and this year was proving to be no exception despite a legal injunction against the lumbermen's dam that, unfortunately, allowed the sawmill a seven-month grace period to cease and desist in the damming.

Alvin pulled the wagon to a stop in front of the barn. From the blacksmith shop behind it, he could hear the clanging of steel on steel. He hopped down and was followed by Kip who stayed by his side as Alvin walked through the huge, open sliding door on the barn's front and continued toward the clanging sound. When he reached the open doorway at the rear of the barn, he shouted, "Hey, Jeb, we're home."

In the blacksmithing shop, a separate building, the hammering stopped. Jebediah Washington tossed the red hot implement he'd been pounding on into a large vat of water, quenching it in order to stop any tempering that might take place as it cooled naturally in the afternoon air. As the water sizzled, he laid his hammer on the anvil and shouted back, "Good trip?"

"Well, got everything I went for," Alvin said, and then added with a grin, "and maybe a little more."

Jebediah Washington was like the older brother Alvin never had. Nellie Price had nearly died giving birth to Alvin. The doctor had told her, after mother and child somehow miraculously survived, that she'd never have children again. He'd been right, until Alvin and Jeb had come home from the war together. They had not fought in the same battles, but nonetheless they'd been comrades in arms, fighting on the Union's side for the same cause.

Jeb was an escaped slave brought north on the Underground Railroad. As an eighteen-year-old, he'd managed to escape to Montreal, Canada, in 1855. There he'd flourished as a typesetter after he'd spent the first two years of his freedom learning to speak French and read both English and French. Then, in 1860, as the American Civil War broke out, he made the choice to return to the US and fight on the side of the Union. He wanted to see slavery ended. He'd met President Lincoln once at Fredericksburg after Lincoln spoke to a group of Black Union soldiers. Less than six months after that inspiring event, Jeb was badly wounded at Chancellorsville. The doctor dug a lead ball out of his hip, but the damage it had done to the bone and surrounding cartilage left him with a limp. On nights like the previous one, when it was damp and stormy, the hip was painful, but like Alvin, Jeb considered himself lucky. Honorably discharged at Chancellorsville, he'd recuperated from his wounds at the home of the people in Ohio who'd protected him as an escaped slave nearly nine years earlier. Mended as well as he was going to be, he was making his way back to Canada when he met Alvin at a campsite just outside of Toledo, Ohio.

Their meeting was to be most fortuitous. As a young boy of thirteen, Alvin had shown an interest in blacksmithing. He'd been allowed to train with one who lived near their farm, and as his skills grew, so did a blacksmith shop on the Price farm. But now, with his left arm gone, blacksmithing was out of the question. Around the campfire that night outside of Toledo, Alvin had lamented his inability to perform that skill.

Jebediah Washington had resigned himself to returning to Montreal and to typesetting. He'd made a good living typesetting there before he'd returned to the US, but the eager anticipation of freedom that had driven him there before the Civil War was now gone. The bloody war was fought to end involuntary servitude in the US. That night in the late summer of 1863, the war wasn't over, but Jeb was sure the North would prevail in this terrible conflict, absolutely sure of it, and he wanted to be a part of this new land and all that it promised. When Alvin told him he could no longer be a blacksmith, Jeb saw the door of opportunity open up. He'd told Alvin, "If you'll train me, I would like to try my hand at it." They'd been fast friends since then. The two of them had built a cabin for Jeb just a stone's throw from the farmhouse. Ben and Nellie Price, Alvin's parents, were surprised when Alvin showed up with a Black friend, but it hadn't taken either of them long to consider Jeb to be like a second son. Likewise, it hadn't taken Jeb very long to begin thinking of them as if they were his parents as well.

"Where's Pa?"

"Said he was heading to the apple orchard this morning. Haven't seen him since," replied Jeb.

"What's his mood?"

"He isn't happy. He got all the neighbors fired up after the meeting last night. Everybody's losing land to the lake. Not sure what they're thinking, but for sure, folks are fired up." Jeb let that hang there for a moment. Then he asked, "Ready to get that wagon unloaded?"

"Yep. I got some stuff on there for Ma. Ride with me up to the house. We'll unload there, then come back here and put the horses up. I got something I want to tell you about, and maybe it's best not to talk about it when Pa's around."

÷ ÷ ÷

That evening, at supper, Ben Price no sooner had asked the blessing on their meal when he turned to Alvin and said, "Missed you at last night's meetin', son."

Alvin merely nodded, but thought, *Here it comes. That didn't take very long.*

"Folks are right riled up about that damned dam. Everyone's losin' good land to the lake. Ain't nobody in authority doin' anythin' about the injunction that judge issued. There's talk about goin' over to that mill and tearin' the dam out."

Alvin looked over at Jeb who stared into his dinner plate as he raised a spoonful of potatoes up to his mouth. Alvin asked Ben, "Taking matters into your own hands, huh, Pa?"

"There's talk of it, yeah. Don't know what else we can do."

Alvin said, "You do that and watch how long it'll take the constable to get out here and start asking questions about who did it." Out of the corner of his eye, Alvin could see his mother nodding, but she said nothing.

Ben shook his head. "That's the whole point, son. The law's lookin' the other way, but us farmers ... well ... We got the law on our side with the injunction, but the constables, the court, none of 'em seem to care one bit about it ... about us. So, if they ain't gonna do their job ... "

Alvin said, "Lumber's king and—"

Ben slammed a hand down on the dinner table.

Nellie said, "Ben, you brought this up at the dinner table, and now you're gettin' mad about it. That ain't right." Nellie Price was perhaps the only person in the world who could settle Ben down when he flared like this.

Ben looked in her direction, but before he could say anything, she cocked her head to one side. That head cock was like some kind of signal between the two that warned Ben that perhaps it was time to consider discretion as the better part of valor. "Sorry, Nellie. You're right." Things fell silent around the dinner table for a moment, and then Ben said, "I got one more thing I want to say to Alvin, and then I'll let all this go for the time bein'."

Nellie laid her knife and fork down on either side of her plate and gave her husband a look. "If you can lose that tone like you been beat down worse than a stray dog, then say what you gotta say and let's enjoy this meal God's given us."

Ben nodded, turned his attention to Alvin, and asked, "Know how many people were at that meetin' last night?"

Alvin took a guess based on his past experience. "Ten ... maybe twelve."

"There were twenty-five of us there, Alvin. Twenty-five!

And if it weren't such a miserable night last night, I bet there would have been thirty or more."

That number was a bit of a surprise to Alvin, but he hid it well.

Ben continued, "One thing's for sure, after the war ended and the government started offering free land around these parts for homesteading, people are comin' here to settle. That ain't gonna stop. When there was just a few farmers, the lumbermen could get away with ignorin' us. They ain't gonna be able to just keep doin' that. Our numbers are growin'. No sir, if the law won't do somethin' about it, then us farmers will."

Alvin gave his mother a glance. He knew she was not expecting him to continue this discussion at the dinner table. So, he simply said, "I got that pipe tobacco you asked for."

A smile crossed his father's face. "Good. I'm completely out. After supper, I'll smoke a bowl of it on the front porch, and we can pick this up somewheres it won't upset your ma."

Alvin knew how relentless his father could be, especially about the issue of the dam. But an evening on the front porch rehashing the meeting he'd been careful to avoid, was not something he was looking forward to. Rather, he hoped to spend the evening at Jeb's cabin telling him more about Lydia.

It was late when Alvin approached Jeb's front door, but before he got to it, the door opened and Jeb said, "You see it any differently than I do? He's gotten them all fired up, Alvin. Trouble's brewing unless we can do something about it."

"Were there really twenty-five farmers here last night?"

Jeb nodded, "My guess is that number is about right. They met in the barn to get out of the weather. It started out all right. They were just discussing going to the constables, the court, and talking to the judge; things like that. At first, I thought they were using pretty good common sense about it. But at some point, six or eight jugs of shine showed up."

Alvin laughed. "Oh, yeah. Pa left that little detail out."

Jeb continued, "I can't be sure exactly how many jugs there were, but it seemed like quite a few. They started passing them around. I got out of there, but I could hear them. They got pretty loud. I think maybe Ben spent the night in the barn. Nellie wouldn't let him in the house the way he was as the evening wore on." The two laughed, and then Jeb added with a big smile, "Thought for a minute he might show up here and want to bunk in with me, but I think there might have been a little shine left in one of those jugs in the barn, so he went back there."

Alvin laughed again, "Pa doesn't drink enough to have much tolerance. Ma won't even let him have the stuff in the house. I think she probably saw him with a snootful when they were younger, and she put the quietus on him drinking if he was going to court her. Guess it was lucky for me that he knuckled under. Otherwise, I might not have ever come into this world."

As they both sat in front of the dwindling fire in Jeb's cabin, the laughter over Ben's sobriety, or lack thereof, subsided. More serious now, Jeb asked, "So what are we going to do, Alvin?" When there was no answer, Jeb added, "You know folks 'round these parts respect you maybe even more than they do your pa. I know you don't like going to these meetings, but after what I saw last night, I think it's best if you don't miss too many more of them. These folks need someone smart like you, a voice of reason, to add to their discussions... and maybe, someone to tell them to put the shine away until the business is concluded."

Alvin Price wasn't seeking to be a leader, but it seemed that role was looking for him. He never considered himself smart. He had been home-schooled by Nellie, who'd been taught the same way by her mother. Life on the farm kept them away from any kind of easy access to schools, and as Alvin got older, work on the farm simply didn't allow time for it. He could read, write and cipher. Reading, however, was his favorite pastime, and it was while reading *Uncle Tom's Cabin* he first realized the terrible horror of slavery. Alvin looked at his friend and shrugged his shoulders. "I guess I'll just have to be there whenever they're meeting. Be there with me?" Alvin asked, smiling at Jeb.

Jeb nodded and then changed the subject. Fluent in French from his time in Montreal, he had to make himself use the language or allow his skill with it to perish. One of the ways he'd learned he could use it was to teach a bit of it to Alvin, who was an eager student. Smiling at his friend as the embers in the fireplace slowly diminished, he said in his best French, *"Dites-m'en plus au sujet de la femme fatale que vous avez rencontré."*

It had been a while since they'd last practiced. It took Alvin's mind a moment to translate. But when he'd gotten what he thought was the gist of it, he looked across at his friend, a broad smile covering his face, and began, "Ah ... *la femme fatale.*" Reverting to the more comfortable English, he said, "Lydia Cockrum is the most beautiful woman I have ever met."

CHAPTER SIX

MOTHER-DAUGHTER BOND

Sunday, June 5, 1870

Lydia and her mother stood in the sewing room at the rear of the Cockrum house. A gentle breeze wafted through Manistee off Lake Michigan, and the day had already warmed to a comfortable 72 degrees. The walk to church earlier had been a pleasant one for the family; the walk home, less so. Irene knew Lydia was fuming mad at her father, who now sat happily content with himself in the drawing room in the front of the house. Irene pointed to the small platform in one corner of the sewing room. As she grabbed her measuring tape, she said to Lydia, "Step up there and let's get started." Wordlessly, Lydia complied. As Irene began to take measurements, she said to her daughter, "I know how infuriating it can be."

"The two of them talked about me as if I was some kind of prize," Lydia said, referring to the conversation she'd witnessed between Herb Fletcher and her father following the church service. She'd walked away from her parents and the Fletchers at church when her father asked Herb if he knew yet exactly when Richard was coming home. There was little doubt in Lydia's mind that the only reason her father and Herb Fletcher were planning this little get-together was so Richard Fletcher and herself could become better acquainted. Frustration evident in her voice, Lydia lamented, "Richard Fletcher went to university when I was ten years old. I don't think I've seen him more than four or five times since then; only when he comes home during the summer and then only at church. How can father think that I could ever have any feelings for him?"

"I don't know," was her mother's short, to-the-point answer as she stood behind her daughter and carefully measured the width of her shoulders.

Lydia felt her mother shift the tape from the width of her shoulders to the length of her spine between her neck— about where the upper edge of a coat collar would strike her—and her waist. When she felt her mother move the tape again, she spun around and asked, "Is he doing this in hopes that I will marry Richard instead of going to college?" Not giving her mother a chance to answer, she continued, "You know that isn't going to happen."

"I know, Lydia."

Lydia knew full well her mother was her best ally, even better than Lydia's friends her own age. Manistee's high school was a good one, but small. Lydia was her class's valedictorian, and in her address to those assembled at their recent graduation, she'd proudly told the six girls and twelve boys graduating with her that the world stretching out in front of them was at its fullest for possibilities. She truly believed that, but Lydia's idea of what might be possible differed from most of her classmates. Four of the six girls she'd graduated with were already betrothed to four of her male classmates. Wedding dates had already been set. Lydia would be here for two of them before setting out for East Lansing and The Agricultural College of the State of Michigan.

Irene reassured her daughter, "You are going to college. Nothing your father or Herb Fletcher can do is going to change that."

"Then why do we have to have this absurd gathering?"

Irene laid her tape down and spread out the dozen or so fabric samples they were considering for Lydia's winter coat. When she was through, she turned to Lydia. "I wanted to go to college, you know."

The hint of regret in her mother's voice was not lost on Lydia. "But you didn't. You married Father instead."

Raising an eyebrow, and with an uncompromising edge to her voice, she looked at her daughter and said, "Before you start feeling like you've been too put upon, young lady, I'd point out that your father has provided quite nicely for the both of us. Wouldn't you agree?"

That stung. Lydia nodded. She adjusted her tone to be more conciliatory and looked her mother in the eye. "I'm sorry. I am thankful for him, for our lives, but I'm still curious. Why didn't you go to college?"

"Because I fell in love," Irene said with a smile and a nod toward the drawing room. "After that, our life together took over completely." She stopped there for a moment, trying to gauge Lydia's reaction, and when she was unable to, she added, "Lydia, I have no regrets. It's important that you know that."

Lydia said, "But, Mother, I don't love Richard Fletcher, and the likelihood that I'm going to after this get-together that Father and Mr. Fletcher are concocting is well below zero." A long silence persisted between them before Lydia asked, "So, what should I do? I don't want him to think that anything is going to come ... "

Irene held up a hand and said, "If there's one thing I've learned about your father over the years, it's that he can be awfully stubborn about some things. This thing with Richard Fletcher, appears to be one of them. Lord knows I've tried to change his mind about your college education, but that is also one of those things that he holds particular views about."

"So now he doesn't want me to go to college?"

"Honestly, I don't think it's a matter of not wanting you to go, but more a matter of why you should go at all."

Lydia threw her hands up in frustration. "Wonderful! So, what should I do?" she repeated.

Calmly her mother replied, "Some women see faults in the men they marry and believe they can change them. Other women see faults in the men they marry and are sufficiently smart to know they will likely never change them. I am one of those who is sufficiently smart. So, I go about my own way, and sometimes that requires me to detour around him when his mind is made up in a wrong direction." She gave that just a moment to sink in, and then proceeded, "So, I suggest two things. First, you enjoy the lunch you and Alvin Price are planning." Irene watched what she thought was something of a conspiratorial smile spread over her daughter's face. "Then, I suggest you spend some time alone with Richard when the Fletchers are here. I suspect that in between the time he actually gets home and this get together that your father and Herb Fletcher are insisting upon, Richard will be feeling the same kind of pressure you are. So, when it's just the two of you, I'd ask him about it. Be honest with him. Tell Richard of your plans for the next four years. Find out what his plans are. My hunch is that the two of you are smart enough to come up with something that will placate both of your fathers until it is time for Richard to return to Ann Arbor and for you to head off to college."

Lydia said nothing. Instead, she stepped over and gave her mother a hug, followed by a whispered, "Thank you. I don't know what I'd do without you."

CHAPTER SEVEN

FIRST, THE LAW, AND THEN, LYDIA

Wednesday, June 8, 1870

L ydia Cockrum was constantly on Alvin Price's mind. If it were up to him, he would have gone to Manistee before this and roamed around River Street just on the off chance of bumping into her again. But chores on the farm prevented that, as did his father's impatience and his insistence on another meeting with the surrounding farmers to decide what to do about the flooding which, by now, was nearing its peak. Thus, this short trip to see the constable in Portage today was a welcome diversion in the middle of a long two weeks for him. He'd intentionally and carefully hidden the trip's purpose from his father, lest he insisted on coming along. When they'd parted ways that morning in front of the barn, Ben was headed to the orchard on the southeast side of the farm with a plow and two mules. Alvin, ostensibly, was headed to the northwestern-most fields to inspect the corn they'd planted there a month earlier.

In fact, Alvin had done just that. He'd driven past those cornfields carefully looking down each row as the wagon rolled by. But when he pulled to the top of a hill that more or less marked the end of their farm, and where he could see Lake Michigan through the forest, he turned the wagon down a bumpy, little-used trail that turned due north across a narrow isthmus of land separating Portage Lake from the big lake. His destination was the settlement of Portage. His purpose was to make himself clear on the facts surrounding the injunction issued by the Manistee County Circuit Court against the damming of Portage Creek by the sawmill owned by Porter & Company.

The constable had tried to be helpful; he even appeared to be sympathetic to the flooding caused by the dam, but at the end of the day, there was little the constable was able to do except allow Alvin to make a handwritten copy of the circuit court's injunction. He was careful to make sure he got every word of it.

Nathan P. Pierce, complainant versus
Lee Porter, Henry Porter, William Coffin.

The case was held at the last term of court, was argued by counsel and upon consideration was decreed that the complainant has sufficiently established in evidence the grievance described in his bill, that the defendants have not established any right to raise or maintain the dam on Portage Creek and to flow back the waters of Portage Creek and Portage Lake upon the lands and tenements of complainants in any of the claims of rights set forth in the defendants' answer and that the raising of the said dam, insofar as it hath injured the complainant, in the matter set forth in his bill, is a nuisance to complainant and ought to be abated and from hereafter, keeping up, continuing, or after abatement, from again raising said level. And it is decreed that the said defendants abate and educe the said Portage dam so that it shall not raise the waters of Portage Lake above their natural level within seven months after the entering of their decree. And it is hereby ordered that a writ of injunction be issued against the defendants commanding them to comply with all the premises so enjoined upon them and it is further ordered that complainant do recover his costs in the premises to be taxed by the register.

J. G. Ramsdell, Circuit Judge
Sworn to William Dunham, May 25, 1870

Bullis and Cutcheon for the Complainant
Ramsdell and Benedict for the Defendants

After he copied it, he reread it, this time very carefully. Then he went to find the constable who had left him to his copying. Finding him poring over a ledger in his office, Alvin knocked lightly on the door frame. When the constable motioned him to come in, Alvin gave the original copy of the injunction back to him. "Thank you, but I do have a few questions." Alvin thought he saw the constable grimace slightly, but he went ahead anyway. "Even though it took the court two years to issue this injunction, the mill operators have another seven months to stop damming Portage Creek. That means the earliest farmers will see any relief from the dam's flooding will be next year. Is that right?"

"That would be right, but I still have to serve the injunction on Mr. Porter, the mill's owner."

That answer spawned another question. "And when will that be?"

"I don't know. When I first received the injunction from the court for the purpose of serving it, I went to the mill to see Mr. Porter. I was told he was not there. I asked when he would be there; I was told by the mill's manager that he did not know. Mr. Porter lives in Chicago."

Wary at this point, Alvin pursued the point. "And in what way does Mr. Porter's absence hold up the serving of the injunction?"

The constable, as if preparing for an argument, leaned back in his chair, crossed his arms over his chest, shrugged his shoulders, and said, "The law requires that I serve the injunction on the mill's owner, Mr. Porter, and that I must do that in Michigan."

"What if Mr. Porter chooses not to arrive in Michigan? What if he simply remains in Chicago? What would you be able to do about any damming of Portage Creek next year in violation of the seven-month deadline established by the court?"

"I cannot bring enforcement to any injunction that has not been properly served on the named defendant. In this case that is Mr. Porter who is not here ... who is not even in the state."

Now Alvin was really thankful his father was not with him. There would have been a cataclysmic eruption of temper. Alvin, however, managed to maintain his rationality. Changing course, he asked, "Do you know Judge Ramsdell?"

"I do. He's been the circuit court judge ever since I was hired into this job."

"And what is your opinion of him?"

The constable replied, "He's fair and honorable."

"And it is he who has advised you that this injunction must be served against Mr. Porter as the mill's owner and only Mr. Porter, not his designated representative at the mill?"

"It is."

As Alvin climbed aboard the wagon for the trip home to the farm, he made the decision he would not disclose any of what he'd learned here today to his father. Not yet anyway. He and Jeb would discuss it, and between the two of them decide what their next course of action should be.

June 15, 1870

A week had passed since Alvin's trip to Portage to talk with the constable about the injunction. He and Jeb had decided that Alvin should go into Manistee and seek out Judge Ramsdell, who'd issued the injunction. Nellie Price looked at Alvin across the dinner table and asked, "What time will you be off in the morning?"

Before he could answer, Ben Price piped up, "Where ya goin', son?"

Nellie intervened, "I got some supplies I'm needin' from town. I asked him to go in and get 'em for me." It wasn't a lie, but it was a contrived truth she and her son had carefully worked out.

Ben said, "So, you'll be back on Friday." It was phrased as a statement, not a question.

Alvin looked over at Jebediah, who was staring into his plate. Alvin put his knife and fork down and turned his attention back to his father, "Not back until Saturday, most likely."

"Whoa. I was plannin' on usin' them horses on Friday and Saturday. Why gone so long?"

Alvin swallowed and replied, "Meeting someone on Friday?"

"Who's that?" Ben inquired.

"A friend of mine."

"This friend more important than my purposes with them horses, son?"

Nellie jumped in. "Honest to God, Ben Price, sometimes you're denser than maple syrup in the middle of winter. Alvin's friend's a young woman he's met. Don't make no big deal out of it. He's got some errands to run for me, and when he's through with them, he's meetin' her for lunch. You ain't so old are you that you don't remember those days?"

Ben sputtered something at Nellie, and then to Alvin said, "Okay, son. I was just thinking ... "

Nellie burst out in a laugh, "Now there's a surprise. Ben Price thinking."

Ignoring her, Ben asked, "Who is she, Alvin?"

Again, Nellie spoke up on her son's behalf, knowing Ben would keep asking questions until he got to one about Lydia's parents. "What's it matter to you? Give the boy some room, for Pete's sake. It's only the second time they've met up. Don't make no big deal out of it," she reiterated.

Alvin changed the subject. "What did you need the horses for, Pa?"

"Was gonna pull some stumps in that acre above the orchard." Glancing over at his wife whose look had softened, Ben said, "But that's okay. I got some plowin' in them orchard rows to do. I can use the mules to get that done. You go on into town. The stumps will be here when you get back."

Time and time again Alvin had seen it. No one had a way with Ben Price like Nellie did. He could be the wildest of mustangs, but she could tame him with just a look, a cock of the head, or a smile.

June 16, 1870

When Alvin reached Manistee the next day, he discovered that finding Circuit Court Judge J. G. Ramsdell was more difficult than he thought it should be. He'd spent a couple of hours just finding the circuit court's office. Manistee had not yet built its own courthouse. One person told him they thought it was located in Ellis Hall. But when Alvin got there, the place was locked up, empty. Someone else suggested he look at Thurber Hall; they thought the circuit court had moved there from Ellis Hall a couple of months ago. Thurber proved as fruitless as Ellis. Finally, Alvin stumbled on a sign that read *Manistee City Hall,* where a helpful clerk inside advised him that the circuit court had indeed been a moving target, but was currently housed in an office just off the vestibule of the newly built Congregational Church. The clerk was even so kind as to offer Alvin directions.

Now, as Alvin stood in the doorway of that office inside the church, a man with oily, slicked-back hair, parted in the middle asked, "Do you have an appointment with the judge?" His upper lip hid behind a thick, black, waxed handlebar mustache and his tone was an impatient one.

"No. I'm from Portage. I live on a farm there. I would like to speak to the judge about the injunction he issued against the damming of Portage Creek."

With a certain finality, the clerk told Alvin, "The judge isn't here right now."

Alvin was thankful, again, his father was nowhere around, but the clerk's unhelpful, almost condescending attitude was beginning to ruffle even Alvin's patience. He asked, "Will he be back today?"

The clerk shrugged his shoulders and replied, "Um, maybe, but I have no idea when that might be."

At that point Alvin plunked himself down in a chair outside the clerk's office and said, "I'll wait."

Two hours later, a well-dressed, distinguished-looking man opened the church's narthex door and walked down the hall toward Alvin who stood up as he approached. "Judge Ramsdell?" Alvin noticed him stare at his missing arm. The judge nodded but didn't say anything. "My name is Alvin Price. My family has a farm on the south side of Portage Lake."

Ramsdell was a busy man. In addition to his duties as circuit judge, he was also a businessman with varied interests in Manistee ranging from lumber to bridges. Busy men can be blunt, dismissive sometimes, but Alvin's disability now afforded him an advantage. The war was over, but it wasn't forgotten. Pointing to Alvin's arm, the judge asked, "That happen in the war?" Alvin nodded. The judge asked, "Who'd you serve with?"

"24th Michigan Volunteers."

The judge seemed to soften. "How'd you get signed up with them? They were from downstate, weren't they? Detroit, if memory serves."

"Yes, sir. Traveled down there to join up."

The judge was familiar with the 24th Michigan Volunteers and knew they'd suffered tremendous losses at the battle of Gettysburg. Pointing again to the missing arm, he asked, "That happen at Gettysburg?"

"Yes, sir."

"How can I help you ... Alvin ... that's right, isn't it? Alvin, you said your name was?" Alvin nodded. The judge motioned for him to follow him into the small office, whereupon the judge asked the clerk to go get him some pipe tobacco at the tobacconist down on River Street. "I'm completely out," the judge said, flipping a coin in the clerk's direction.

Ramsdell pointed to a straight-backed wooden chair in front of the desk and said, "Have a seat." The office was small and sparsely furnished. A wooden filing cabinet stood in the corner. Ramsdell stepped behind the desk and took the chair just vacated by the clerk. "Bet you want to talk about the injunction I issued on Porter's mill and their dam on Portage Creek."

"Yes, sir. Did you know the constable hasn't been able to issue it to Mr. Porter?"

"Was not aware. He give you some reason?"

"Said it has to be issued to Mr. Porter himself. He told me it can't be issued to his mill supervisor. Is that right, Judge?"

Ramsdell spun his chair around facing away from Alvin and stared out the small window behind the desk. When he spun back around, he said, "And Mr. Porter isn't here to be served is he?"

Alvin answered, "He lives in Chicago."

The judge issued an expletive under his breath. "That hearing was a long and contentious one. The lumbermen had a couple of attorneys representing their side of the case and they were good. The farmers had one lawyer representing them, but he called some pretty good witnesses. My decision to issue the injunction was an easy one by the time it was all over, but I've got to tell you, Alvin, it cost me quite a few friends in the lumber business. The one thing I can't get around, though, is the provision in the law that injunctions like this one must be issued against the land's owner; in this case, Mr. Porter. And it has to be done here in Michigan. I can't send the constable to Chicago to issue the writ. First, he has no authority there. Second, the land... the mill... is here in Michigan. My hands are tied at this point, Alvin."

Alvin dropped his head and shook it. "That just doesn't seem fair to me, Judge."

"Fair... now there's a word for our times. It's got almost as many meanings as there are people, yet it's the basis of our legal system." The judge pointed to a statue on top of the filing cabinet in the corner of the office. "Take a look at her. She's the blindfolded lady of the law standing there balancing the scale perfectly. She's meant to be a symbol of the law's fairness. Yet, here we are, Alvin, and you're right, if I look at it from your viewpoint, it doesn't seem fair that injunction hasn't been served." He paused and then continued, "The law that allowed me to impose that injunction came out of Lansing just a year or so after the war ended. I can't recall the exact details except some business was doing something that made money, but some other business was being hurt by what the first business was doing. I can't say for sure—it's been too long—memory's too light on the details—but my guess is that whatever it was, it went on for some time before the lawmakers got involved in it. Then, when the issue got big enough, they figured they'd better start getting their heads together—representatives and senators there in Lansing. So, a bill was introduced. But then, Alvin, you've got to remember what the mood of the country was back then—what the mood of folks here in Michigan was—right after the war. Everyone was sick of it. There'd been so much death and destruction. People wanted prosperity to return, and for that to happen, business had to improve, and that's still the mood today. So, the lawmakers found themselves in a real bind. They had to figure out a way to be fair. As that bill worked its way through the state capitol, some of those men who were going to have to vote on it were also businessmen. I know some of them and I know how they think. They reasoned 'now if the law and the courts are going to start playing around with my business interests, then by God, I want to be the one who they inform of any decisions they reach—no one else, just me.' So, the lawmakers put that stipulation in the bill before it was passed into law. My injunction hurts Porter and Company's sawmill at Portage Creek. Mr. Porter's the owner. So, Mr. Porter—and only Mr. Porter—is the one I am obligated to inform of the injunction. If you look at it from Mr. Porter's point of view, it's fair. Point is, Alvin, fairness is a matter of perspective."

Alvin, once again glad his father wasn't around to hear this, said, "Farmers are right riled up about that lake rising again this summer, Judge. We are all losing tillable land to that dam. Just as important, it creates havoc with us when they start to use the water to operate the mill like they're doing right now. The lake slowly drains and we're left with stagnant pools of water everywhere. Mosquitoes, flies, maggots, all kinds of vermin form in those pools. People get sick from it, Judge."

Ramsdell nodded. "I heard testimony to such. That's one of the reasons I issued the injunction, but I can't make Mr. Porter come to Michigan."

Alvin said, "The farmers have been meeting. My father's one of the organizers. They are threatening to go over and tear out the dam on Portage Creek."

The judge's tone turned quite serious now, and, with an unmistakable sternness, said, "You know I'd advise them against taking matters into their own hands."

Alvin leaned forward in his chair as the judge continued.

"If they were to do something like that, the mill's owners would be within their rights to prefer charges. The constables out there in Portage would be required to investigate. If it could be proved that ..." Ramsdell let that hang there. "The lumbermen are powerful around here. When they complain, people listen ... I listen. I know these men. They are businessmen and they will use the law any way they can to weaken the position of the farmers. Do you understand what I'm trying to say to you?"

Alvin nodded. "I know, Judge. That's why I came to see you today. I wanted to know if there was anything you could do."

Ramsdell shook his head, "I'm sorry. But unless Mr. Porter comes to Michigan and we can serve that injunction on him legally, there's nothing more I can do."

Alvin stood.

The judge added, "I wish there was more ..."

"I know. I thank you for taking the time to talk with me."

"It's been nice meeting you. If there's ever anything else I can do ... all you have to do is ask. Please know that. I am a proud American, and I appreciate your service in defense of the Union."

Alvin left thinking that the issue he'd come for was no closer to resolution than before, but that he'd made a friend of Judge J. G. Ramsdell.

June 17, 1870

Alvin had camped for the night in a clearing surrounded by half a dozen huge oak trees next to Lake Manistee. It was just east of downtown, but far enough away that he knew he, Kip and the horses would be alone. Mid-June in northern Michigan was still cool in the early mornings, and the morning after his meeting with Judge Ramsdell there was a light fog rising off the lake's surface. He undressed and waded naked into the cold water. Kip followed him, oblivious to any cold, wagging his tail. Through chattering teeth, Alvin muttered, "Damn, this water is cold." Standing waist deep now, he splashed several handfuls over his upper body before lathering up with the bar of strong lye soap his mother had made. No matter how cold the water was, he was not going to meet Lydia in a few hours without having cleaned up. When he'd finished with himself, he called Kip to him. Reluctantly the dog waded in his direction. Alvin lathered him up. "We both have to bathe before we meet her, Kip." Kip disliked the bath part, but while Alvin vigorously rubbed him, Kip enjoyed his touch and his attention.

Alvin possessed one suit, as did Jebediah. One suit, however, was one more than his father owned. After he dressed, he took the gold pocket watch and chain from a wooden box and placed it in the vest's watch pocket.

No fire was built, no coffee brewed, no breakfast prepared except for Kip's, which was always served cold. He was not going to show up smelling like smoke. He took a long hour to hitch the horses to his wagon, partly not wanting to break a sweat, partly rather enjoying the anticipation of his long-awaited second meeting with Lydia. Before climbing up on the wagon, he pulled on the final piece of his ensemble, a loose-fitting sack coat and fashionably buttoned only the top button, leaving it open as it fell over his flat stomach to just below his waist. Exposed were the gold chain and the stem of the gold watch extending just above the watch pocket. Alvin Price was not a vain man, but he wished he had a full-length mirror to see how he looked.

He rolled the reins over the horses' backs. He and Kip rocked easily back and then forth on the wagon's seat as it began to move forward. There were a few errands to run before heading to his meeting with Lydia, and Alvin's stomach rolled with the adrenaline rush of anticipation as he thought of seeing her again.

It had been two full weeks since Lydia Cockrum had last seen Alvin Price. She stood in front of the full-length mirror in the corner of her bedroom, smoothing the folds on the dress she'd chosen for her much anticipated meeting.

Behind her, her mother was smiling at her daughter's image in the mirror, "Your hair looks lovely, dear. I love the flowers you've woven into it." The white dwarf daisies with their deep orange center had been growing in her mother's flower garden just an hour earlier. They contrasted perfectly with her auburn hair which she wore up in a bun. The sun streaming through the bedroom's window shimmered off it like a beam of light. "Do you think I might meet this young man while he is in town to see you?"

Lydia flashed her mother a smile and asked, "Is it coincidence or did you have something to do with father being gone overnight tonight in Frankfort?"

Her mother waved a hand nonchalantly, "Completely coincidental. You know I only manage your father's business accounts, not his travel schedule." They both chuckled.

"I am excited to see Alvin again. Aunt Liliane said he stopped by her store after bumping into me. She thought it took some gumption on his part to introduce himself like he did. She liked his sense of humor. So, if everything goes as well as I expect it to, I will certainly invite him to stop and meet you." She paused for just a brief moment and then added, "I think he's aware that father may be difficult."

"Ummm ... well, yes," Irene murmured. "You go and have a good time and let me worry about how best to deal with your father. He's gruff, but he's manageable."

54

First Street at its western terminus turned abruptly into an expanse of sand that eventually became a beach stretching to the south for miles and miles along Lake Michigan. To the north, however, the beach was interrupted by the wide mouth of the Manistee River as it met Lake Michigan. This was the Port of Manistee, and in the hour or so that Alvin had been there, he'd watched three or four schooners arriving or departing. Those arriving carried all kinds of cargoes from Chicago to this otherwise rather remote part of northern Michigan. Those departing were mostly headed for Chicago laden with thousands of board feet of lumber, the thirst for it in the Midwest seemingly unquenchable.

He judged he was within half a mile of several steam-powered sawmills. Billows of smoke rose against the blue sky and wafted eastward over the city, pushed by the breeze off Lake Michigan. Alvin liked none of it. The mills were ugly; pumping smoke that would have to come to ground somewhere and ... *what ... create some kind of nuisance?* He wasn't sure. All he knew for sure is that these mills never shut down except when the lakes and rivers, upon which the logs floated, froze. Alvin knew the lumbermen wanted railroads as soon as they could get them. Then, ice be damned! Logs could come to the mills year round.

Maneuvering his wagon and horses as far away from the sawmills as he could get, he pulled under the shade of a huge maple tree off to one side of the expansive sandlot. A stand of trees sheltered his view of the mills, but there was no reprieve from the clouds of smoke they were belching into the sky. He climbed down from the wagon and began setting up their spot when Kip let out several excited barks and ran toward the Cedar Street hill. Preoccupied with his preparations, Alvin paid little attention to his dog, figuring it was a squirrel or some such thing that had his attention. But as he sat their lunch basket down on the tablecloth he'd spread out for them, Kip ran back to him, barking even more excitedly and then ran back toward Cedar Street, looking back and forth between Alvin and something Alvin could not see. "What is it, boy?" Kip stood looking up the hill, barking furiously. Alvin walked the few hundred feet over to where Kip stood barking, looked up the hill, and saw Lydia, still at some distance, carrying a basket at least equal in size to the one he'd just taken off his wagon.

Kip continued to bark alongside his master as Alvin ran up the hill. "Lydia, please let me take that." Kip ran excited circles around the couple, still barking, as Alvin relieved her of her burden.

"Who's this?" she asked, as she knelt down and held her hand out to Kip who immediately went to her.

"I've never seen him like this with anyone else, except maybe my ma. He saw you coming, and even though he's never seen you ..." Then Alvin added, shyly, but with an ear-to-ear smile, "But he has heard of you."

Lydia stood, with Kip still at her side, but quiet now. She cast a playful look at the dog and then back to Alvin. "Oh, so you and he have been talking about me." Alvin nodded. Lydia asked, "What's his name?"

"Kip."

"Well, Kip, I hope I'm worth all this excitement."

Alvin answered for his dog. "Oh, you are, Lydia. You are."

Together, the three of them walked down the Cedar Street hill and then to the beach. They sat on the canvas tarp Alvin had taken from the seat of his wagon and ate their lunch. Occasionally, Alvin would toss a scrap of one thing or another to Kip who would catch it in midair. Lydia seemed to delight in both of her lunch partners.

After they'd eaten, the three of them went for a long walk on the beach. For the first hour, the conversation had been light. She learned how Alvin and Kip met. She laughed with delight as the dog brought her stick after stick to throw into Lake Michigan, where Kip literally dove into waves to retrieve them, presented them to her, and then, quite unashamedly, shook vigorously, throwing water and sand all over them. The first time he did this, Alvin scolded him for ruining Lydia's beautiful dress, but when she playfully scolded Alvin for scolding Kip, Alvin let it go.

During the last half of their beach walk, however, the conversation turned more serious. Alvin told her of his friend, Jebediah, a story that inevitably revealed some of the horrors both had faced on Civil War battlefields. Lydia told Alvin of her plans to leave Manistee in the fall to attend college in East Lansing. At one point, Alvin asked Lydia about her aunt. "She goes by Burke. Is she married?"

Lydia gave a sigh and then explained, "Aunt Liliane is a widow. My Uncle Charley was first mate on a schooner. The accident happened ten years ago this November. His ship was sailing from Green Bay to Manistee. A storm caught them in the middle of Lake Michigan. All hands were lost. She's owned the millinery shop for the last eight years. It's made a difference for her; it's given her purpose in life again, I suppose."

It was late in the afternoon when Lydia opened the clasp on the watch pinned to her dress and noted the time. Their time together had flown by. Closing the clasp, she looked at Alvin and asked, "Are you in a rush to get home?"

He immediately responded, "I am not."

She reddened slightly, but confidently asked, "I was wondering if you'd mind giving me a ride home? I'd like you to meet my mother."

Her request surprised him, but he jumped at the chance to spend more time with her. "Nothing would make me happier."

They packed up the wagon. Kip jumped into the back. In an effort to be his most polite, Alvin asked, "May I help you up?"

Smiling she said, "Please."

From the wagon's seat, she watched Alvin's accomplished gracefulness as he climbed aboard in spite of his disability. She was curious to see how he would handle the reins of the giants that stood in front of them. She was impressed again with his gentleness and his ability to control the two draft horses with only one hand. "These are the biggest horses I've ever seen."

"That's Amos on the left," he said, "and Tom. They're brothers. Amos is a year younger than Tom. They were both foaled on a farm not far from ours. My father bought them just after I got home. We decided we wanted to plant an orchard. We knew there'd be a lot of stumping to do."

"Stumping?"

Alvin nodded. "It's not just as simple as cutting down a tree. If you want to farm the land around where that tree grew, you've got to get the stump and as many of the roots as you can out of the ground. These two get that work done in about half the time it would take with a team of mules, so you can pull more stumps in the course of a day. Plus, it's a lot easier on the animals. These two boys were made for that kind of work. Mules, well, mules get used up much quicker if you use them a lot for stumping."

Lydia had just had her first lesson in farming just a few months before she was to head off to the state's agricultural college. "Sounds like really hard work, this stumping."

"It is. Farming is. But it's going to get easier. There's a new invention, just a few years old. It's a steam-powered tractor. We don't have one yet, but maybe someday..."

As they reached the top of the hill on Cedar Street, Lydia directed Alvin to turn the wagon west down the second cross street they came to. "I live just a short distance down here," she said.

It was time for Alvin to ask the question that had been burning on the end of his tongue since she'd suggested she would like him to meet her mother. "Will your father be home?"

This time Lydia really reddened. "No, he's traveling."

It was an easy conclusion for Alvin to reach. She was comfortable asking him to take her home because she knew her father wouldn't be there to disapprove of him. Looking at her, he said, "Lydia, I don't want to be a problem for you."

Returning his look, Lydia laid her hand on his right arm, "My mother's a friend, Alvin. She understands a lot of things that my father doesn't. She's asked to meet you. My Aunt Liliane ... from the millinery shop ... she's told me about meeting you. I'm glad you went in there. I'm glad you introduced yourself to her. She and my mother are wonderful women. I know Mother is going to like you as much as I..." She caught herself up short as she felt the heat of embarrassment color her face.

He looked into her eyes, and with all the sincerity he could muster, said, "I'm looking forward to meeting her."

CHAPTER EIGHT

THE DECEPTION

Sunday, June 19, 1870

The day Lydia had been dreading finally arrived. She stood at the kitchen window looking out at her father sitting in a chair reading his Sunday paper under the shade tree on the side of the house. Scornfully, she said to her mother, "I was never so embarrassed in my life. I felt like a prize heifer father was offering up." Her mother said nothing. "Of all the places to do that, church ought not to be that place," Lydia continued. "I'm not sure I can go through with this gathering today. What's the point, Mother? I'm not going to throw myself at Richard Fletcher, and he didn't exactly seem thrilled about coming over here this afternoon."

Irene Cockrum waited until Lydia was finished venting, and then turned to her and said, "This is something that Herb Fletcher and your father have gotten into their heads. I think Richard is a fine young man, but I can certainly understand your opposition to the way Herb and your father are going about this. But I know your father, and I know that if he sees you aren't even willing to give it a try, he won't give up. I suspect Mr. Fletcher will be the same way with Richard. So, let's be realistic. Richard is home for how long? A month? And you leave for school in September. Neither of these are interminable lengths of time, Lydia," Her mother's tone had become a bit scolding.

"However unpleasant this may be for you, it isn't something that is going to last forever, is it? And I must say, I am a bit surprised at your infatuation with Alvin Price. Like Richard, he seems to be a very nice young man. But again, you are going to be leaving soon."

"So, now you don't approve of my seeing Alvin?"

"That isn't what I said, Lydia, and you know it."

Lydia sulked for a while after getting only partial sympathy from her mother but snapped out of it after the Fletchers arrived. Raised to be a proper lady, she knew not to spoil the day for everyone else. Lunch had gone well from the perspective of the two fathers. The fare was simple: ham and cheese sandwiches on bread Irene baked just yesterday and served with generous helpings of her delicious potato salad. The afternoon had warmed nicely, and there was noticeable humidity in the mid 70s temperature, prompting everyone to comment that summer couldn't be very far off. In fact, the summer solstice was only a few days away, but no one put much faith in the belief warmer weather was inevitable with its arrival, not this far north. They ate at a table under the same tree where Reilly Cockrum had read his paper earlier. The seating arrangement had been carefully worked out by the two fathers well in advance of lunch. Reilly sat at one end, Herb Fletcher at the other. Aleta Fletcher sat on one side closest to her husband. On that same side, Irene sat closest to Reilly. Richard and Lydia were then directed to sit on the side of the table opposite their mothers. Reilly Cockrum asked the blessing.

Lydia had actually enjoyed the meal. Reilly would have preferred that his daughter not mention her college enrollment in the fall, but it became the dominant subject between her and Richard as lunch progressed. Lydia wanted to know all about what college life was really like.

After everyone had eaten their fill, it was Richard who

turned to Lydia and said, "I don't know about you, but after that lunch, I feel like I need to get up and move around a bit. Would you like to take a walk with me, Lydia?"

From their respective ends of the table, Reilly Cockrum and Herb Fletcher smiled broadly at one another.

Once Lydia and Richard had put enough distance between them and the house, Richard turned to her and said, "I'm glad you agreed to walk with me. I don't know what I would have done if you had said no."

"Richard, I..."

He interrupted her, "Lydia, we both know what our fathers are trying to do."

Lydia, though surprised by his frankness, welcomed it.

Richard said, "I must tell you something, and I hope you will keep it just between the two of us."

Lydia found this element of intrigue rather appealing. "Of course. What is it?"

He paused as if working through some kind of second thought. Then he blurted out, "I'm married."

Lydia was speechless. She didn't know whether to laugh at the humor in this or cry at the desperation she thought she could hear in his voice. After she managed to come to her senses, she sputtered, "But...but, your father..."

He shook his head and completed her thought, "Would not approve."

"Your mother...does she know?"

He shook his head. "My wife is a freed slave."

Again, Lydia found herself at a stultifying loss for words. All she could manage was a benign, "Oh."

"We met two years ago. I was halfway through medical school. She was working in the university library and I must say it was love at first sight."

Lydia could easily understand, but had to ask, "Then why are you alone here?"

"It's a terrible deception, I know, but one I must keep

up for another year until I've completed my training. Father pays for my school, and he would never do that if he knew..." He paused as if he regretted how ruthless what he'd just said sounded, and then added, "My father is a good man, but he has certain ideas about right and wrong. My marrying a Negro may never set well with him. But she's a wonderful mother to our son..."

Lydia blurted out, "You have a son?"

Richard smiled. "A year old and he's the joy of our lives. After I've completed medical school and start to practice, Abigail will enroll at the university, just as you have done at the agricultural college. The University of Michigan has just this year opened up its enrollment to include women. Abigail may be the first Negro woman to be admitted. I don't have to tell you that women should be able to attend college. It shouldn't matter if they are White, Black, or Indian; I know men of each of these races who are attending. Why shouldn't women?" They had stopped walking, and Richard stood ramrod straight as if he were standing in defiance of everything that was wrong with the world. "Abigail wants to become a teacher and start her own school, for our son, Samuel, and other sons and daughters of former slaves. We will stay in Ann Arbor. I hope to teach at the university as well as practice in the city. At some point, after I've established myself, I'll tell my parents about my wife and child. I'll bring Abby and Sam to Manistee to meet them, but in the meantime..." He paused and then confessed, "I've told you something that is very important to me. I hope I can trust you to keep my secret."

Smiling back at him, she said, "It's safe with me. I wasn't sure how I was going to tell you, but it was going to be my suggestion that we let our fathers think there is a possibility that we are..." she searched for the right words. "What's the harm in letting them think we are interested in each other?"

They walked for another hour, and in that time, Lydia told Richard about Alvin. In her own kind of confession, she admitted, "I find myself thinking of him often."

Richard asked, "But it remains your intention to attend college?"

Lydia immediately and emphatically replied, "Yes, absolutely."

"College isn't easy. It isn't enough to be smart. I think you have to have a vision of what you want to become. For women the traditional role of wife and mother is all that there has ever been, but that is changing. What is it you want for yourself, Lydia? That's what you have to think about."

"It won't be easy, I know. Alvin is a complication I had not anticipated. My father completely objects to him, and my mother has expressed some reluctance in my getting involved in a romance if I'm going to be leaving in the fall. But I really enjoy his company. He is hard working, sweet, smart in a very common-sense kind of way. I think a lot of that comes from his wartime experiences."

"He was in the war?"

"Yes. He lost his left arm at Gettysburg."

"I didn't go." There was a hint of regret in his voice. "I couldn't go. My vision was then and is now to become a doctor. To help people who are afflicted. I was called to serve once by the government, but once I proved I was in college with the intention of becoming a doctor, I didn't have to go. Maybe I should have ..."

She interrupted him, "I think you made the right choice." She took his hand. "The thing about Alvin is that I don't think he regrets going, but now that he's back from war, he never wants to see it happen again."

"Well, it did put an end to slavery. The cause was a noble one ... a just one. But, that damned war cost so many lives and then there are the many who lost limbs like your Alvin."

"Yes."

"So, maybe I can help him someday."

"How do you mean?"

Richard explained to her he intended to go into ortho-pedic surgery involving all too frequently the necessity to amputate limbs, but that he was interested in the growing field of prosthetics. "Maybe someday, I can look at Alvin's situation and be of help."

All of this was a bit overwhelming to her. She was over-joyed she didn't need to worry about Richard falling in love with her; he was married and a father. She didn't know whether or not she loved Alvin Price, but she certainly hadn't gotten him out of her thoughts since they'd met. And now this! A doctor holding out the hope that someday Alvin's missing limb might be partially restored. Never, for even the slightest of seconds, did it ever enter her mind that this deception of their fathers they were about to pull off was the wrong thing to do. No, it was, in fact, the only thing to do.

The Fletchers had left about 4:00 p.m., shortly after Rich-ard and Lydia returned from their walk. In the last hour, Lydia had purposefully and carefully avoided her father; but as she and her mother stood in the kitchen doing a few dishes remaining from their lunch that afternoon, Reilly Cockrum finally cornered her. "You and Richard were gone quite some time on your walk. I'm taking it that the two of you found each other's company enjoyable."

She knew this was coming and she'd used the hour to pre-pare her answer to his inevitable inquiry. "We did. He will call on me next week and we will go for another walk." She noticed her father's broad smile, and then she added, "He is giving me some very good advice and information about college."

Her father's smile faded, and he shook his head. "Lydia, I wish you would come to your senses ... "

Irene was standing at the kitchen sink finishing up a few dishes. Lydia's back was to her, and Reilly's attention was focused on his daughter. Both of them jumped as Irene smashed a large serving spoon down on the metal counter next to the sink. She didn't scream, but the volume of her voice was certainly raised and there was a stern edge to it that was very much unlike her. "Reilly Cockrum, stop that this minute. She has done your bidding with Richard Fletcher. They enjoy one another's company. Be happy with that small accomplishment. Do not think for an instant, however, that I am going to stand here and have you discourage her from this greatest opportunity of her young lifetime. She is going to college in the fall and that is all there is to it!"

Reilly Cockrum nearly made the fatal mistake of challenging Irene, but at the last minute he thought better of it. Instead, he turned and left them standing there in the kitchen.

Lydia turned to her mother and mouthed, "Thank you."

Irene, nearly in tears, stepped over and embraced her. "You will have this chance, Lydia. No one will stand in your way, especially not your father."

Lydia, now herself bordering on tears, had been struggling with how much she should tell her mother. Still in Irene's embrace, Lydia whispered in her ear, "Richard and I talked about it. We both agreed that a little deception is called for." She'd decided just now in this moment that Richard's secret would be safe with her. There was no need in further burdening her mother with it; there was still, apparently, a battle she would need to fight on Lydia's behalf here at home.

Irene pushed her daughter back to arm's length, smiled and said, "Good for the two of you."

CHAPTER NINE

BAD NEWS

Sunday, June 19, 1870

It was the day before Ben Price's fiftieth birthday, and
Nellie's preparation for this landmark event was well
underway when Alvin walked into the kitchen. She
was kneading a huge ball of dough and without stopping, she looked up at him, smiled and said, "When did you
get home?"

"Late last night. The house was dark. Thought you and
Pa were probably asleep and I wanted to talk with Jebediah, so Kip and I went to his cabin."

Nellie gave him a knowing smile, "So, the visit with
Lydia went well?"

"It did. I think you would like her. I met her mother."

"You did!"

He could see Nellie was beginning to let her imagination
run away, so he tried to rein his mother in a bit. "Yes, but
don't read a lot into it. Lydia had this big basket she'd carried all the way from her house to Creeping Joe ... "

"Creepin' Joe?" Nellie interrupted.

"It's what folks in Manistee have named that sand dune
down at the end of River Street. We met there, had lunch
and then walked the beach. After that, she asked me if I
could take her home. I was happy to because I didn't want
her carrying that big basket back up the Cedar Street hill.

Her mother was very gracious, but I doubt Lydia would have invited me to her home if her father had been there."

"Ever met the man?"

"No."

"But you're thinkin' he's already judged you?"

"He builds railroads, Ma. He's partial to lumbermen, not farmers."

Nellie shrugged her shoulders, "And how did the other reason for your trip turn out?"

"Not good. Jebediah and I had a long talk about it last night. I spoke to Judge Ramsdell. I think he's on our side, but there is only so much he can do. The injunction against the dam has to be issued to the mill owner and it can only be served here in the state. The owner lives in Chicago, and I think he knows not to come to Michigan."

"Your pa still doesn't know about your visit with the constable or the judge?"

He smiled at her. "You haven't heard any explosions, have you? No, I'll wait until the birthday party is over. I need to talk to Jebediah some more, too. Once I tell Pa, it'll be up to me and Jeb to calm him down. We both know that."

Tuesday, June 21, 1870

Ben's birthday celebration had been one to remember, but now it was the morning after the night before. Jebediah led Amos and Tom to the front of the wagon by their bridles. He handed Tom off to Alvin. The two began hitching up the pair of horses. Jebediah asked, "Are you going to tell him this morning?"

"I am, but I'm going to wait until we get to the orchard. He's less likely to want to start stirring up trouble with the other farmers if he's away from the house and he's got a full day of work staring him in the face."

Jeb walked around to Alvin's side of the wagon. "Sounds like a good plan." He pointed in the direction of the farmhouse, "Here he comes. Let's hope for the best, and that he holds his temper."

Ben Price's eyes had that swollen look of an alcohol-induced sleep and a redness that Jeb and Alvin attributed to having had too much shine. Perhaps it was the occasion that allowed Nellie the tolerance to overlook her husband's condition last night and permit him to spend the night in the farmhouse.

"How are you feeling this morning?" Alvin inquired, a big smile plastered on his face.

Managing something of a smile, Ben replied, "Glad fiftieth birthdays don't happen more than once in a lifetime." The three got a good laugh, and then Alvin and Ben headed for the orchard while Jeb set off toward the blacksmith shop.

Once they'd reached the orchard, Alvin pulled the two draft horses to a halt. "Pa, I've got something to tell you, but before I do, I want you to promise me you won't go off half-cocked."

Ben looked over at his son. "This got somethin' to do with that lady friend of yours in Manistee?"

Alvin only wished that he could talk about Lydia rather than the subject of the injunction. "It does not. It has to do with the injunction Judge Ramsdell's issued against that dam."

Ben scrunched his face up, his skepticism obvious. "Well?"

"I've met with the constable and with the judge ... "

Ben held up his hand, "Whoa. Stop right there. Ya met with these people and ya didn't take me along?"

Alvin was prepared to explain his purposeful omission. "That's right." He watched Ben begin shaking his head, a characteristic behavior Ben always exhibited as he was starting to get angry. "Before you explode, let me tell you why. I wasn't trying to put you off, nor was I trying to make you angry. I had some of my own questions that I wanted to get answers to, and I figured the best way to do that was to go it alone."

"So, what kind of questions did ya have that ya thought I wouldn't want to know the answers to myself?"

Alvin hung his head. His father could be quite stubborn, especially when it came to matters of that damned dam. Casting a glance toward Ben, he said, "Pa, have you read the injunction in its entirety?" It was a question he already knew the answer to. His father was brought up on a farm; there had been no time for formal education. Reading wasn't something Ben liked to do, and he only did it when it was absolutely his last recourse—and, as far as Alvin knew, that never included things like legal documents.

"It's just a bunch of words that no workin' man can understand. All I know is that the judge said they can't dam up Portage Creek. Ain't nothin' else I need to know."

"Well, that's where you're wrong." That was strong language for Alvin to use and he knew he was running the risk of further angering his father, but it was time—maybe even a little past time—for this confrontation to take center stage. "You need to know that the injunction gives the mill seven months before they have to stop damming the creek."

"Don't matter, Alvin. Knew they wasn't gonna stop this summer. But next summer they best—"

Alvin didn't let his father finish. "There's another technicality that I learned about that you aren't going to like, but it's the law."

"What's that?"

"The injunction hasn't been served, and it's not likely that it ever will be."

To Alvin's surprise, rather than erupting like a volcano, his father just sat there as if he hadn't heard him. Ben sputtered, "It's...it's the law. The judge has to issue..."

"The judge issues the warrant; the constable serves it. But in this case, it has to be served directly to the mill's owner." Alvin waited, but still the expected eruption didn't occur. "And it has to be served here in Michigan. The owner lives in Chicago and I'm pretty sure he knows to stay there."

Ben turned to Alvin, the fire in his eyes real now. "Give me the reins," he demanded.

"Why?"

"We're goin' back home. I gotta get the farmers together. They gotta hear ... "

"Hear what, Pa? You're hopping mad right now and that's not going to help matters at all. I saw it in the army. If you make decisions about things when you're angry like you are, generally they aren't good ones. You need to take some time and cool off before you go riling up the farmers more than they're already riled."

Ben, the reins now in his hands, slapped them hard over the horses' backs. He pulled hard on Amos's reins and turned the wagon to the left. "You're damned right I'm angry. We counted on the law to treat us fair and from what you're tellin' me, they ain't gonna do nothin' about it." He stopped ranting for a moment, but then added, "You're too young to understand."

Alvin expected the rant, but the final criticism caught him off guard, and it stung him to his core. "Stop the wagon," he demanded.

Ben kept urging the two horses on.

"I said stop the wagon. Me and Kip are getting off."

"You gonna walk home?"

"That's right. Look at you! You just turned fifty and you still haven't learned patience and reason are more effective than getting mad. I am not going to be any part of whatever hell you are fixing to raise with the other farmers, and I don't think Jebediah will either when he sees what you're up to."

Ben started to ask, "Ya just gonna let the lumbermen get away with..."

Alvin interrupted him. "You're assuming that, and that proves my point that good decisions aren't reached when you're mad about something."

"So, what the hell are ya thinkin'?"

Alvin shrugged, "At this point, I'm not exactly sure. But what I'd like for you to do, since we already know we aren't going to see any relief from the flooding this summer anyway, is to let me and Jebediah talk about it. We'll come and talk to you when we think we've got something. But in the meantime, you have to stop riling up the other farmers. I spoke to the judge about this. He says that right now we have the law on our side, but if you and the others go over to the mill and start tearing things up, we lose that advantage."

"Don't seem like much of an advantage to me..."

"I know it doesn't right now, but that's why you need to give me and Jebediah some time to think this thing through." He saw his father pull back on the reins. Amos and Tom came to a stop. Alvin had the thought that maybe, just maybe, he'd gotten through to his father. "Now, why don't we turn this wagon around and let's go back to the orchard. We've come all this way to work, so let's get something done, seeing as how we can't do anything about the dam until next spring anyhow."

Ben was silent, but he handed the reins to Alvin. They worked the orchard rows until mid-afternoon. On the ride back to the farmhouse Ben made one request, "When you and Jebediah have come up with a plan, I want to know about it. No more secret meetings behind my back."

Alvin's first reaction was to flare at the "behind my back" remark, but he bit his tongue, nodded, and instead said, "I promise."

CHAPTER TEN

NO TIME TO WASTE

June 23, 1870

Two days had passed since Ben had his blow up, and Alvin had bought Jeb and him the time to talk about things. The rhythmic clang of hammer against anvil told Alvin Jebediah was back. When he and Ben had returned from the orchard, Jebediah had disappeared. Alvin had asked Nellie if she knew where he'd gone, but she didn't, and his disappearance wasn't all that unusual. In the last seven years, Jeb had become an accomplished blacksmith. He took orders from other farmers, even a few lumberjacks, who'd come to know his work was high quality and done at a fair price. Often, Jeb would deliver a job he'd done for someone. This work created a cash flow for the Price farm that was unusual among the homesteaders, and Alvin, Ben and Nellie all knew Jeb was generous with the money he made from his blacksmithing. After all, it was Alvin who'd taught him everything he knew about that line of work. All of this made Jeb more of a partner in the farm operation than just some hired hand who had to ask permission to be away from the chores. Standing at the doorway to the shop, Alvin said in between hammer beats, "Everything all right with you? Missed you the last couple of days."

Jeb looked up, flashed a smile, beat the hammer down

on a red-hot piece of metal, and said, "Yep. Just fine. How 'bout you? How did it go with Ben?"

"There was a minute there when I thought he might have shot me if he'd had a gun handy, but he seemed to come around after a while. I came to see you Tuesday night, after we got back from the orchard, but you weren't here."

"Sorry. You and Ben were in the orchard and I didn't want to bother Nellie. Something came up that needed takin' care of."

Alvin recognized this answer as somewhat vague, but their understanding was implicit; neither probed into the other's affairs. If you wanted advice, then one would ask it of the other. Otherwise, leave it alone. "You around this evening? I could use your help. I think we need to write Mr. Porter, the mill's owner, a letter. Need your thoughts on that, and then maybe you can help me with writing it, if you think it's a good idea."

"Sure. Happy to help."

Jeb and Alvin sat on the front steps of Jeb's cabin after supper. Jeb observed, "Ben didn't have much to say at supper tonight."

Alvin replied, "I think he's still mad at me. I think he sees himself as the appointed leader of the farmers and he's still peeved about my visit with the constable and the judge. I'm sure he thinks I was interfering more than helping him solve the problem."

"Naw, I think you may have that wrong. You know that meeting you missed a few weeks ago, the night it stormed?"

"Yep. That wasn't accidental, Jeb. I really didn't want anything to do with that."

"I know, but at that meeting Ben kind of put us—you and me—out there. He told the others that he was sorry you weren't there. Then he pointed to me. I was just standing in the back. He told everyone that he was counting on us to help him fix the problem. He told them that we weren't quitters. Just look at what we'd both gone through in the war, and that we'd help him come up with a plan to make sure the lumbermen stop flooding us out every year."

Alvin hung his head, "Well, that explains a lot."

"I probably should have told you about this before now. But I wasn't sure how it might all play out. Now that you've talked with the law, I guess we are in for a fight."

"Yeah well, don't worry over it." Alvin paused for a moment to collect his thoughts and then asked, "Do you have any idea how many of the farmers at that last meeting fought in the war?"

"Can't be sure, but I suspect a lot of them are vets. I didn't hang around too long after the shine started flowing. Almost everyone I talked to, though, were new to the area and new to farming now that Michigan has opened up homesteads to vets. None of the vets I saw at the meeting the other night carry the scars like you and me. To be honest, the ones I talked to, I think, look up to us because... well, because of what happened to us. Kind of a terrible way to get respect, but that seems to be what's happened."

Alvin reached over with his right arm and grasped the stump where his left arm should have been. Jeb walked with a terrible limp and some days Alvin knew it hurt him more than others, especially if it was wet or cold. He shrugged his shoulders and said, "Well, old friend, like it or not, seems like you and I are going to have to be the cooler heads that prevail."

"I've been thinking on it, and I agree that a letter to the mill's owner in Chicago is the right way to go. What's the worst that could happen?" Jeb paused for just a moment and then answered his own question, "He won't answer our letter. At least then we'll know where we stand on the injunction ever having any force."

"Help me write it?"

"Of course, but before we get too serious, tell me about your visit with Lydia. Are you going to see her again?"

Alvin smiled, "I am. We have plans to watch fireworks together on the 4th of July."

Smiling back, Jebediah said, "I heard you met her mother."

Alvin chuckled, "Ma tell you that?"

"She did."

"I've met both her aunt and her mother. I'll say this, the women in the Cockrum clan are very gracious."

More serious now, Jeb asked, "How about her father?"

Clapping him on the shoulder, Alvin said, "Now that, my friend, is another matter altogether. But it's not one I'm going to worry about at this point. Lydia and I enjoy one another's company, but she's got a plan for her life that's going to take at least the next four years to play out. She's going to college."

Jeb whistled.

"Yeah, so you see there's no need for me to really think of Lydia as any more than a friend right now, no matter how much I'd like to think of her as something more. So, I'm going to enjoy this summer and see her as often as she will allow."

"That's good, Alvin. I'm happy for you!"

Alvin smiled, then asked, "Are you ready to start that letter?"

Jeb paused. "Uh, yeah...but before we do that, there's something I want to tell you. And you're the first to know." Another pause and then Jeb disclosed, "I met someone."

"What?" *You rascal,* he thought. And then, Alvin added, "Jeb, that's great news. Tell me more."

"Well, I'd gone over to a farm on the other side of the lake to deliver a plow blade and a few other items I'd been asked to make. On the way back, I stopped at the mill store in Portage. There was a woman in there and, it turns out, my arrival was timely. She was going to have to put back some things she wanted to buy because she didn't have enough money, and the storekeeper wouldn't extend her credit. She had a baby with her, a boy, and I could see a lot of the things she was buying were for the child. I told the storekeeper to wrap up everything she wanted and then gave him another twenty dollars to put on an account for her."

"You are a good man, Jebediah Washington."

"Yeah well, that storekeeper took one look at me, and I could tell he was wondering how someone like me was going to have that kind of money. But when I laid the gold coins on the counter he got a lot nicer. I hate going in that store. They overcharge everyone that comes in there, including the millworkers. I heard they just take any money owed out of their pay at the end of the month without even asking, and that they charge an extra amount if they have to do that." Jeb shook his head and added, "It just doesn't seem right that they can meddle with a man's hard-earned money like that."

"Goes along with what I've heard. The mill's kind of a heavy-handed operation. But tell me about the woman you met."

"She's an Algonquin Indian from Quebec. Her name is Dancing Flower. The baby's father is a French-Canadian fur trapper, Claude DuBois. Ever heard of him?"

Alvin shook his head. "Can't say that I have."

"Yeah, me either, and I can honestly say, I hope I never meet him. He bought Dancing Flower from her father— making her father another person I hope I never meet." Alvin could only shake his head. Jeb shrugged and continued, "Anyway, DuBois brought her down here with him on a trapping trip, but when she got pregnant, he told her he didn't want anything to do with her or the baby and up and left them. She doesn't speak much English, only Algonquin and French. The Ottawa around here don't shun her, but they don't give her much help either. That may be because the baby is mixed blood. I don't know. So, she lives in a ramshackle old cabin about halfway between Portage and Bear Lake. She says the place doesn't really belong to her and she has no idea if it legally belongs to DuBois. It probably doesn't. She didn't say it, but I know she's afraid he'll show up there any time."

Alvin said, "She's in a tough spot."

Nodding, Jeb continued, "I asked if she'd allow me to help her get everything home. She was on foot and there was a lot to carry and the baby isn't of walking age. I was on one of the mules, so we loaded ol' Jasper and we walked to her cabin. I spent the night there." Jeb caught Alvin's expression and put up a hand, "But it's not what you think. The place needs a lot of repair and I got started on what I could. She fixed us dinner and I slept on the front porch."

Alvin asked, "So, you're going to see her again?"

"Absolutely. She's beautiful, and she said she hopes I'll come back. But I don't want you, Nellie, or Ben to worry. I'll take care of all my responsibilities around here, including doing what I can to help you with keeping the farmers in line and negotiating with the mill's owner. But in between chores I may be making myself a little scarce."

Alvin could easily sense his friend's joy. "If you need a hand helping to get her place in order, you know all you need to do is ask."

Jeb turned very serious at this point, "Thanks, but her place is pretty much falling down." Then he pointed to his cabin, "I could use some help in fixing this place up. It would be a better use of our time and money."

Alvin was somewhat stunned as he realized what Jeb was implying. He managed to ask, "You're that serious about her?"

Jeb smiled broadly at his friend and began to move toward the cabin's front door, "I am, Alvin. I'm not getting any younger, and that boy deserves to have a father while he's growing up."

If it were anyone other than Jeb, Alvin might have expressed some caution. But he knew this man as well as he knew himself. "I'm happy for you."

He cast a sheepish glance toward his friend. "Thanks, Alvin. Now, let's go take a crack at that letter."

They settled around the table in Jeb's cabin, but before they began to write their letter, Alvin asked, "Are you going to tell Ma and Pa about Dancing Flower?"

Jeb gave that some thought and then said, "Wanted to let you know first. You think they'll be all right with this?"

Alvin thought for a moment and then said, "I do. I think they'll be very happy for you, just like I am."

"I'll do that first thing in the morning then. After all, it does mean I'm adding two more mouths that need to be fed by this farm."

Alvin smiled, and in his most respectful tone, said, "Like I said, you're a good man, Jebediah Washington, and good men deserve to be happy. I think Ma and Pa will see it that same way."

CHAPTER ELEVEN

IT IS OFTEN THE UNEXPECTED THINGS IN LIFE THAT OFFER THE GREATEST PLEASURES

July 4, 1870

Anxious to see Lydia again, Alvin pulled away from the farm just after first light. It was a beautiful, cloudless morning and he snugged his straw hat low over his forehead to shield the sun from his eyes. He was wearing his old bib overalls over a short-sleeved shirt. It was the start of the dry season and the trail to Manistee would be dusty. Carefully folded in a canvas bag in the rear of the wagon, however, was his black three-piece suit, his good boots and the small wooden box containing his gold pocket watch. Again, he'd had a bit of a skirmish with his father over being gone with Amos and Tom for a couple of days, but again, with Nellie's help, they'd worked things out. He held the horses at a slow gait. There was no reason to rush. He was to meet Lydia at the same shady spot at Creeping Joe where they'd met the last time, but not until five o'clock this evening.

Alvin arrived at the camp site southeast of town on Lake Manistee that afternoon. It was the same spot he'd used the last time he'd come to town to see Judge Ramsdell and to meet Lydia. He pulled the horses and wagon well into the shade and carefully helped Kip down from the wagon's bed before preparing to take a bath. Alvin couldn't be sure how old Kip was when they'd found each other seven years ago, but he thought he might have been one or two at that time. If he was right, that would mean Kip was now eight or nine, and he could see his old friend was slowing down. A week or so ago, Kip had a run in with a wily old ram who'd managed to sneak up on his blind side and send the dog ass over tea kettle with a solid head butt, catching Kip squarely on his right hind hip. Nellie had spent a lot of time nursing him back to health and this is the first time he'd been out of her sight since the incident. Nellie's last words to Alvin as he'd left the farm were ones of caution. "Don't be lettin' him jump around too much. He can walk now. He's mendin' but you'll undo all the good I've done if you ain't careful."

The lake water over the last few weeks had warmed nicely in the summer heat. The two of them bathed, Alvin taking a much greater pleasure in the experience than Kip. When he was dressed, Alvin pulled the watch from his vest pocket. *4:00 p.m. Time to go.* Kip's silky coat had dried almost completely. As he sat next to his master on the wagon's seat, Alvin gave the dog several good strokes down his back to smooth his fur and said, "Well, I think we are both presentable enough to make a good impression." He rolled the reins gently over the horses' backs and steered toward River Street and Creeping Joe sand dune.

Alvin's plan called for another long walk on the beach, then perhaps a bite to eat. The evening's finale would be to watch the fireworks display from their spot at Creeping Joe. But there was a concern. It would be late when the fireworks were over and he would not be able to either drive or walk her home, since her father would likely be there. The two of them had not discussed her father very much, except to say Alvin was aware he was not in the man's good graces. So, exactly how Lydia would get home that late at night would be something the two of them would have to decide.

At the sand dune, he parked the wagon in the stand of trees where he and Lydia had enjoyed lunch the last time and walked back toward the Cedar Street hill. Kip was with him, but Alvin remembered how the dog had reacted the last time he'd met Lydia, and his mother's warning was still in his ear. This time Kip was leashed. The two were standing at the foot of the Cedar Street hill when Kip let out his first joyous bark. Alvin, who had momentarily been focused on his pocket watch and the time, looked up the hill and saw Lydia walking toward him, but she was accompanied by someone else, and as they came closer together, Alvin could see her companion was another man about his own age.

As they met, Lydia flashed a dazzling smile. Kip barked excitedly and Lydia knelt to greet the dog. "Hey, Kip. Good to see you ..." then, glancing up at Alvin, she added, "and you as well, sir!" She stood back up. "Alvin, I'd like you to meet Richard Fletcher."

His heart sank. *Oh, no. The pharmacist's son. Her father, his father... they must have...*

Fletcher extended his hand, "A pleasure to meet you, Alvin."

Alvin managed to stammer out, "Uh, yes, well, very nice to meet you, too, Richard."

Lydia turned to Fletcher. "Thanks so much, Richard. I'll meet you back here about eleven o'clock. Enjoy your evening."

Richard Fletcher doffed his hat to them both. "See you then."

As Fletcher walked away, Alvin could only stand there with a confused look on his face. *What just happened?*

Lydia stepped close to him, stood on her tiptoes and kissed his cheek. "Not to worry, Alvin. You're the one I'm looking forward to spending the evening with. But for that to happen, Richard and I had to work a little deception on our fathers."

Her delicate touch as her lips touched his cheek made his heart leap from its depth of depression to a soaring new height. He squeezed her hand in his and said, "I...I am so happy to see you. I'm not sure exactly what just happened, but I'm sure you'll explain it all to me." Kip yanked on his leash and let out a bark as he pulled toward the sand dune and Lake Michigan. "Care to walk with us on the beach?"

"I'd love to." She put her arm through his.

The fireworks had been spectacular from their vantage point on Creeping Joe. Kip had sheltered close to Lydia during the frenetic overhead lights and booms. Now that it was over, he'd returned to his old self as Alvin lifted him up into the back of the wagon. Lydia walked over to the dog, took his head in her hands and said, "You take it easy, Kip. I'll see you soon and I expect you'll be ready to chase some sticks into Lake Michigan by then."

Alvin issued an order to his dog. "Stay here, Kip. I'll be back soon."

Lydia said, "He is an amazing dog."

"He is, isn't he? He's been a really good friend to me."

She took his hand in hers and they headed back toward Cedar Street. But before they emerged from the edge of the shelter of the oaks, he stopped, turned to her and said, "I don't know where the time goes when I am with you. May I see you next Saturday?"

"I would be disappointed if it were longer. Let's meet at my aunt's shop. I'll fix dinner there for us."

"She knows..." He paused, then began again, "She knows you are seeing me?"

"She does, as does my mother."

"And they approve?"

"My mother and my aunt are, well..." she paused to choose her words. "I think I can best describe them as ahead of their time. They believe women should be able to vote, work, go to college, and decide who they step out with." She paused again then added, "They're both very independent-minded. I take after them. And they have both told me they are looking forward to getting to know you better."

From the bottom of the Cedar Street hill, Alvin could see Richard Fletcher approaching. He was not nearly ready to say goodbye to Lydia, but that time was just a few foot-steps away. They were still holding hands, and he pulled her closer to him. "Dinner with you next Saturday sounds just wonderful." Lydia looked up at him. Dropping her hand, Alvin put his right arm around her and pulled her into their first real kiss.

As Richard and Lydia walked up the Cedar Street hill, Alvin watched them. When Lydia turned and blew him a parting kiss, his heart leaped. If this is what love felt like, he was undeniably in it.

Kip stood on the wagon's seat when he saw Alvin approaching out of the darkness. He gently grumbled, his tail wagging furiously as his master climbed aboard. Alvin settled onto the seat next to him. Looking into the dog's eyes, he petted Kip's head. "I'm going to marry her some-day, Kip. You just wait and see."

Early morning, July 5, 1870

It had been a slow ride home on a comfortable summer, their trail lit by a full moon. Alvin took comfort from Kip's rhythmic breathing as he slept on the wagon's seat next to him, and he continued to revel in the memory of Lydia's kiss. First light was just breaking as he pulled to a stop in front of the barn on the Price farm. Amos and Tom stood very still as Alvin unhitched them. He was about to put

them up for a well-deserved rest, when he found a beautiful saddle horse in Tom's stall.

From behind him, Alvin heard Jeb say, "His name's
Valiant."

Startled, Alvin turned around. "Where? Who...who
does he belong to?"

"He's yours."

"No..."

"Yes. I wasn't expecting you until later today. I have
the things to build a small corral over there," Jeb said,
pointing to a small area of pasture just beyond the barn.
"Thought I'd get that done or at least a good start on it
before you got home. What are you doing here so early?
Everything go well with Lydia?"

"Yes, we had a wonderful time, but Jeb, I can't..."

"Yes, you can. One of these days Ben's going to start
winning the argument that you can't be gone all the time
with the wagon, Amos and Tom. Valiant here can get you
to town and back in half the time, and my guess is you will
want to be going to town a lot more than you have in the
past." He smiled. "Am I right?"

"You are exactly right," Alvin said. But then he let his
practical side creep into their conversation. "But how am I
going to afford to keep him?"

"Already taken care of, Alvin. His saddle's over there,"
Jeb said, pointing to a sawhorse with a fine leather saddle
laid over it. "His feed's paid for the next year. Got him
from the Geppersons, just two farms north. I've laid in
a good supply of feed for him and there's more growing
in the Gepperson's field right now. When the time comes,
they'll harvest it and deliver it here over the course of the
winter. In the meantime, we can decide where we might
want to plant some hay and oats next spring, so we don't
have to depend on anyone else for his upkeep."

He's thought of everything. How can you ever repay him?
"You shouldn't be spending your blacksmithing money on me. You've got Dancing Flower and Daniel to think about ... "

Jeb held up a hand. "Alvin, you let me worry about the money. I got some stashed away. It'll be fine. So, do you need to get some sleep, or do you want to get started on that corral?"

"The corral."

"Good. I'll stake Valiant under the maple out behind the barn while you put Amos and Tom up."

"Yep." Alvin took a moment and then added, "And maybe while we're working on the corral we can talk about the fixes you'd like to make to your cabin. Am I right in assuming you are still planning on Dancing Flower and Daniel moving in here?"

"Saw her yesterday on my way back with Valiant. I asked her ... " he paused. "Told her I'd sleep in the barn. She and Daniel can have the cabin. Told her it would be up to her if and when that was to change."

He's moving fast—but who am I to point that out—not any faster than Lydia and I are, I suppose, he thought. "What did she say to that?"

"Well, she didn't say no. But she didn't say yes either. If you don't mind, I'd like to take Valiant this evening and ride over to her cabin. She's fixing dinner for me and promised an answer."

"Yes, of course, he's *our* horse, not just mine," Alvin said.

Jeb headed into the barn to put a bridle on Valiant while Alvin turned to fetch one of the draft horses. As he grabbed Amos's bridle, Alvin shouted into the barn, "I hope she says yes, Jeb. I really do."

"Me, too," Jeb called back.

CHAPTER TWELVE

A REASONABLE APPROACH

Early evening, Monday, August 1, 1870

Ben Price stood in front of the barn door and stared at the ever-darkening western sky. "It's an omen, a bad omen," he said to Alvin and Jebediah standing beside him.

"Pa, you don't really believe in ..."

"I do, son. I do. Last time we met, it did this very same thing. Rained so hard that night some of 'em had to stay over. Slept right here in the barn."

Alvin chuckled, "Well, I wasn't here, but I heard about it from Ma. Not sure whether the sleeping over in the barn was caused by the bad weather, or the shine that seemed to flow quite freely that evening." That got another chuckle out of Jeb, but Ben just glowered at the two of them.

The other farmers started arriving at the Price Farm just as the sun was setting. Alvin and Jeb had gone to the trouble of setting up the barn so that it looked more like a meeting place. They'd first tried to use some of the chairs from around the dinner table, but Nellie put a stop to that. "No, you ain't gonna take my chairs out to the barn for them farmers to sit on with their dirty britches!" Instead, they used some tree stumps and planks to set up two rows of seats. If they had as many participants as the last time, it wouldn't be enough. Latecomers would just have to stand. In front of the first row, they'd set up a platform that would elevate the speaker a foot or so above the barn floor. It was their intention to keep things orderly, at least until they'd accomplished what they hoped. Jeb, who'd been around for the last meeting, said to Alvin, "Looks more like a meeting hall. I don't think we'll regret setting it up this way. Makes it more official-looking."

By the time twenty or so other farmers had arrived, the first flash of lightning and bang of thunder drove everyone into the barn. Alvin and Jeb told Ben they wanted him to start things off.

"All right," Ben said loudly and then banged an old hammer against a metal pot that once graced Nellie's kitchen, but now had become a seldom-used container for various things of all sorts in the barn. "All right," he repeated louder and banged the pot a few more times. "Let's get started. We've got some things to discuss this evenin'. Don't know what this storm's gonna do, but any-one's welcome to stay the night if need be." Then he smiled and said, "Especially if you got a jug of shine with you." That comment brought a loud round of applause from the assembled group. Ben held up a hand, "But I promised my two boys here, Alvin and Jeb, that we'd hold off on that stuff 'til they were finished. So, I'm gonna turn things over to them. You all pay attention now. They been doin' some checkin' and I want all of us to understand exactly where we are with the lumbermen before the night's over."

Jeb began by asking the group how many had read the complete writ issued against the Porter Sawmill. Not a single hand went up, so he took a couple of minutes to read it to them. He asked if there were any questions, and one farmer offered a comment. "Sounds to me like we won. Seven months ... well, I guess that explains why there ain't nothin' happenin' this summer, but sure sounds like the mill better not dam that creek up next spring."

At this point Jeb turned the meeting over to Alvin who told the group about his meeting with the constable and with Judge Ramsdell. By the time he got around to the part about the injunction having never been served and why, the grumbling had already begun.

Alvin and Jeb told Ben this would happen and when it did, Ben stepped up to the podium. "I hear you. Knew you wouldn't be happy 'bout any of this but hear these boys out. They got a plan."

Alvin explained, "Jebediah and I have written a letter to Mr. Lee Porter, the mill's owner. We think it's a good step, the right step to take at this time." He read the letter to the group.

One farmer shouted, "We need something to guarantee that Porter is gonna live up to the letter of the law." The name *Porter* came out as a snarl.

Alvin said, "There are no guarantees, but the letter spells out our expectation that he'll stop the damming."

"Or what?" asked the same farmer.

"That's something that we can discuss if Mr. Porter ignores our letter. Until then, Jeb and I think this is pretty fair warning that we expect him to comply with the law." There was some sparse applause which Ben, Alvin, and Jeb took as a good sign.

But as the applause died down, Phillip Maue, another farmer, had something to say. "I work at that mill when it's operatin' in the summer. Got to. It's my family's only source of cash. God knows we ain't makin' anythin' off the land except what we need to survive. But, Jebediah, you know," he said pointing to him, "I need that cash to pay for your blacksmithin'." Several of the farmers murmured their agreement. "I ain't the only one that depends on that work at the mill to pay for the things we can't raise on our land."

Another farmer asked, "What you sayin', Phillip? You sayin' it's all right for them lumbermen to dam up that creek and steal our land?"

"Naw. Ain't sayin' that at all. That mill's a dangerous

place to work. It's old and that Muley saw ..." Maue shook his head, "Saw somethin' there the other day that didn't need to happen. If ol' man Porter would convert that mill to steam, it never would have happened. All the other mills 'round here have changed over. That'd be good for everyone ... "

Jeb listened intently to Maue. He knew the man was a veteran of the war just like he and Alvin. Maue, relatively new to the area, was only a couple of years into his homestead, and Jeb had, in fact, done some blacksmithing for him, some of which he was still owed for. When the farmer had said his piece, Jeb said to Alvin, "I need to change our letter. Keep them occupied and give me an hour or so. I'm going to take Phillip with me. He's got some experience and knowledge you and I lack. I'll be back."

Ben asked, "What you expect us to do with these men for an hour?"

Jeb smiled at him, "Tell them me and Maue went to make the letter better. Tell them to wait for us. We won't be more than an hour." Then he clapped Alvin on the back, "But you have to keep them out of the shine until we get back."

Just over an hour later, Jeb returned and read the letter aloud to everyone.

August 1, 1870
Mr. Lee Porter
Porter and Company
Chicago, Illinois

Dear Mr. Porter,

The undersigned individuals represent a consortium of farmers owning land adjoining Portage Lake in Manistee County, Michigan. Said land is adversely affected by the dam erected by your company over Portage Creek. This letter is written as an appeal in which we request your voluntary compliance with the judgement issued against your company and said dam by the Manistee

County Circuit Court. May we suggest that you do so either by returning to Michigan and signing the writ the Portage Constabulary is prepared to serve upon you, or by advising this consortium in writing that your company will no longer dam Portage Creek, effective spring, 1871.

May we present our reasons for this appeal to your better nature:

This country, especially after its reunification following the Civil War, is a nation of laws, first and foremost, and the Circuit Court has issued a writ against your company prohibiting the damming of Portage Creek.

The dam causes Portage Lake to rise thus costing the undersigned hundreds of acres of otherwise tillable land.

In the spring, as the mill begins to use the risen waters to drive the mill, the subsequent drainage leaves pockets of water that stagnate, causing insect infestations and resultant disease to local residents.

May we further take the liberty to suggest to you that the undersigned would have no objection to the operation of your sawmill if you were to take the initiative to convert the mill to a steam-powered sawmill rather than its current water-driven muley saw configuration. Our reasons for this suggestion are:

Steam-powered mills, while they require water for their operation, do not require water as the driving force of the mill's machinery. Thus, without the necessity of damming Portage Creek, your company would be most welcome to use the water of Portage Lake at its natural level.

Steam-powered mills are much safer for workers. We are aware one of your workers at Porter's Mill recently lost a hand after becoming trapped between a large log and the tray feeding the log to the saw blade. Because of the force of water driving the tray, and that the muley saw cannot be brought to a halt in a timely manner, the worker was dragged kicking and screaming into the saw's blade. This unfortunate accident could have easily been prevented had the mill been steam-powered. Steam, the modern *mill's driving force, as you know, can be turned off by a single worker operating a single valve in a matter of just a few seconds.*

We look forward to your response to our appeal to your fair-mindedness.

Respectfully,

Benjamin A. Price Alvin B. Price Jebediah Washington
August Zosel Christian Smith Henry Fowler
Gottlieb Schimke John Carey John Gordon
Stephen Jones Carl Brandt Henry Brandt
Rudolph Brandt Fred Schultz John Bond
Billie Scott Asa Patch John Bradford
Levi Sherman William Kline Phillip Maue
John Porter Charles Schroeder

The next afternoon Alvin walked into the mill store in Portage, which was also a designated U.S. Post Office. Of concern to him was first, the address on the envelope that carried the farmers' letter, and second, he suspected the integrity of the postmaster, who was also the mill's supervisor. Alvin held out the envelope with the address side up, "Is this address sufficient to get this correspondence to Mr. Lee Porter in Chicago?"

The man took the envelope from him, read the address, and said, "Yeah, s'pose so."

Not at all sure he'd gotten a straight answer, Alvin asked, "Don't suppose you'd know if Mr. Porter was planning a visit to Portage anytime soon? Say before next spring?"

The man harrumphed. "Now why would he want to do that?" He turned his back to Alvin and began sorting a stack of mail, then said, "That'll be a nickel's postage."

Alvin plunked a coin down on the counter. "How long will it take for Mr. Porter to get this?"

"Gotta go up to Traverse City. Ol' Indian Joe'll carry it that far. Then it'll be mixed in with a lot of other mail for Chicago. After that, it's gotta wait for a spot on one of the ships headed that way. Dunno for sure, but probably two weeks after it arrives in Chicago, it'll get to Mr. Porter. Overall, about a month, maybe month and a half. Then when Mr. Porter sees who it's from, not sure how long he might take to read it."

He didn't trust this man. *That's if you don't throw it in the trash after I've left here,* Alvin thought. He was not easily angered, but the supervisor's attitude infuriated him. "I've paid you the rate to make sure this gets in the mail. You best do your job and see to it that this letter gets out." He turned on his heel and stomped out of the store.

CHAPTER THIRTEEN

RUMORS AND LEADERS

Saturday evening, August 13, 1870

The summer was fast coming to a close. Richard Fletcher, Lydia's accomplice in the deception of both of their fathers, was scheduled to leave for Ann Arbor next Monday, but before he left, Alvin decided it would be good for everyone to get together. He was anxious for Lydia to meet Jeb and Dancing Flower who was now living in Jeb's cabin. Under Nellie's watchful eye, Jeb had moved into the barn, but everyone at the Price farm had seen a transformation in Nellie since the new arrivals. Nellie was overjoyed when they'd asked her to keep an eye on Daniel for the evening. She'd never once considered blood to be a factor. Nellie considered that little boy to be, for the moment, at least, her only grandchild. Alvin also wanted to gather as a way of thanking Richard for taking a look at his amputation. Richard had been honest. He told Alvin that the state of the art of prosthetics was lacking in his case since the arm was gone above the elbow joint. But he'd promised to let him know if and when something might be developed that could help him.

The Lake House restaurant sat on the edge of Lake Manistee, on the northwest fringe of town. It was a popular place, somewhat expensive, and Lydia had used her influence to reserve a private room for the evening. Keeping their deception alive, Richard had rented a horse and buggy for the evening and picked Lydia up at her home to the delight of Lydia's father. As he pulled the rented horse and buggy to a stop in front of the restaurant, Lydia pointed to a wagon hitched to two sturdy draft horses. A black saddle horse was tied to the wagon. "Oh, good! They're already here," she exclaimed.

A young woman led Richard and Lydia through to a room at the back of the restaurant, which was busy, but not full. Along the way, they kept a sharp eye out for people they knew. Appearances were important among Manistee's more prominent families and Lydia and Richard wanted to preserve the idea that they were together. Their deception, for the moment, had eased the pressure coming from both of their fathers. Alvin graciously made introductions and they settled into an easy evening in which good food and friendship abounded. Lydia developed an immediate affection for both Jeb and Dancing Flower, and had told Alvin so as he'd ridden with her and Richard to the bottom of the Cedar Street hill where Richard gave Lydia and Alvin a few minutes of privacy.

Sunday, August 14, 1870

Lydia and Richard had sat next to one another at church accompanied by each of their parents. In his efforts to keep pushing them together, Reilly Cockrum suggested that Richard walk Lydia home from church, but he'd declined coming up with some quick excuse. Now, Lydia stood on the fitting platform in the sewing room wearing the winter coat she and her mother had worked on for the past several months. Their discussion had been deeply serious, and Irene Cockrum was trying to organize her thoughts before offering the advice Lydia had asked of her. She flitted around her daughter, pulling a little here, pushing a little there, pinning just a few places. This was the coat's final fitting. When she was finished and Lydia was stepping down, Irene said, "Don't you think you are moving too fast with Alvin? College has been your dream since you were a little girl. It sounds too much to me like you are questioning your own wisdom." Lydia carefully slipped the coat off and placed it on the sewing table. Irene said, "He's a fine man. Liliane and I both like him, but we'd like more time to get to know him, more time to get to know his family. That's the way it should be."

"Was it that way with you and Father?"

"It was. He courted me for over a year before asking me to marry him."

"Yes, but how can Alvin court me when he will be here and I will be in East Lansing?"

"That's not a question I can answer. That's something that you and Alvin are going to have to work out between the two of you. So, I'm just going to be very blunt about this. You cannot—you should not give up your dream of going to college for Alvin Price or for anybody else at this point in your young life." There was so much more she wanted to say, but she didn't. This was not like the point she'd been at in in her life twenty years ago; Irene had not been accepted into any college, nor had she even applied. Twenty years ago, college for women was virtually out of the question. But things were changing, and for the first time, well-recognized state colleges and universities were accepting women, and her daughter was to be one of those early pioneers. She'd heard there was even a college exclusively for women opening its doors in Massachusetts, Wellesley College.

Lydia slumped into a chair in the corner of the room. "Four years is such a long time."

Irene said, "If he loves you, he'll wait. What do you think he'd say if he knew you're even thinking about not going to college because you think you are in love with him? Have you asked him?"

"Is that a fair question for me to ask, Mother?"

Irene looked her straight in the eye and said, "Lydia, it is a very fair question. Don't wait until it's too late—after you've given up on your dream, after you've brought children into this world."

The rest of Sunday and half of Monday passed with Lydia pondering her mother's advice. It was a gorgeous summer day, hardly a cloud in the azure blue sky. A breeze off Lake Michigan quelled the day's high humidity somewhat. Lydia walked down River Street rather aimlessly, lost in her thoughts. She stopped at the entrance to Manistee General Mercantile. *A piece of hard rock candy would taste good,* she thought. Stepping inside, she immediately noticed the stultifying heat of the store's interior, undoubtedly made worse by the radiant heat emanating from the tin ceiling above her head. As a courtesy to shoppers, the owner had placed some folded-paper fans on one of the counters, just inside the door. These were meant to be used by shoppers only while in the mercantile. Lydia knew that. Phineas Gutkowski, the store's owner, never missed an opportunity to advertise. When the fans were opened, lettering read, "WE KNOW IT'S HOT. COOL YOURSELF WITH THIS." Then in smaller letters across the bottom of the fan, "Property of Manistee General Mercantile. Do not remove from store." Waving it briskly in front of her face, she made her way over to the candy counter. As she looked over the varieties, she couldn't help but overhear the conversation between Gutkowski, whom she knew, and another man, whom she did not.

Gutkowski asked the other man, "So what's happening with you farmers?"

"Don't exactly know, to tell the truth. We're just waitin'. Got some faith in Alvin Price and Jebediah Washington.

Both them boys is vets, ya know, shot up pretty good in the war."

Gutkowski nodded, "Know 'em both. They trade here regular. Been knowin' Alvin since he was a little boy. Heard tell, Jeb's a freedman, come back to the states from Canada to fight against the Confederacy and slavery. Didn't have to do that, I guess, but shows me some gumption, for sure."

The farmer replied, "Didn't know his roots, but I do know the man can read and write. Jeb and Alvin wrote a letter to ol' man Porter in Chicago on behalf of us farmers around Portage Lake. We're askin' him to do the right thing; comply with the law and stop dammin' Portage Creek."

Gutkowski asked, "Yeah well, what's the plan when he doesn't?"

The farmer shrugged and replied, "Alvin and Jeb says we just have to wait and see. I trust 'em both. Besides, can't do a damn thing 'til next spring anyways. Might just as well put my faith in them two boys as worry my fool head off about it."

Gutkowski lowered his voice slightly, "Heard ol' Jeb got hisself a squaw livin' with him now. Heard she's got a baby." He let out a lecherous chuckle, "Guess Jeb's tired of livin' like a monk out there on the Price farm."

Lydia had heard every word, despite Gutkowski's poor effort at discretion. Her mood was dark to begin with and now she'd heard enough. She stopped fanning herself and closed the distance between them. Nodding in Gutkowski's direction, she greeted him, "Mr. Gutkowski."

Somewhat embarrassed, Phineas Gutkowski managed, "Miss Lydia, how are you today?"

Ignoring his question, she went right to it. Looking back and forth between the two men, she began, "Couldn't help but overhear your conversation. First of all, Dancing Flower isn't a squaw, she's a woman, a human being. More important, she's a good mother to her son. You should know that." Then she turned her attention to the farmer. "And you, sir," Lydia extended her hand and said, "I'm Lydia Cockrum." She could see her boldness was unexpected. "And you are?"

Surprised, the farmer managed to stammer out, "Asa Patch. Uh...pleased to meet you, miss."

"Likewise, Mr. Patch. I'd take it as a true favor if you wouldn't spread any rumors about Dancing Flower and Jeb. For the time being, he's sleeping in the Price barn and she's occupying Jeb's cabin with her young son."

Patch glanced over at Gutkowski and then back to Lydia, "We didn't mean to offend."

She looked Asa Patch squarely in the eye and said, "Well, you did, sir. Alvin Price is a gentleman friend of mine." Immediately she read more surprise in Patch's eyes. *You can't believe that Alvin and I are friends, can you?* Lydia's anger went up a notch and that inspired her to add, "...a very special gentleman friend of mine." With that, she bid both men good day and headed for the door.

After taking a few steps down the street, she realized she still had the mercantile's fan in her hand. *Not taking it back.* She neither regretted taking the fan nor standing up for Dancing Flower, Jeb, Alvin and the Price family in general. *Those two wouldn't know a rumor from the truth and could care less about spreading a lie.* In her soul she felt good about what she'd just done—all of it.

After Lydia left the two men standing there in the mercantile, Asa Patch turned to Phineas Gutkowski and said, "Well, now, don't that beat all. How's Alvin Price know someone like that?"

"Dunno," Gutkowski said. "Lydia's in here a couple of times a week. She's from good stock. Family's got a nice place up the hill at Cedar Street. Her father builds railroads."

Asa Patch thought for a minute and said, "Then he's in cahoots with them lumbermen."

"Yeah, I suppose so. Funny thing is, though, Herb Fletcher was in here the other day braggin' about his boy, Richard, who's gonna be a doctor soon or some such thing. Told me his boy is seeing Reilly Cockrum's daughter. Don't know what to make of it. Guess, I'll ask Herb about it next time he's in."

CHAPTER FOURTEEN

TIME TO SAY GOODBYE

Wednesday, August 17, 1870

The anger in Reilly Cockrum's voice betrayed his anger and frustration. "You knew about this? You were part of her deception?"

Irene Cockrum stood at the kitchen table focused on the bread dough she was kneading. She was expecting this tirade. Yet she was surprised at the efficiency of Manistee's network of gossip. Lydia had told her about her conversation at the mercantile with Phineas Gutkowski and Asa Patch. Without looking up, she said, "I did, and I was."

He was not prepared for her blunt, unremorseful honesty. "You can't be all right with this ... this person she's seeing. He's a farmer, Irene." Reilly waved his hand around the room overdramatically, "Lydia has no idea what she's getting into. Look at everything she has. Do you think she'd have any of this if she were to marry a farmer?"

If he could be infuriating, so could she. Irene stopped kneading, stood up straight, and looked him in the eye. "Listen to you, Reilly Cockrum. Aren't you the privileged one? Aren't you the one to be judging how another man earns an honest living?" She gave that a moment as she watched him just stand there, unapologetic. She continued, "What do you know about Alvin Price other than he's a farmer? Do you even know what he looks like? Do you know he lost an arm in the war?" She saved her best salvo for last, "Do you know that right now I'd consider him a much more honorable man than your privileged self, Reilly?" She watched him turn to leave the room, but she was not about to let him off the hook so easily. Following him, she scolded, "All these Sundays spent at church and you are willing to dismiss another man simply because he's a farmer. You should be ashamed of yourself."

"Herb Fletcher—"

She interrupted him, crossed her arms over her chest, and said, "Ah yes, Herb, your accomplice in the scheme to marry your daughter off to Richard."

Ignoring her, he continued, "Phineas Gutowski at the mercantile told Herb Fletcher Alvin Price is leading the farmers in their efforts to close down the sawmill on Portage Creek. That will not be good for lumber, Irene, not good at all."

"And did Mr. Gutowski or Mr. Fletcher, either of them, inform you that these farmers have a legal writ in their favor prohibiting the damming of that creek because it floods the farmers' land and causes disease?"

Dripping with sarcasm, Reilly said, "You seem to be well informed."

"Lydia has told me of the problems at Portage Lake and the farms that surround it."

His face reddened. Reilly took a deep breath, then went off on another tangent. "The more important issue here is what are we going to do about Lydia and this Price fellow? She's much too young ..."

Her hand shot up in his face and her voice took on an uncharacteristic shrillness as she posed a question, "She's too young to be seeing a farmer who just happens to be the same age as Richard Fletcher, but not too young to be considered by you and Herb to marry Richard? Honestly, Reilly, listen to yourself!"

"I forbid her to see Price."

Irene dropped her hands to her side but stood ramrod straight in front of him shaking her head. "In that case, Reilly, you will be on your own until Lydia leaves for college." This time it was Irene who left the room.

Saturday, August 20, 1870

The last week had been excruciatingly long for Lydia. She endeavored every way she knew to avoid her father, but every time he saw her, he harangued her about both her deception and the man she wanted to keep company with. And though she found some sympathy from her mother, Irene was always careful to point out that being too serious about Alvin was not advisable with her departure for East Lansing and college just around the corner. Without saying goodbye to either of her parents, she left the house an hour early for her five o'clock meeting with Alvin. She was waiting on him at their meeting spot on Creeping Joe sand dune as he pulled the wagon to a halt under the trees. Kip had begun barking as soon as he saw her. Alvin had no sooner stopped than the dog jumped off the wagon and rushed to her. Lydia bent down to nuzzle him, then standing back up, she fell into Alvin's embrace as soon as he caught up to them. She held him tight and sobbed into his chest.

"What is it, Lydia?" he asked. "What's the matter?"

"Take me away from here, Alvin."

"Of course. Tell me where? We'll go there."

"Take me to the place out of town where you said you camp, the place on Lake Manistee."

Pointing to the west, he said, "There's a storm coming. That's a ways out of town. I don't want you to ..."

Lydia shook her head, "I don't care. I just need to get away for a while with you ... and Kip. Please let's go there."

As they rolled down River Street toward Lake Manistee and then turned slightly southeast heading out of town, she told him of the past week's events.

Alvin was quiet as he stared at the trail ahead of them. When he did speak, he was calm, sincere, "Lydia, it would be unfair of me to be angry with your father. I haven't met him." He smiled at her. "Perhaps, if I were the father of someone like you, I would be like him. What truly is upsetting to me is that I am the cause of such a rift in your family."

She reached over and put her hand on his arm, "Don't be upset. It has been a long time coming. Father has forever had a certain expectation of what my life will be. It's been only these past few years I have realized his expectations and mine are at odds with one another."

There was still a lot of daylight remaining as they reached his camping spot. Unhitching Amos and Tom, Alvin led them to a nearby stand of trees and tethered them loosely so they could graze on the lush grass that grew along the edge of the tree line. Then he suggested a walk along the lake's shore. It wasn't like their walks along the beach at Lake Michigan. This was more of a walk through the woods, down a narrow trail that necessitated at some places they had to walk single file rather than side-by-side where they could hold hands. Kip accompanied them, of course. Lydia tossed sticks into the lake for him to fetch as breaks in the woods between their path and the water's edge permitted. For the hour or so they were gone, her tensions melted away like the day's fading sunlight.

By the time they returned to their camp, a light rain had begun to fall. "Should we get you home?" Alvin asked.

"No."

"But it's going to start raining harder..."

"I don't care. I don't want to go home just yet."

"Okay, but we're going to need some shelter."

She watched him pull the canvas rolls from the wagon and

followed his instructions as she helped him cover it. When it was done, the three of them crawled under the wagon. As Alvin fed Kip, she said to him, "This is perfect."

"It is nice, isn't it?" Alvin said. Just then a loud crack of thunder spoiled the serenity of their cozy place. Kip pinned his ears back. Alvin pointed skyward, "But it's going to come up a pretty good blow, is my guess. We're going to be stuck here until it's passed us." Alvin felt compelled to ask, "Are you all right with that? Do you think it wise that ... ?" He struggled at tactfulness. "Does your mother know ... does she know about this?"

Lydia nodded. "She knows I'm with you. So does Father for that matter. There's no more hiding the fact that I'm seeing you. Those days are over. Richard's the lucky one. He doesn't have to be here to face his father's ire, although I'm sure a scathing letter is headed his way. Mother's concerned I might do something rash. So is Aunt Liliane. Both have given me talks about what I should and shouldn't do."

He offered her a piece of jerky which she accepted with a look that spoke of both interest and trepidation. She bit off a piece, chewed it for a moment and said, "It's good, Alvin."

"Straight from the farm. It takes some getting used to, but it's really nourishing." Pausing, he smiled at her, "And the stuff never goes bad." He pulled out a jar of honey. "Dip it in this before you try your next bite."

"You have bees too?"

"Not me. Ma raises them and she won't let me, Jeb or Pa anywhere near the hives. She says we scare the bees," he told her as he dipped a piece of the jerky in the jar and tossed it to Kip who caught it in midair. Lydia squealed with delight.

By the time they'd eaten their fill, darkness was setting in, sped up by the storm still raging over their heads. Alvin retrieved a candle from a sack and lit it.

Lydia's voice was low with a huskiness that surprised

even her a bit. "Lie down with me, Alvin. Hold me. There's something I want to ask you."

He took a blanket from a canvas sack and pulled it up over them, then rolled up another one to make a perfect pillow for them. Lydia spooned next to him as Kip, lying on top of the blanket, took up his spot in the crook of Lydia's belly. Alvin lifted his head sufficiently to peer at his dog over Lydia's shoulder. "He doesn't even know I exist when you are around."

She pulled an arm from under the blanket and put it around Kip who gave out a long sigh.

"See what I mean," he said. She chuckled.

Her voice still low and husky, she asked the question that had been on her mind all week long. "Alvin ... will you ..." She paused, pondering for a moment exactly how she should phrase it. "Will you wait for me?"

Without hesitation he replied, "No matter how long you might be gone from me, the one thing you can always count on is that I will be here when you come back."

"I will miss you so. I've thought about not going away. Mother and Aunt Liliane have told me whatever I decide, it must be my decision. I've thought about little else." Another pause, and then, "I've decided I have to go to college. It's something I've planned on for so long. If I don't go and see for myself, I think it would be something I'd regret for the rest of my life."

He whispered into her ear, "I will always be here. You have things you must do with your life. I have things I must do with mine. These are things we can't turn our backs on. If it means we must be apart for a while, then that is the price we must pay for these things of importance to each of us. I believe you will come back to me. I know I will be right here waiting for you. So instead of dwelling on this challenge to our future, why don't we talk about our lives together after you've gone to college and the Price farm has begun to thrive."

She said nothing. Instead she pulled his right arm over her and snugged his hand against her chest.

Alvin awoke with a start. Under the wagon it was pitch black, the single candle long since burned out. Next to him he could feel Lydia's rhythmic breathing. Reaching over, he felt Kip curled next to her. *Oh my God! What time is it?* He didn't have his pocket watch with him and even if he had, he wouldn't have been able to see the time. He listened for the rain, but it had apparently stopped. Gently, he awoke Lydia. "We have to go. We must have fallen asleep. Your parents must be worried sick. How will you ever be allowed ... how can I explain this to them?"

Lydia, still groggy from sleep, pulled him close to her, kissed him deeply and said, "No more deceptions. We'll just tell them the truth. We fell asleep."

Alvin, stunned by her calmness, said, "Maybe your mother and your aunt will believe that, but your father ... "

Together they rolled up the canvas tarps and boarded the wagon. Lydia had a key to her aunt's millinery shop. Their plan was to start with Liliane by explaining to her what had just happened. Lydia would spend the remainder of the night with her aunt and then undertake explaining to her parents tomorrow. All of it made Alvin quite uncomfortable.

Saturday, August 28, 1870

A long week had passed since Alvin had left Lydia at her Aunt Liliane's millinery shop somewhere around midnight on August 21. This morning, mounted on Valiant, he'd left the Price farm just after dawn. As he reached the Maple Street bridge over the Manistee River he checked his pocket watch. *10:00 a.m.* Lydia's stagecoach was scheduled to depart Manistee for Muskegon at eleven on the first leg of her trip to East Lansing. Liliane would accompany her niece on the three-day trip downstate. Alvin had been very glad to hear that Lydia would not have to make this trip, at least for this first time, by herself. He tied Valiant to a hitching post just east of the millinery shop and walked the short distance back to it. Lydia was not there, but at the front door; Alvin could see her packed bags. Inside the shop, Liliane greeted him and told him Lydia would be back shortly, that she'd just walked home to pick up something she'd forgotten.

Feeling like he owed her an apology, somewhat sheepishly, Alvin said, "Liliane, I'm very sorry for keeping Lydia out so late last Saturday."

"It did cause a stir," Liliane replied. "Reilly is still quite angry with the both of you."

"Can't say that I blame him."

"Yes, well, if it helps at all, I'm glad you just didn't try and act as if it didn't happen. Your apology is accepted."

"How about Mrs. Cockrum? Can she ever forgive me?"

"I think she has. I know she's forgiven Lydia for the misstep. But, just a suggestion, if the opportunity presents itself, I'd suggest you apologize to Irene just as you have to me." She paused and then added, "However, if you should happen to encounter Reilly don't expect your apology to go very far. He is dead set against the two of you seeing each other."

"Thanks for the advice and the warning."

Behind him he heard the shop's door open and Lydia stepped in. She glanced at her aunt and then made a dash for Alvin. Throwing her arms around him, she said, "I'm so glad you made it. I wasn't sure ..."

"Nothing could have kept me away."

"I ... I will miss you desperately ..."

"And I, you."

"It's all so complicated."

"It is and it isn't. I will think about you every hour of every day. Yet I know this is what you were meant to do."

From the stairway leading to the second floor apartment where Liliane lived, Irene appeared. "Hello, Alvin. Good to see you again. Glad you could come to see Lydia off."

"Mrs. Cockrum..."

"So, it's Mrs. Cockrum now is it? What happened to Irene?"

His sheepishness returning, "I wasn't so sure you'd ever want to speak to me again."

Irene looked first at Liliane and then to Lydia before coming back to him. "Lydia tells me nothing happened. What do you say?"

"I...I...we fell asleep. As soon as I woke up..."

She waved a hand in his direction, "Then I believe the both of you. But that is not to say that I approve of what happened."

"No...neither do I, Mrs. Cock...uh...uh, Irene. It won't happen again. I can assure you of that."

The stagecoach pulled to a stop in front of the shop and the driver hopped down. Irene said, "Ladies, the stage is here. Let's get your things loaded." Liliane and Irene supervised the loading, leaving Lydia and Alvin alone to say one final goodbye.

Alvin asked, "Your father's not coming to see you off?"

She shook her head. "I said my goodbyes to him just now at home. He asked if you were going to be here. When I said you were, he refused to walk down with me."

"Lydia, I'm so sorry. I shouldn't have..."

She interrupted him. "Alvin, this isn't just about last Saturday night. Oh, he is furious about that. But what really bothers him is that I refuse to stop seeing you." She kissed him and when the kiss was over, she said, "As long as he remains stubborn about that, he and I will have a fractured relationship."

Irene called, "Lydia, they're ready to go."

"I will miss you, Alvin."

"I will see you at Christmas."

Irene and Alvin stood in front of the millinery shop and watched the stage roll east down River Street, heading out of town.

CHAPTER FIFTEEN

LIFE ON THE FARM GETS HARDER IN THE FALL... AND THEN THERE'S WINTER

September 12, 1870

Two weeks had passed since Alvin had seen Lydia off to college. This morning at first light, Alvin, Jeb and Ben had gotten an early start on their chores. Jeb sat in the middle of the wagon's seat holding the reins. Ben and Alvin were squeezed in on either side of him. The rear of the wagon was stacked with orchard crates eight high and tied down with multiple ropes from front to back and side to side. The Price farm was hard work every day, but this time of the year, the fall, the hard work had a deadline. Things had to get done before the harsh northern Michigan winter weather set in. There were a variety of crops to be harvested, including oats, hay, and corn. Amos and Tom, the two draft horses, were prodigious eaters by themselves, but then there were the two mules, six hogs, six sheep, two dairy cows, and two head of beef cattle. All of their feed needed to be laid up. Valiant's feed, at least for this upcoming winter, was part of his sale price and would be delivered each month by the farmer Jeb had bought him from. The focus today, however, was the apple harvest, important for a reason other than subsistence; these apples were worth cash to the Price farm.

Today was just the beginning. Next week, half a dozen Native American men, whom Jeb and Dancing Flower were able to find, would arrive at the farm to commence the picking. They would sleep in the barn at night. Nellie and Dancing Flower would provide breakfast, lunch and dinner to them, and they would be paid one dollar a day for at least twelve hours work each day. Ben would supervise the pickers, and each of them had been warned that work would commence just after first light each day come rain or shine. The picking of the apples, however, was just the first step. They'd have to get to market. The plan was for Alvin and Jeb to load the filled orchard crates on the wagon and take them to town where they had contracted with three different cider mills to provide each with five hundred crates of fresh picked apples. Seven other merchants in town had contracted with them for ten crates of apples each, which they would sell as fresh produce over their counters. For all of this effort, the Price family calculated they would be paid seven hundred fifty dollars which would make this year's apple harvest their first cash crop in twelve years of farming their homestead.

The orchard crates had been last year's winter project for Alvin and Jeb. They'd bartered some fresh steaks, pork, eggs, and chicken for some time on the muley saw at the Portage Creek sawmill last fall, just before the mill ceased operation for the winter. The mill supervisor had thrown the logs in for free. There weren't a lot of them left; it had been a productive season for the mill. By the spring, when Portage Lake thawed out and the mill opened up again, he wanted these last few remaining logs gone to make way for new logs cut during the previous winter. Jeb and Alvin took the supervisor's generosity as a sign that the mill was planning for next spring to be business as usual and that gave both of them some second thoughts about using the mill. After all, there was a legal injunction against it. It was their enemy, so to speak. But they'd heard of a dozen other farmers who'd used the mill for various projects on their farms and decided it was much easier than trying to cut the logs into boards by hand. They allowed necessity and convenience to placate their consciences. It had taken them less than a week at the mill to cut and transport to the farm enough board feet of pine to make what they thought would be about a thousand durable, reusable orchard crates, each one about four feet long, two feet wide and eighteen inches deep.

Jeb, working sometimes through the night last winter, had fabricated nearly ten thousand strong metal fasteners to attach at each corner of each box, one at the bottom and one at the top, eight fasteners per orchard crate. He'd gotten so efficient at making them he could hammer one out about every two or three minutes or so. The screws they'd needed for assembly were bought with money Jeb had made from blacksmithing. Just a few weeks ago, the last crate had been put together and added to the ones now stacked neatly outside, against the barn's back wall.

As they approached the orchard, Ben said, "Just look at them trees, boys. Their branches are just loaded with apples. If we don't get some of that weight off, they's gonna snap for sure." That gave them a further sense of urgency to get things ready for the pickers. One of them would drive the wagon down the strip of land between two rows of apple trees. The other two walked behind the wagon, pulling an orchard crate off the wagon about every twenty feet or so and placing it on the ground on alternating sides of the path.

Today, they'd also get a start, small as it might be, on the picking. One would stay in the orchard and pick, while the other two would return to the area behind the barn where the empty orchard crates were stacked, reload the wagon and return to the orchard. It wasn't a lot of picking, but it kept every available hand engaged. It was Alvin who preferred to stay in the orchard and pick. He was busy and that was good for him. It made time pass faster; his thoughts seldom straying from Lydia. *Did they get there safely? Where does she stay? Who does she stay with? Classes? What is she taking? Does she like it? How does she get there each day? Does she miss me as much as I miss her?* To this last question he sincerely hoped the answer was "no" because if she did, *how would she ever be able to study?*

September 23, 1870

Not quite two weeks into the apple harvest, the work was progressing well. This was their third trip into Manistee, and Alvin and Jeb had just finished delivering a load of apples to one of the cider mills. Alvin had the reins and asked, "Mind if we take a little detour by the millinery shop? Ma gave me a list just before we left this morning, and I'm hoping Lydia's aunt is back. I just want to hear that their trip went well."

"Not a problem," Jeb said. "Give me the reins. Maybe while you're in there I'll swing by the Congregational Church. Got something I'd like to ask the Pastor."

That piqued Alvin's curiosity. While everyone at the Price farm was God-fearing, Sunday church was a privilege too far away. Ben Price, somewhat cynically, had once observed, "God may have rested on the seventh day, but he wasn't no farmer. Fact is, a day lost to farmin' might be the day that cost you the farm." Instead, everyone at the Price farm worshipped in their own way, whenever they could, with the notable exception of hands held around the dinner table every evening as Ben asked the blessing.

Alvin took a shot in the dark. "Have you asked her yet?"

Matter-of-factly, Jeb replied, "I did. Couple of nights ago. She said yes."

Alvin let out a loud whoop and slammed his right hand down on his knee before asking, "When are you thinking?"

"Well, the answer to that question is going to depend a lot on the Pastor's schedule, but soon, I hope." He hesitated for just a second and added, "We decided we were only going to be at this point in our lives once, so neither of us saw much reason to wait. I thought we should have a preacher marry us. Dancing Flower agreed." Another hesitation and Jeb continued, "But Dancing Flower and I don't want it to be a big wedding. Of course, you, Nellie and Ben ... maybe we'll invite a few of the other farmers to come over ... "

Alvin broke in, "C'mon, Jeb, you know Ma isn't going to let this just come and go."

Jeb nodded and smiled at him, "Yeah, I was pretty sure of that too. But I won't let it get too big. We still got a lot of work to be done before winter."

"Now you sound like Pa," Alvin said, but he also knew Jeb was right.

Jeb pulled the horses to a stop in front of the millinery and the two parted ways. Liliane Burke, to Alvin's surprise and hope, was indeed home from taking her niece to East Lansing. She greeted Alvin warmly.

Eagerly he asked, "How is she doing?"

Liliane beamed at him, "She's right where she wants to be." Motioning for him to follow her, she led him to the counter. Stepping behind it, she retrieved an envelope. "Lydia spent a lot of time on this letter. Her address in East Lansing is in there," she said, tapping the envelope. "I know she can't wait to hear back from you."

He took the envelope and fought the instinct to open it right then and there. He genuinely liked Liliane Burke and he also knew she was on his side. He looked up from the precious letter and asked, "She's settled? She's started classes?"

She smiled and said, "Alvin, she's read a lot of that letter to me... but not all of it, I'm sure. She tells you all about her life in East Lansing. You should hear all about it in Lydia's words, not mine."

His eyes averted, he said, "Thank you, Liliane. I...I..."

"She's fine, Alvin. I promise you, she's just fine... except that she misses you desperately."

For a moment, his heart soared, but then there was a second thought, a cloud of concern. "How's... how's Mrs. Cockrum?"

In her most reassuring voice, Liliane Burke answered him. "She told me to tell you, she's doing just fine. She said she knew you'd ask, and she also told me to tell you, you are not to worry in the least about her or concern yourself at all about Lydia's father." She threw her hands up in the air in a kind of mock disgust, but with a smile, said, "Oh, that man... sometimes Reilly Cockrum can be the sweetest man on the face of the earth and other times..." She didn't finish. She didn't need to.

Alvin asked her to assist him in picking up the few things his mother needed from the millinery shop. As Liliane gathered them, they seemed to Alvin to be quite incidental and then the thought hit him, *She knew... somehow Ma knew I should stop by here today.*

Alvin was quiet on the ride back to the farm. Lydia's letter was tucked in the front pocket of his bibs. He was dying to read it, but Jeb couldn't stop talking. The Pastor would be out on Sunday afternoon, October 2, to marry them. There was much to do between now and then. But that evening, at dinner, when Jeb and Dancing Flower broke the news to Nellie, everything else on her list of winter preparations became less important. "Joyful things like this have to be proper celebrated," she'd said and no one at that dinner

table that evening thought she should be otherwise reck-
oned with.

November 21, 1870

Not quite a month later, as Thanksgiving was fast approaching, Ben pronounced the harvest complete. They'd kept the
hired hands longer than anticipated, and while that had
cut slightly into the profits from the orchard, their help
had been indispensable in getting things buttoned up tight
for winter. Last week each had been paid their due, and
Alvin and Jeb had driven them to their homes with prom-
ises that they would be needed again come spring planting.

But no one at the Price farm was prepared for what was
coming. Claude DuBois, the French-Canadian fur trapper
who'd left Dancing Flower alone and pregnant over a year
ago, was looking for her. There were better places to trap
than around Portage or Bear Lakes, but he'd come to have
a hankering for her, so he'd trekked south. At his ramshackle shack near Bear Lake, there were no signs of her.
He'd headed for the Portage Mill store in need of supplies
and information, and to DuBois's satisfaction, the clerk at
the store seemingly couldn't wait to engage in some gossip.
In heavily accented English, the French-Canadian trapper
asked if the clerk knew "an Injun squaw by the name of
Dancin' Flower?"

The clerk nodded. "She trades in here sometimes." Then
in a more lecherous tone, he added, "Got a Negra feller
from the Price farm that pays some of her bills too."

"Where's this Price farm?" the trapper asked.

A light skiff of snow covered the ground and hung from the
boughs of the trees in a dense stand of hemlocks a hundred
yards or so east of the farmhouse. Hiding among them,

Claude DuBois observed the goings-on at the Price Farm. He'd seen Ben depart to the northwest toward Lake Michigan with a team of two mules. Shortly after that Alvin and Jeb hitched up a team of good-looking draft horses and headed to the southeast, a load of apples on the back of their wagon.

DuBois was just about to break his cover and head to the farmhouse looking for Dancing Flower when he saw Nellie come out and walk the short distance to a neat little cabin. Dancing Flower came to the cabin's door to greet the older woman. He hadn't seen her in a long time, but the sight of her immediately aroused him. The two women spoke briefly, and then Nellie returned to the farmhouse.

In the farmhouse kitchen, Nellie tended to some baking. Kip had not made the trip to Manistee with Alvin and Jeb and his staying home proved fortuitous. Nellie noticed his ears perk up and he suddenly set to barking. "What is it, boy? What's got you all riled up?" When Kip kept barking, she went to the door, opened it and, thinking he was after a squirrel, a rabbit or some such thing, paid little attention as he rushed out and she closed the door against the cold. Other more important things needed tending in her kitchen.

Claude DuBois was just a hundred feet away from the cabin's door when he saw the dog charging toward him. The wide leather belt around his waist held a large, heavy hunting knife in a sheath, the end of which was strapped to his right leg. The knife was his preferred weapon, but his musket was strapped over his right shoulder and it covered the knife rendering it difficult to get at. He realized quickly he didn't have time to pull the musket around, aim it and squeeze the trigger before the dog would be on him. Instead, he grabbed the muzzle, swung it off his shoulder, and as Kip lunged at him, DuBois angrily swung the old rifle around, the musket's walnut stock catching Kip on the skull, squarely at the point between his right ear and eye. The dog let out a loud yelp and fell to the ground motionless. DuBois instinctively wanted to turn the musket on him and finish him off, but from the blood he could see coming from the dog's head he figured he was dead already and not worth wasting a musket ball. He continued to move toward the cabin's door.

Nellie heard Kip yelp. When she looked out the kitchen window, she saw him lying on the ground, a blood stain marring the skiff of snow around his head. And then she saw what, at first glimpse, she thought was a bear. But as she focused in, she could see it was a man dressed top to bottom in animal fur ... a bear of a man.

Nellie ran to the kitchen fireplace, grabbed the Winchester repeating rifle Ben kept there above the mantle and scrambled out the farmhouse door. By the time she got to the cabin, the man was standing in the open doorway. Past him, just inside the cabin, Nellie could see Dancing Flower. The loud conversation between her and this man was in French, so Nellie had no idea what was being said, but she could tell by her tone that Dancing Flower was scared. Nellie could see she was holding up a frying pan which did not seem to faze the stranger at all.

Nellie shouted at him from behind, "I don't know who you are or what you're up to, but if you don't skedaddle on out of here, I'm gonna shoot you."

DuBois turned around toward Nellie and started to move toward her speaking in French.

"Stop right where you are, or I'll shoot."

DuBois didn't stop. Dancing Flower continued screaming, but in French. Nellie had no idea what she was saying.

They were only about twenty feet apart when Nellie saw the trapper's hand settle on the knife's handle, and as he began to extract it from the sheath, Nellie pulled the trigger. Dubois was at least six feet tall and standing on the cabin's first step. He towered over Nellie who stood just a little over five feet tall. Nellie's bullet traveled on an upward trajectory and hit the intruder in the cheek just below his right eye and exited through the back of his head. He stood there for a moment, a disbelieving look in his eyes, his hand still poised on the handle of the knife that was halfway out of its sheath. To the two women it seemed like an eternity. Nellie had already chambered another round and was ready to fire again when DuBois fell straight forward onto the snow-covered ground. Within the next few seconds, the snow around his head had turned to a bright red slush. Her ears rang from the gunshot and adrenaline coursed through her like a shot of Ben's moonshine.

Nellie managed to ask Dancing Flower if she was all right.

Dancing Flower managed a nod.

Once she was sure Dancing Flower was all right, Nellie walked over and stood over Dubois. She wasn't sure if he was dead or not. Noticing the pool of red slush around his head, she reasoned, *Well, if you ain't dead just yet, no one here is going to be able to save your miserable life.* Half of the trapper's head in the back was gone. *Who is he? Why are you here?*

"Bring the boy! Go to the farmhouse. I'll be right there!" Nellie shouted to Dancing Flower.

Nellie turned and ran the twenty yards or so to where Kip lay, still bleeding and unconscious in the snow. The dog's breathing was labored, shallow, but he was still alive. Scooping him up, she whispered to him as she carried him to the farmhouse, "Okay, boy. You'll be okay. Nellie's gotcha now. Let's getcha inside and let me take a look atcha."

Ben pulled the mule team and the small wagon to a stop in front of Jeb's cabin and alongside DuBois' corpse. *What the...?* Jumping down, he ran and pounded on the door of Jeb's cabin. There was no answer, so he ran to the farmhouse. Throwing the door open, he shouted, "Nellie...Nellie!" She was in the kitchen tending to Kip, but at the sound of his voice, she dropped the cloth she was using to clean his wound and ran to Ben. She threw herself into his arms and it surprised him even though he was prepared for the worst after seeing the corpse outside the cabin. He could feel her trembling. Holding her tightly, he asked, "Are you all right? What's wrong? What happened?" Dancing Flower, who'd gone upstairs to put Daniel down for a nap, came down the steps. Nellie was sobbing so hard she could hardly catch her breath. Looking at Dancing Flower, he asked the same questions. He watched and listened as she tried to explain, but her English was poor and his French nonexistent.

Nellie spoke softly into Ben's chest, "I think he's someone Dancing Flower knows, but she can't tell us. Her English ain't good enough." There was a long pause, and then she began to sob harder, "I shot him, Ben. He didn't give me no choice in the matter. I told him to get outta here. He wasn't going to leave." She repeated, "I shot him."

The farmhouse door flew open and Jeb and Alvin rushed in. As soon as Dancing Flower saw them, she ran to Jeb. Alvin went over to Ben and Nellie who were still holding onto one another. "Jeb and I heard the shot. Sounded like it came from here. We rushed back as quick as we could. What happened?"

Jeb and Dancing Flower held one another and spoke in French. In between sobs, she slowly began to explain what had happened. When she was finished, Jeb turned to Nellie and asked, "Did he pull his knife?"

Ben broke in before Nellie could answer. "A knife! He'd'a had to been crazy. Nellie had the Winchester. I've seen her use it and she's knows what she's doin. What's wrong with that feller? Who brings a knife to a gunfight?"

Jeb held up a hand and asked again, "Nellie, did he pull his knife?"

Nellie nodded. "He was reachin' for it. That's when I pulled the trigger."

Jeb walked over to her and laid a hand on Nellie's shoulder. "It's a good thing for all of us that you did what you did, when you did it. Dancing Flower says if he'd gotten that knife out he'd have killed you with it. She says she's seen him kill a rabbit running away from him using that knife. She says one day he threw it at her. She could hear the blade spinning past her ear, and it stuck in the wall behind her. She was furious at him, but he laughed it off and told her if he'd wanted to kill her, that knife would have been in her heart and not the wall. He's Daniel's father and one nasty man."

Ben shook his head. "He's the father of that sweet boy?"

Jeb glanced at Dancing Flower and then back to Ben. "Not anymore, he's not."

They left DuBois where he was, but covered him with a canvas tarp to keep the scavengers away. No one ate dinner that evening. Jeb comforted Dancing Flower as they sat around the farmhouse's kitchen table. Dancing Flower kept Daniel cradled in her arms, reluctant to put him in his crib for the night. Ben, Nellie and Alvin positioned their chairs around the kitchen fireplace where Kip lay. Nellie had stitched up his head wound with needle and thread while Alvin had held the dog still and tried to comfort him through the excruciating process. Kip had regained consciousness, but had not gotten to his feet yet, his tongue lolled lazily out of one side of his mouth. Nellie moved to the floor next to him, something that would have normally started Kip's tail wagging, but not tonight. She applied a poultice to his wound, "This'll help keep infection down."

When it became apparent that nothing more could be done for anyone, including Kip, Jeb, Dancing Flower and Daniel headed to their cabin. Ben and Nellie retired for the evening. Alvin gathered his pillow and blankets and made his bed on the hardwood floor in front of the slowly dying fire in the kitchen fireplace. He'd keep vigil over his old friend tonight.

November 22, 1870

The next morning, Alvin rode Valiant over to Portage and found one of the constables to report a murder in self-defense. Together they rode back to the Price farm where the constable took notes as he listened to the details of what had transpired the previous day. The constable did not know Claude DuBois except to say that he had heard of a French-Canadian trapper who sometimes trapped in the area and supposedly had a ramshackle cabin around Bear Lake somewhere.

The constable asked Nellie and Dancing Flower some questions about what had happened. He asked Dancing Flower if she knew if DuBois had any family around here or perhaps in Canada. Her response to both questions was negative.

He then asked Ben if he'd take care of the remains, to which Ben agreed that he'd see to a proper burial but would not mark the grave. He didn't think anyone would ever want to remember Claude DuBois or what had happened at the Price farm.

November 24, 1870

Thanksgiving was a relatively new holiday, created under President Lincoln in 1863 during some of the darkest days of the Civil War. That was the same year Alvin had returned to the Price farm along with Jeb. The holiday was normally a day of celebration for them for that reason, but this year, events of just a few days before took their toll.

Kip was back on his feet, but Nellie warned everyone

not to get him excited. He still had a lot of mending to do. She'd determined Kip was likely blind in his right eye, a result of the blow he'd taken from DuBois. She determined this by tossing scraps of meat to the dog when his back was turned to her. If she tossed the snack on Kip's left side, he immediately saw it, even managed to catch it sometimes in midair. If she tossed it to his right side, he made no attempt to snatch it out of the air. Instead it would land on the floor. He wouldn't even move his head in that direction in response to the sound it would make hitting the floor. Kip would use his nose to find the morsel. From this she also speculated the dog was probably deaf in his right ear too. These injuries to the dog were sad, but if not for Nellie's nursing skills, Kip likely would not have survived.

That night in his room, with Kip lying at his feet, Alvin sat at a small desk, a single candle burning. He'd just finished rereading his last letter from Lydia in which she'd invited him to join her at her Aunt Liliane's for dinner on Christmas Eve. Taking out a sheet of paper he wrote back to her.

I am sorry I haven't written to you sooner. There was an incident here that rattled everyone. I will tell you about it when I see you at Christmas but be assured everyone here is just fine. Nothing could keep me from seeing you on Christmas Eve; you may count on me being there.

Now I have something to ask. Would you consider spending New Year's with me on the farm? I very much want you to meet my mother and father. This invitation is meant to cover several days... December 27th through January 2nd or 3rd, depending on how quickly you must leave to return to school. Tell your parents not to worry. My mother is very strict. Please say yes.

I miss you so much. Christmas cannot get here soon enough.
All my love,
Alvin

December 1, 1870

One week after Thanksgiving, Asa Patch knocked on the front door of the Price farmhouse. Ben invited him in, but Patch declined. "Me and some of the others have been talkin'. We think we should have another meetin'. Some of us are wantin' to know what's come of the letter we wrote Porter. We ain't heard nothin' from either Alvin or Jeb. We're startin' to lose faith, Ben."

While it was no secret around Portage Lake that Ben Price was not too difficult to anger, Asa Patch had a reputation as even a bigger hothead. Yet this visit and the message was a surprise to him. "Losin' faith? Why's that, Asa? I'm pretty sure Alvin said Jeb didn't expect to hear nothin' til after the first of the year. Seems to me we just need to be ... "

Patch interrupted, "It's not just that, Ben. Me and some of the boys been wonderin' about Alvin and the girl he's been seein' in Manistee. Her daddy's in cahoots with them lumbermen, so naturally," Patch rubbed a hand over his chin, "we're wantin' to know where Alvin's loyalties are a-lyin' these days."

His temper on the edge of flaring, his voice up a notch, Ben replied, "Let me set you straight and put an end to any rumors. He's been seein' Lydia Cockrum. Her daddy builds railroads, so he's with the lumbermen because that's where his money comes from. But, as far as Alvin's concerned, it makes me madder than a rattlesnake-that's-been-stepped-on that you are questionin' his loyalty. That boy's loyal as the day is long to gettin' that mill owner to do the right thing."

"All the same to you, Ben, I think we'd like to hear that from Alvin's mouth. Call a meetin' Ben, or I will. We need to be talkin' anyways about what we gonna do next when that mill's owner ignores us in the spring and our land starts to flood out again."

December 5, 1870

Four days later, in response to Patch's demand for a meeting, Alvin and Jeb set the barn up just like they did before, but the place was a lot more crowded this evening with the livestock in out of the cold and crammed into their various pens and stalls. The western sky looked like snow was on its way, and that could mean a shorter meeting, but Ben, Alvin and Jeb also thought this one could be more rancorous. As expected, Asa Patch started it off straight and to the point, "Alvin what's goin' on with you and Lydia Cockrum? We all know her father's a railroad man and in these parts that also makes him a lumberman. He ain't changin' your loyalties is he?"

Attendance tonight was much lighter than previous meetings. Alvin thought that was because ten homesteaders were the most Patch had been able to sufficiently rile up. But it still concerned him. Their group was only about twenty-five to thirty homesteaders at most, so any fragmentation at all could seriously hurt their cause. Alvin stepped up on the platform, took a deep breath, and began, "I'll be honest with you gents. I don't know that I like all of you having such an interest in my personal affairs, but if it means keeping us farmers together, then I'll answer both those questions. Up to you if you believe me or not, but I haven't told you a lie yet, so don't know why you'd question my loyalty now. I am seeing Lydia Cockrum when she's home. She's in college right now in East Lansing. Yes, I am aware her father is allied with the lumbermen. That, however, is a problem I must deal with in my relationship with Lydia, and nothing that you should concern yourself with. My allegiance is to us farmers as far as the Portage Mill is concerned."

Patch started to ask another question and Ben interrupted him, "Asa, you asked your questions. Seems to me my boy answered them. Now how 'bout the rest of you? Any of you got questions you wanna ask us?"

There was silence and some shuffling of feet for a minute, and then someone from the back of the gathering asked, "What we gonna do next if ol' man Porter ignores our letter jus' like he's ignored Judge Ramsdell's injunction against the dam?"

Alvin, who still was standing on the platform, looked over at Jeb who nodded at him. "That's a fair question. Jeb and I have been talking about that. If we haven't heard anything from Porter and Company by the middle of January, I will ride into Manistee and see Judge Ramsdell and ask him to send another letter, maybe even a stronger one than ours, if he's willing. I think he will be."

"Seems reasonable," came the response from what sounded like the same voice from the back of the barn.

Doggedly persistent, Asa Patch wasn't satisfied, "And if Porter don't answer the judge's letter, then what?"

Alvin stared hard at Patch and the tension in the room ratcheted up a bit. "Asa, like I have been telling all of you, there are no guarantees with any of this. If the judge writes a letter and it doesn't do any good, then we'll cross that bridge when we come to it, and that will be about March or April as I figure it."

Ben stepped up on the platform. "Take a look outside, boys. It's startin' to pound down the snow. If you want to get home to your warm farmhouses tonight, you better get goin'. Anyone's welcome to stay here in the barn tonight, but I don't think there's enough shine to take the chill ... or the smell, out of the air." That got a smattering of chuckles. Then Ben added, "And anyone who stays tonight would be welcome to stick around in the mornin' when it's time to muck out these pens and stalls." Four of the farmers in attendance apologized to Alvin on their way out. Asa Patch left without saying a word. After everyone was gone, Ben lit up his pipe, the three men passed around the shine jug, and each took a draw on it. Ben asked, "So what will we do if Judge Ramsdell's letter don't work?"

Alvin shrugged. He didn't have a good answer, so he said, "Give me and Jeb until the end of January, first of February. We'll let you know." Alvin and Ben headed for the farmhouse. The downstairs coal-oil lamps were still burning, a sign that Nellie was up unusually late. Jeb headed for the cabin where Dancing Flower would be waiting to find out what went on in the barn.

CHAPTER SIXTEEN

'TIS THE SEASON ...

Christmas Eve, 1870

Alvin Price pulled Amos and Tom to a halt in front of the millinery shop just in time. Liliane Burke was about to close up for the day, but when she saw him, she unlocked the door and stepped to the sidewalk. Alvin jumped down and, while brushing snow from his canvas jacket, greeted her with a smile, "I've got Lydia's Christmas present. I was hoping I could drop it off before I take the horses to the livery for the night. Would that be all right?"

"Of course." She watched him as he began to unload something of considerable size. "May I help you with that?" she asked, still standing in the shop's doorway but out of the snow that had started to come down harder.

Alvin pulled back a canvas tarp covering the gift. "No thanks. You stay inside, out of this stuff." He grabbed a handle with his right hand and pulled the chest toward him, then twisting his hand with his palm up, he hefted it onto his right shoulder and moved toward the open doorway. Once inside, he pulled it slowly around toward his front and steadied it with his right knee as he lowered it to the floor.

Liliane exclaimed, "Oh, Alvin, she will love this!" The chest was crafted out of beautifully grained oak, each board sanded to perfect smoothness. The edges of the lid and the chest were covered in a hammered copper. The lock and the handles on each side were bronze. "You made this?"

"Jeb and I did. He did the metal work. I'm the carpenter," Alvin said, the pride in their combined craftsmanship apparent in his voice.

"Let's take it up to the apartment and find just the right spot for it. I'm assuming Lydia has no idea?"

He shook his head, "None."

"Perfect."

Liliane watched as he maneuvered the heavy chest up the rather steep stairway leading to the apartment above the store. She wondered how in the world, with only one arm, he'd been able to craft the wood so skillfully. The chest was a beautiful gift, but also a testimony to his positivity. *He doesn't take no for an answer!* she thought. After they'd found just the right place to put the chest, Liliane said, "I have some ribbon downstairs in Christmas colors. Would you like me to fashion a bow to put on your present?"

"I'd be much obliged." He happened to glance out the window and noticed the snow accumulating on the horses. "I should get the horses down to the livery. The snow is starting to come down pretty hard..."

"You go and take care of them. Lydia isn't due until about five o'clock, so you have plenty of time."

At the livery, the owner had given his help the evening off and was on his way out to begin the holiday celebration with his family just as Alvin got there. So the task of settling the horses into their stalls fell to Alvin. Removing his long canvas duster, wet from the snowy ride into Manistee, he spread it over a rail in one of the stalls. He was in no rush. It was just a little after four o'clock. When he was satisfied the horses were set for the cold evening ahead of them, he fetched a wool overcoat from a canvas sack in the back of his wagon, pulled it on and departed the livery for the twenty minute walk back to the millinery shop. He couldn't wait to see Lydia.

In her bedroom, Lydia stood in front of the full-length mirror and finished her final primping. Irene Cockrum stood behind her, looking at her daughter's image in the mirror. In a tone barely above a whisper, she said, "Lydia, you look beautiful and you and Alvin have made Liliane's Christmas Eve special by spending the time with her. She is very much looking forward to it. It's hardly all she's talked about since you got home."

Smoothing the folds in her outfit, which reached to the floor, Lydia asked, "Are you sure I look all right? I'm so nervous."

Irene gave a little laugh and then said, "You've never looked prettier, and I'm sure Alvin is just as nervous."

Irene grew serious. "I've asked Liliane to chaperon the two of you this evening. I do not want a reoccurrence of what happened the week before you left for school. That cannot happen again, Lydia." She watched as Lydia reddened. "I have not told your father about your plans for after Christmas, and I must confess, I am concerned as well. We don't know anything about the Prices."

"But you know Alvin. You see what a good man he is. He is who he is because of his parents. Honestly, Mother, sometimes you and Father ... "

Irene shot back, "Be careful, Lydia. I would tend to agree with you, but your father will not tolerate a flippant attitude. You know he's not going to allow you to go to the Price farm after Christmas for even a day, much less for a few nights."

Lydia's tone became sharp. "And you, Mother? What will you allow me to do?"

Irene Cockrum shook her head. She knew her daughter was headstrong, smart, logical, and now that she was away at school, she knew she was also used to being on her own.

She trusted her, but she also knew how strong the effects of your love could be. "I haven't yet decided. The two of you haven't seen each other for quite some time. Tonight will be a test for you. It will be a test for Alvin. Let's see how it goes. We'll talk tomorrow."

"The three of us … you, me and Father?"

Irene shook her head again. "There's no point in talking this over with your father. I know what he will say. You and I will find some time to talk."

"I'm going to the farm with Alvin, Mother."

Irene's voice took on a sternness very much unlike her. "You will go to the Price farm if I say you're going, young lady, and that is all there is to it."

Choosing not to further challenge her mother, Lydia turned and pulled on her winter coat and picked up a small bag she had carefully prepared. Leaving the bedroom, over her shoulder, she said, "Nothing's changed between Alvin and me, but we will talk tomorrow." She took a few more steps and then turned to Irene and said, "I love you, Mother."

Irene followed her daughter through the house to the kitchen. Lydia left through the back door and Irene busied herself preparing Christmas Eve dinner for Reilly and herself.

Reilly Cockrum was somewhere in the house, sulking, angry that Lydia was going to see "that damned farmer." Those had been his exact words when he'd found out. He was equally outraged at his wife and her sister for facilitating the occasion.

It was the perfect Christmas Eve as the snow was pelting down harder now, and Alvin didn't want to unbutton his overcoat to check the exact time, but he was sure it was five o'clock give or take a minute or two. The millinery shop was dark, deserted. Cupping his hands around his eyes, he peered through the glass but saw no one. He tried the door and to his surprise, found it unlocked. He stepped inside.

From the shadows off to one side of the shop, Lydia emerged into the low light provided by the streetlamps and the open door, "Alvin, I've missed you so!" There was no awkwardness, no hesitation on either of their parts. They moved toward each other and fell into an embrace and a long-anticipated kiss.

The dinner Liliane prepared for them was delicious; both ham and turkey, yams in a thick maple syrup and brown sugar mix, some pickled asparagus she'd put up last spring when the asparagus was fresh. She'd baked and carefully decorated some delicious sugar cookies for dessert.

This was Alvin's first chance to really get a look around Liliane's apartment above the millinery shop. It possessed conveniences he'd only heard about, but never really seen. Radiators under each window emanated heat. The kitchen and bathroom had hot water. Then there was the toilet. On the farm the outhouse sat at some distance from the farmhouse. In the summer it was hot and it stank...and then there were the flies, thousands of them, lingering there in wait for the next person in need of this terrible, but necessary place. In the winter, the stink and the flies were replaced by the extremely cold temperatures, and if you were the first or second person to use it after a snow, it meant you'd be the one breaking the trail through what often was a knee-deep accumulation.

After dinner, everyone pitched in for the clean-up, and then gifts were exchanged. Lydia loved the chest Alvin and Jeb had made for her. Her present to Alvin was a small, flat gold fob. Engraved on one side was his name and on the other, hers. Alvin gathered another package he'd brought with him and gave it to Liliane. "This is for you. My ma made it."

"Oh. You...she shouldn't have...there was no need..."

"She insisted. She thinks it was very nice of you to allow me to come here tonight for dinner," Alvin blushed slightly, "and to see Lydia."

Inside the package was a wool scarf, about six feet long and a foot wide, dyed a beautiful dark red. "Oh my ... it's ... it's just beautiful." Liliane threw it around her neck. "It's so soft and warm. How did she ..."

"The wool is from our sheep. She spins it into yarn and then knits the scarves. The color for yours comes from beet juice. I can't explain more than that. I don't know how she does it exactly. Everyone at the farm has one. Nothing is warmer," he pointed to the scarf, "than having that wrapped around your neck when you are out in the cold."

"You thank her for me. Tell her I will wear it often in anticipation of meeting her sometime. It's just beautiful." She fondled the scarf for a moment and then said, "Tell me about your family, Alvin."

"My pa, Ben, is a farmer. That's all he's done all his life, even as a boy. I'd venture to say he's forgotten more about farming than I will ever know. My ma, Nellie ..." It took him a moment to organize his thoughts. "Where do I begin? She's a great cook. She's a teacher who taught me how to read, write and work numbers. She's a nurse when one of us is sick or hurt. She and Pa have been married for nearly thirty years." He looked over at Lydia. "I think the two of them love each other more every day they are together." Then he laughed and said, "I know she can back Pa down out of a bad mood with just a glance or a cock of her head. No one can do that except Ma. Believe me, I've tried and it's never worked for me the way it does for her. I don't know where our family would be without her around."

Lydia spoke up, "Aunt Liliane, I need your help ..."

Liliane held up a hand in her direction. "I know." She was nodding her head. "You need my help in convincing your mother she should allow you to go with Alvin to the farm for a few days and meet his family." Liliane turned her attention back to Alvin. "Lydia's told me about Jeb. She says he's like a brother to you."

"Yes, ma'am. He's a member of our family just as much as I am."

Liliane smiled at him, but then turned suddenly stern, "So, tell me, if her mother allows Lydia to go meet your family, Alvin, what will be the sleeping arrangements?"

The blunt question surprised him, but he managed to stammer out, "Lydia...I will sleep..." He realized he was fumbling around and paused to collect his thoughts. "Lydia will sleep in my room, by herself. I will sleep on the floor in the kitchen in front of the fireplace. It's really not a problem. I've done that before."

A silence filled the room. Lydia tried to lighten the mood. "Why do I have to sleep by myself? Can't Kip sleep with me?"

Alvin looked at Liliane and clarified, "Kip's my dog. And yes, you know how he is around you. You won't even need to ask him."

Liliane laughed and said, "Lydia's told me about him, about how the two of you met. It's a beautiful story."

At somewhere around nine o'clock, Liliane excused herself. "It's getting late. I'm tired and tomorrow is Christmas. Lydia, your mother tells me we are expected at your house by ten. Does your family have Christmas plans, Alvin?"

"We do. I'll sleep in the livery tonight with the horses and we'll head home early in the morning. Ma will have Christmas dinner ready by noon."

Lydia protested, "Sleep in the livery! You can't do that." Turning to her aunt, she said, "We can't turn him out like that."

Liliane smiled, "Well, there's a cot in the storeroom

downstairs." Turning to Alvin she said, "You'd be welcome to spend the night down there. It isn't much, but it will be better than a night spent in the livery."

"I...I...can't. I shouldn't..." Alvin stammered.

"Nonsense." Liliane left them to gather a pillow and some blankets. When she returned, she handed them to Alvin. Then she turned to her niece and said, "I've told your mother, Lydia, that I would chaperon the two of you this evening." To both of them she said, "I'm going to leave you now so you may have some time to yourselves. But hear me when I say that I believed you once when you said you both fell asleep and lost track of time. I'm not likely to believe such a mistake a second time." Liliane took their nodding as an implicit understanding of her warning.

Her curiosity nearly consuming her, Lydia was compelled to ask, "So will you help me convince Mother to let me go with Alvin to the farm?"

Glancing back and forth between the two of them, Liliane merely nodded and then bade each of them goodnight.

CHAPTER SEVENTEEN

DOWN ON THE FARM

December 27, 1870

Reilly Cockrum's prejudice toward Alvin Price had been trumped by Liliane Burke and Irene Cockrum's consent which allowed Lydia to spend a few days on the Price farm. Alvin had promised Lydia a long, cold ride from Manistee and he had not exaggerated. While the snow had stopped, the temperature hovered around twenty degrees and there was a light breeze blowing out of the north. Lydia expressed her surprise that Kip wasn't with him when he picked her up at the millinery shop. So, the story of Claude DuBois, Dancing Flower and Nellie that he'd withheld from her on Christmas Eve, unfolded. It was an unsavory event he hated to dwell on. Yet it was something he felt obligated to tell her about. Both Nellie and Dancing Flower still had occasional nightmares about what had happened that day in November. He didn't want either of them to have to tell Lydia about it, and he certainly didn't want it to come up accidentally once she got to the farm.

As they pulled onto the farm trail, Alvin and Lydia could hear Kip's barks get louder as he plowed through the nearly unblemished snow that covered the ground. Alvin slowed the wagon and got down. Kip came to his call and Alvin lifted him up into the rear of the wagon. Then, ignoring the one who'd put him aboard, Kip rushed up to the seat and put his front paws up on the back of it, still barking with joy at seeing her, his tail wagging furiously. Lydia reveled in the dog's attention. Alvin climbed into the wagon's rear, stepped behind Kip and lifted him over and onto the seat where Lydia pulled him close to her. Alvin stepped over the seat and took the reins from the brake handle. Looking over at the two of them, he said with a laugh, "He used to be my dog ... now I think he's yours."

She ran her hand down over the top of his head, "He's our dog, Alvin, and I love him."

Lydia fell under the spell of both Nellie Price and Dancing Flower Washington within minutes of her arrival at the Price farm. She had taken some French in high school, so she and Dancing Flower had a comfortable connection. Nellie, on the other hand, wanted to know everything about what it was like living in the big city and going to school there. No formal education of her own, she'd been taught the basics of math and reading by her mother, a farmer's wife. Like her mother, Nellie Price had never lived anywhere else except on a farm. Lydia would barely finish answering one of her questions, before Nellie fired the next one off.

Three meals a day were taken together in the farmhouse kitchen. On Lydia's first full day at the farm, as they were finishing breakfast, Alvin and Jeb stood and excused themselves to go "muck out the barn." Lydia excitedly asked, "Can I come, too?"

Jeb looked at Alvin and shook his head. Alvin stuttered, "Ah ... Lydia ... I ... I don't think you should ... "

Nellie interrupted, "Now, you two boys, stop thinkin' just because Lydia here didn't grow up on a farm that she ain't strong enough to muck out a barn. My bet is she'll throw as much manure as either of you will."

Lydia hadn't known exactly what it meant to "muck out" a barn, but after Nellie's admonition of Jeb and Alvin, she sure figured it out.

Nellie asked her, "I'm dyin' to know why you are wantin' to study farmin'? I mean, we're sure glad you came out here to meet us. You're always welcome, but I'm curious."

Lydia smiled at her. "You mean I'm a city girl. And that's true, Miss Nellie. But ..." she paused and thought for a moment. "Two women have led me to it. First there's my mother. She's a gardener, Miss Nellie, like no one you've ever seen before. It's not like farming, mind you. She's a flower gardener, and her garden is as beautiful a one as you'll ever see. I've watched her since I was a little girl. It's like she's painting a picture with her flowers—so much color, so many different kinds of flowers, vines, grasses. Sometime this summer Alvin will have to bring you into town so I can show it to you. The other woman is Mrs. Bonnie Brown, my science teacher in high school. She's the one who made me curious about the how and the why of growing things; she got me interested in subjects like botany and biology. But the more I studied those, the more I thought, no, I want something more practical. I didn't want to know only how or why things grew. I wanted to see how we can use the things we grow to make our lives better. Mrs. Brown's the one who suggested I apply at the ag college. She helped me with all the paperwork and encouraged me to pursue it." Lydia laid her hands on the table, looked at Nellie, and said, "Yep, two very strong women ..." and then she added, "a lot like you, Miss Nellie." For a moment, Lydia thought Nellie was going to cry. To lighten the mood a bit, Lydia said to Jeb and Alvin, "Yeah, so c'mon, you two. Sooner we can get to muckin' out that barn, the sooner we can move on to the next chore."

Nellie, who'd pawed away a tear, clapped her hands loudly and said, "See what I'm a tellin' ya? This here gal's got some kind of spirit. Lydia, when you're through helpin'

Jeb and Alvin, me and Dancin' Flower gonna boil up some soap. We'd be much obliged to have your help."

The farmhouse had no running water. Every ounce of water had to be brought into the house in large, stone jugs which, when full of water, weighed somewhere in the vicinity of fifty pounds. This job belonged to everyone living on the farm, especially if you were the one who noticed the farmhouse's water supply was running low. The source of the water was a naturally flowing artesian well about forty yards away from the kitchen door. On her first trip to the well, Lydia asked Alvin, "How long has it been flowing like this?"

The water bubbled up through a pipe Ben Price had sunk in the middle of the well when he'd first discovered it. The farmhouse had been built where it stood because of its proximity to this source of water. Alvin replied to her question, "Can't be sure, but we've been taking water from it ever since we started homesteading here; that's about twelve years now." From the well, the water flowed a short distance and then collected into a small pond that Ben had dug out by hand.

"The well never freezes?"

"Not since I've been living here," was Alvin's response.

Lydia pointed to the pond, which was now frozen over and snow covered, "How deep is that?"

"The middle of it's about up to my chest. Dad, Jeb and I have been known to just strip right down to nothin' in the summer and cool off in it. You see how cold this water is coming out of the well. It isn't much warmer in that pond."

"I love how this little stream just meanders from the well into the pond, so natural-like," Lydia said.

And with that simple observation, she gave Alvin an idea that could prove to be the answer to the question Asa Patch

had thrown at him at the last gathering of farmers. *If ol'
man Porter don't answer Judge Ramsdell's letter, what we
gonna do then, Alvin?* The answer had been right in front
of him all this time. It just took Lydia to point it out to
him.

The week on the farm had flown by for Alvin and Lydia.
He'd given her a tour of it on horseback. She'd been particularly impressed with the apple orchard. Lydia helped
Nellie and Dancing Flower make soap, bake bread, fetch
meat from the smoke house, and this time of year, when
the temperatures were well below freezing, fetch frozen
meats from the shed everyone at the Price farm called the
coolin' shed. She helped with the meal preparations and
the cleanup. When it was just the three women alone, they
gossiped about the idiosyncrasies of the men.

On the next to last night, after dinner and clean up, Dancing Flower and Jeb had gone back to their cabin. Ben and
Alvin had gone to check on a flare-up at the chicken coop.
Thinking it was a fox, coyote or wolf after the chickens, Ben
had snatched the rifle from the mantle. It was just Nellie
and Lydia alone. "You know, darlin', my Alvin is crazy in
love with you." Lydia could feel the redness coming to her
face, but she wasn't going to deny the truth of what Nellie
had said. She nodded. Nellie continued, "I know it's been
hard for you to stay in that room of his up there," and she
pointed to the steps. Lydia reddened some more. Chuck-
ling, Nellie added, "Been just as hard for him to keep to
that hearthstone over there." She pointed to the kitchen
fireplace where Alvin had already laid out his bed for the
night. "But I respect the two of you for bein' proper. He
tell you my thinkin' on bein' proper before you've tied the
knot?"

"He has, Miss Nellie."

"What you got to say about that?"

"I respect it."

"I know how hard it can be."

Lydia reached across the table and put her hands over Nellie's. "Alvin and I haven't … we …" This was not so easy to talk about. Lydia swallowed hard and tried again, "Alvin and I have not, nor will we ever be, completely intimate until I've graduated from college. That's a long time from now. And if I've got anything to say about it, we will be tying that knot you spoke of, just as soon after graduation as possible."

"But in the meantime, you have to be content with just holdin' onto each other, kissin', and not much more."

"That's right."

"Well now, just so you know, that's how me and ol' Ben made do, in the year or so he courted me." Lydia smiled and laughed along with Nellie. "So if'n I understand things right, Alvin's takin' you back to Manistee in the mornin' so you can get ready to head back to school."

Lydia nodded and said, "I can't believe how fast the time's gone, Miss Nellie."

"Well, you study hard when you get back to school. The time'll pass. It will. If you are busy there, it'll go faster than you think. Alvin … well, he, Jeb and Ben, they got the farm and they got that thing with the sawmill. Alvin's told me your father's dead set against what the farmers are doin'. I understand why he thinks that way, but I don't agree with him. That dam causes the farmers around here a lot of heartache. What I want you to know though, is that you're always welcome out here. We've loved havin' you. You and Alvin keep behavin' yourselves and soon enough, darlin', you'll be a permanent part of the Price farm. I can feel it in my bones."

Lydia squeezed Nellie's hands. "Thank you, Miss Nellie. I do love your son. And we will behave ourselves. Don't you worry about that. My mother and my aunt have had this same talk with me. Neither Alvin nor I would ever want to disappoint any of you."

January 3, 1871

Just before first light, Alvin saddled Valiant and got on. Lydia put a foot in the stirrup and he helped pull her up. She sat sidesaddle, squeezed between Alvin and the saddle's horn. She put her arms around him and held him tightly as they rode through the muffled silence of a snow-covered hemlock forest to a bluff just west of the Price farm overlooking the vastness of Lake Michigan as the sun rose behind them. There were no words between them. Each knew how difficult this day was going to be. Lydia laid her head on his chest and murmured, "I love you." It was the first time she'd said that.

Alvin kissed her and when their lips parted, Alvin said what he hoped she already knew, "I love you, Lydia, with all my heart."

When they returned to the farm, Alvin gave her the chance to say goodbye to everyone and the two set out for Manistee. On Valiant, the ride would take half the time, a certain saving of time that neither of them relished, but it was time for her to get back. The rest of her life was calling her away from him, away from this farm, away from Manistee.

CHAPTER EIGHTEEN

TAKING ADVANTAGE?

January 16, 1871

Two weeks had passed since Lydia had gone back to school. Alvin Price entered the Congregational Church and walked down the hall to the circuit court's office. The clerk, the same one who'd been so dismissive of Alvin at his last visit, was seated behind the desk. He looked up and then returned to scribbling something in a ledger. Alvin asked, "Is Judge Ramsdell here?"

In a tone rife with sarcasm, the clerk responded without looking up, "Do you see him?"

So, this is how it's going to be? Biting his tongue, Alvin asked, "Do you know if he will be in today?"

"No," came the terse reply.

"No, he's not going to be in, or no, you don't know when he might be here?"

The clerk dropped the pencil on the ledger page and looked up this time, "Don't know where he is or when he might be here."

"I'll wait."

The clerk looked up, his voice up a notch, "I said, I don't know if the judge will be in today."

Alvin returned the clerk's bad attitude, "And I said I'll wait." He took the very same seat in the hallway where he'd waited for the judge the last time.

Alvin had just heard the church's bell toll twelve o'clock noon. The church's outer door opened. Alvin stood when he saw Judge Ramsdell approach.

"Alvin Price," the judge said as he extended his hand.

"Judge Ramsdell, good to see you again, sir."

"Everything all right at the Price farm? I was very sorry to hear of your mother's trouble with that intruder a few months ago."

Surprised, Alvin stammered, "You...you heard about that?"

"The constables in Portage are required to file a report of felonious incidents with me, and the actions they have taken in regard to each of them. So, yes, I heard about it, and I must say I have no difficulty with the constable's decision. It was self-defense, and from what I read, your mother's quick action likely saved lives."

"Thanks, Judge. Ma and Dancing Flower are doing better." Alvin paused, appreciative of the judge's support, but he was ready to get on with the purpose of this visit. "I was wondering if I might ask a favor?"

"I think I told you the last time that I would help in any way I could." He motioned him into the office. The clerk, not looking up, kept scribbling in the ledger. "Can you do that somewhere else?" the judge said to him.

The clerk shot Alvin a look, who returned it with a smile. The clerk quickly closed the ledger, grabbed his pen and ink, and shuffled out of the office. When he was out of ear-shot, the judge said to Alvin, "He can be a bother, but he pays careful attention to the details. A fair court needs to keep track of details."

Alvin took a seat in front of the desk, and the judge settled into the chair vacated by the clerk. "Judge, we sent a letter from the farmers to Mr. Porter about the mill and the dam last October."

Ramsdell nodded and said, "Seems like an appropriate move."

"I thought so...and so did the farmers. I had most of them sign the letter." Alvin paused briefly then added, "But there's been no response."

"Does that surprise you?"

"No." Alvin paused for a moment and then continued, "But I can't be sure Mr. Porter even got the letter. The postmaster in Portage is also the mill supervisor. When I dropped off the letter, he knew it was about the dam and your injunction. There's a chance he never put it in the mail."

"Do you have any proof of that?"

Alvin shook his head. "No, just a gut feeling."

The judge cupped his chin in his hand and thought for a moment, "What did your letter ask of Mr. Porter?"

From the front pocket of his bibs, Alvin produced a paper. "Jebediah and I kept an exact copy."

"Jebediah?"

"He's a freedman. Fought for the Union. Badly wounded at Chancellorsville. We met when we were both heading home after our discharge. He was on his way back to Montreal where he was a typesetter. I asked him if he wanted to be a partner in my family's farm. We've been the best of friends since. He's like a brother to me."

"I see." The judge turned his attention back to the copy of the letter, and Alvin gave him all the time he needed to read it. "So, what is it you'd like me to do?"

"I...we...the group of farmers around Portage Lake, would like you to write a letter to Mr. Porter, remind him of your injunction and let him know you expect him to abide by it come this spring whether it's been properly served or not."

"All right. But what makes you think Mr. Porter will pay attention to my letter?"

Alvin shrugged, "Don't know that he will, Judge. But seems like the next logical step to me and Jeb."

Ramsdell asked, "And what will the farmers do if he dams the creek?"

Alvin's eyes brightened a bit. "Well, that's something I was hoping I could talk over with you. I've got an idea, but I haven't talked to anyone else about it. I wanted to wait until I got some expert legal advice."

Ramsdell pursed his lips and said, "I'm a judge, Alvin. I'm not supposed to give legal advice. That's what attorneys do."

For a moment, Alvin feared he'd pushed his friendship with the judge beyond its breaking point.

"But since you and Jeb gave a lot for this country, and since you came all this way...go ahead. But understand, I'm listening as a private citizen, not as your lawyer and certainly not as a judge. What's your idea?"

Alvin brightened again. "What if we farmers cut a ditch across the isthmus between Portage Lake and Lake Michigan? The mill could dam the lake as much as they wanted, but our cut would allow the water to drain. So, it won't matter if they dam Portage Creek."

After a pause, Ramsdell asked, "Do you own the land your cut would be crossing?"

"No, not yet." Alvin reached back in his bib pocket and produced another piece of paper. Unfolding it, he laid a platted map in front of the judge and pointed to a particular plot, "So this is our farm. Here's our boundary line to the west, right here." Then moving his finger to the adjoining plot, he said, "This is where we would make the cut. It's the narrowest part of the isthmus."

"Who owns that land now?" was the judge's next question.

"I stopped at the Registrar of Deed's office before I came here, Judge. The land is owned by a Mr. Albert Shanks."

"And is Mr. Shanks willing to sell this piece of land to you, Alvin?"

"I don't know the answer to that question, but before I begin inquiring of him, I was wondering, if we owned that land, could we legally make the cut?"

Judge Ramsdell took a moment to think, then said, "Remember, I'm not your lawyer, but I don't see why not. The land would be yours to do with what you wanted. The lumbermen are going to argue that you're diverting water and, of course, you are. But it seems to me, your diversion of water through your cut would not be illegal." He paused and then asked, "When would you propose making the cut?"

"The spring... April or May."

"The seven-month moratorium provided to the mill owner in the injunction is long past. No, I don't see any problem with your plan as long as the Register of Deeds has issued you the deed to that land."

A broad smile on his face, Alvin stood up and extended his right hand, "I can't thank you enough. Jeb and I have been struggling with what to tell the farmers if Porter refuses to abide by the injunction. There's still talk about just going over to the dam and tearing it down. I've told them of your caution against doing that. So, this offers us a way to do things legally. The cut will be our backup plan if he doesn't respond to your letter."

Ramsdell asked, "May I keep this copy of your letter? I'd like to enclose it with my letter to Mr. Porter. I intend to tell him I am not happy that I must write my letter, that he could have just responded directly to you, but that I now expect him to respond to me about his intentions. If I hear something, I will be sure to let you know."

"Thanks, Judge, I appreciate the advice and the support."

Alvin retrieved Valiant from the livery and set out for home. He was anxious to tell Jeb about his plan and the judge's opinion of it. From the Registrar of Deeds, he'd gotten the contact information for Albert Shanks, who lived in Muskegon. Contacting him would be a bit difficult, but, as he rode toward home, Alvin knew there was a bigger issue than just contacting Mr. Shanks. Where would the money to purchase the land come from? He knew he didn't have it.

CHAPTER NINETEEN

THE INVESTMENT

February 16, 1871

A month had gone by since Alvin's conversation with Judge Ramsdell and in that time he'd faithfully checked at the Portage Mill's store for any letter from Porter and Company, despite the fact that he'd already pretty much given up hope of any response. Alvin was beyond tired as he sat down at the dinner table. The trip today had been a short one, only a couple of miles each way across the isthmus to Portage, but the weather was brutally cold, with a north wind blowing constantly and a deep snow on the ground. But it had been worth it. A letter from Lydia had been waiting for him. He hadn't opened it yet. It was a game he played with himself, a way of coping with the long and lonely days without her. He wouldn't open it until he went to bed tonight, and then he'd spend his last waking hours hanging on her every word.

"Any news from Lydia?" Nellie Price asked after Ben had asked the blessing.

Alvin merely nodded.

"Well, what did she have to say?"

"Don't know. Haven't had the chance to read it yet."

Ben Price inserted himself into their conversation, "Haven't had the chance! By God, if it was me and I had just gotten such a letter, I'da read it the first minute."

Nellie chided, "But it ain't you, ya ol' fool, so just let Alvin handle his letters as he sees fit."

Jeb spoke up. "Dancing Flower and I have some news."

Ben kept eating. But Alvin and Nellie put their knives and forks down and looked at the couple in anticipation.

"Dancing Flower's expecting."

Nellie's voice rang out, "I knew it. Could feel it in my bones. Oh, Jeb, Dancin' Flower, I'm so happy for the two of you."

Alvin smiled and said, "Congratulations, Jeb...Dancing Flower. That's great!"

Ben, still chewing a mouthful of food, managed, "Good for you two!"

"When is the little critter expected to get here?" Nellie asked.

Jeb shrugged. "We think she's about three months along. Barely showing. So that would make it July...August at the latest."

Ben piped up, a smile spread across his face, "Well, Jeb, that didn't take you long..."

Nellie immediately rebuked him, "Now what kind of a remark is that, ol' man. They're married. Don't matter if it takes no time or it takes forever...long as God's blessed their union." Ben immediately went back to eating.

Jeb looked back and forth between Ben and Alvin. "We've a favor to ask."

"What's that?" Alvin said.

"We were wondering if it would be all right with everyone if we took a trip? We'd likely be gone three weeks, maybe a month."

Smiling, Ben asked, "Some kinda' honeymoon? Heckuva time of year to be travelin'."

Dancing Flower, whose English was improving every day, said, "Jeb take me to Montreal."

"That's a long way from here," Ben observed.

Jeb said, "Dancing Flower wants me to meet her mother. She wants her to see how happy she is."

Dancing Flower said, "My mother not see me since I was..." she searched for the English word. Gesturing with her hand held low to the ground, she added, "Little. My father take me away." She began to tear up. "Long time...hope we find my mother."

Nellie looked at her and said, "You should go and find her, Dancin' Flower. I'll keep an eye on Daniel while you're gone. Don't worry at all about him."

It was Ben, the more superstitious of all of them, who observed, "Things happen in threes. Sometimes it's good things; sometimes it bad. These are good things."

Alvin played along. "So what are they, Pa? What are the three things?"

Ben replied, "Don'tcha see? You get a letter from Lydia; Jeb and Dancin' Flower's expectin'; and now she's gonna get to see her Ma again. Three good things!"

That night, Alvin lay in bed, Lydia's letter in his hand, the coal lamp on the bedside table providing just enough light for him to read by. She'd written the letter three weeks earlier; *that's pretty good time for a letter to get from East Lansing to Portage,* he thought. He wasn't sure, but his estimate was the two places were about one hundred fifty miles apart as the crow flies. He'd read through the letter twice now, but one passage in particular had his rapt attention:

Last January, while visiting your beautiful farm, not long after I got there, I was at the well fetching some water for the house, and I happened to look across the lake to a hillside where they were logging. Over the few days I was there, I kept an eye on that hillside and I was amazed at how quickly they managed to strip it bare.

My fear is this will only get worse. The lumber companies want my father to design railroads to make movement of their logs to the mills more efficient. You've told me they only cut logs in the winter, when the ground is frozen and horses can move sleds across the frozen ground easier. But what will happen, Alvin, when trains move the logs and the lumbermen no longer require the ground to be frozen? These beautiful forests of ours here in Michigan won't last forever at the rate they are cutting them down. I fear for the impact their greed will have on all of us at some point in the future. It is this fear that stimulates my studies here at college. I must find a way to, if not stop this destruction, at least abate it, to set some plan for future generations, to make sure that we won't run out of these beautiful trees that bless our part of the country.

He could see it plain as day; Lydia had found her higher calling. He fell asleep that night thinking how lucky he was to have such a woman who could think beyond the present with such clarity.

March 20, 1871

A month had come and gone since Jeb and Dancing Flower had left the farm in search of her mother in Montreal. It was a beautifully bright, sunny day, but still very cool, the temperature not above forty degrees. Kip was the first to see them and had run off barking furiously in greeting, as was his custom whenever there were new arrivals at the farm. By now Dancing Flower was visibly pregnant, but both of the travelers looked well and hardy. Nellie, who'd seen them ride up, emerged from the farmhouse, a shawl pulled tightly around her and Daniel. The boy, just over two, was toddling now, but Nellie was in a rush to greet them and had just scooped him up. Greetings were as profuse as they were profound. The family was united again.

Jeb and Dancing Flower took the rest of the afternoon to

settle back into their cabin with the assistance of Nellie, who helped move all of Daniel's things from the farmhouse to the cabin. Nellie prepared a meal of smoked ham, potatoes, candied yams, and pickled asparagus. An apple pie sat cooling on the top of the stove. After Ben asked the blessing on the meal, Nellie asked, "How's your mother, Dancin' Flower? Surprised to see you, I'll bet."

It suddenly became very quiet in the farmhouse. Dancing Flower hung her head and shook it. Jeb reached over and took her hand before he answered, "We couldn't find her."

It had never occurred to Nellie that they'd fail. "Oh... Oh... I'm so sorry ..."

Jeb said, "We can't be sure what happened to her. Some of the other women in her tribe told us her mother had left them after Dancing Flower's father took her away, but no one seemed to know where she might be. I asked all over Montreal but couldn't find out anything."

It was Dancing Flower who broke the somberness that had befallen their homecoming meal. She said, "It all right." She patted her swollen belly, "Baby back home where he belong. Price farm home for all of us."

Nellie looked at Ben as a tear formed in her eye.

Nellie and Dancing Flower cleaned up after dinner while the three men sat around the dinner table. Jeb matter-of-factly said, "Judge Ramsdell hasn't heard anything from Porter and Company."

"How do you know that?" Alvin asked.

"I was in Manistee yesterday and stopped by the judge's office. Caught him in. He's heard nothing. I've got something I want to show you both." He reached in the front pocket of his bibs and pulled out a folded sheet of paper, carefully unfolded it and laid it on the table facing Ben and Alvin.

BILL OF SALE

The undersigned owner of the land, plot 33, as shown on the included map of the Portage Lake region of Manistee County, Michigan, with this Bill of Sale, signs over complete ownership of said plot 33 to Benjamin Price for the price of $500.

Signed by: Andrew Shanks on this day of our Lord, March 17, 1871.

*Witnesses to signature: Roberta Shanks
    Jebediah Washington*

Below the Bill of Sale was a second annotation:

The Change of Ownership of plot 33 as shown on the included map of the Portage Lake region of Manistee County, Michigan has been duly recorded based on this Bill of Sale by the Manistee County Registrar of Deeds this nineteenth day of March 1871.
    Signed: Bernard Franks
    Registrar of Deeds
    Manistee County, Michigan

The Bill of Sale had the raised seal of the Registrar of Deeds stamped in the lower right corner. Alvin, the quicker reader of the two, snapped his head up toward Jeb, "What? How? You bought that piece of land between us and Lake Michigan? The piece across the isthmus?"

Ben sputtered, "Jeb, where the hell did you get that kind of money?"

Jeb smiled at him, not surprised by Ben's usual bluntness. "Dancing Flower had her reasons for wanting to go to Montreal. I had mine. Remember, before the war I was a typesetter there?" Ben and Alvin both nodded. "Well, back then the newspaper I worked for published three times a week ... maybe four if the Queen's birthday or the anniversary of her coronation happened on a day we didn't normally publish. There were three of us typesetters back then. Today that paper publishes seven days a week, tens of thousands of copies in both English and French. They employ sixty typesetters now. There's somebody setting type twenty-four hours a day, seven days a week."

Alvin asked, "Is there anybody still there who remembered you?"

"A few; not many."

With his usual brashness, Ben, returned to the question that was still bothering him. "So, Jeb, the money ... I hope you didn't spend all your blacksmithing money on this piece of land."

Jeb smiled at the two of them. "Didn't spend a penny of my smithy money. Naw, this money to buy this piece of land came from *The Montreal Ledger.*" Alvin and Ben gave him a blank look. Jeb further explained, "When I started to work for them, the newspaper was a small family-owned business, but they were quickly bought out by a larger corporation. That corporation was taking a chance on a small newspaper operation and they welcomed cash any way they could get it. Back then, I was very frugal, lived very modestly. It was my preference ... " He paused, gave a wry smile and said, "And I guess it still is. So, I invested most of my wages into the company. It turns out that was a very good investment. As the paper grew, so did my investment. There's a lot of money in my account. I always thought it would be there when I needed it, and I haven't needed it until now.

"From Montreal, Dancing Flower and I headed to Muskegon and found Mr. Shanks. Good man. No plans to settle on the land. I think he was happy to sell it to us. I offered him a more-than-fair price and he took it. So, it doesn't matter now whether old man Porter decides to respond to the judge's letter or not. We own that piece of land across that isthmus. We can do with it what we want, free and clear."

Alvin pointed to a line on the bill of sale. "Pa, take a look here. This says the sale's in your name. That means..." Alvin paused and looked at Jeb.

Jeb nodded, "It means the deed is in Ben's name."

Ben started to argue, "Naw, Jeb, that ain't right..."

"Yes, Ben, it is. The Price Farm is now doubled in size." Jeb paused for a moment then turned to Alvin. "I sure am glad you built that relationship with Judge Ramsdell though. The Registrar wasn't going to record the sale at first. Don't know for sure, but I think he was thinking the bill of sale wasn't legitimate. He kept giving me the up and down like it should be Ben getting this done, not some Negro. So, when he refused to record it and change the deed of ownership, I went to find the judge. He marched over to the City Hall and gave that Registrar what for. Stayed right with me until it was properly recorded. Not sure at all what might have happened if the judge hadn't been around to help. Five hundred dollars is a fair amount. I would hate to have lost it just because some bureaucrat didn't like my looks."

Alvin made a mental note that he needed to thank the judge personally, and then he thanked his old friend. Ben was unusually quiet. Alvin and Jeb both thought they saw a tear trickle from an eye, but before it could reach his cheek, Ben took a swipe at it, brushing it away.

CHAPTER TWENTY

THE CUT

May 1, 1871

Alvin, Jeb and Ben stood in the shallow water along the edge of Lake Michigan. Dusk was fast turning to dark. The water was still very cold from the winter just past, and a light breeze pushed gentle waves that only occasionally breeched the tops of their calf-high boots. A work crew of thirteen farmers equipped with shovels and picks stood in front of them. Alvin explained, "All right, here's the first problem we have to deal with. Jeb and I have been experimenting here. In this wet sand, we no sooner dig a trench than a wind comes up and the water fills it in. We've got to cut some trees down and line the trench with logs, at least until we get further up onto the dune."

It made for a slow start. In fact nothing got done that first night except for cutting down some trees. A few of the work crew had brought axes with them. The next night there would be horses, mules, harnesses and chains to move the cut logs from where they fell to the shallow, four-foot-wide trench that slowly began to form over the beach, up over the dune and into the heavily forested part of the isthmus they were attempting to cut through.

May 3, 1871

The farmers had decided to work at night for a couple of reasons. First, they were farmers with farms that required tending to during the day, particularly at this time of the year. Spring planting was upon them. Second, while what they were doing was perfectly legal, they knew the lumbermen would come after them the moment they got wind of what the farmers were up to. It didn't take a genius to know that this cut they were digging was meant to relieve the rising water level in Portage Lake caused by the lumbermen's dam at Portage Creek. So, the decision was made to dig at night, under the cover of darkness, and hope that their efforts might go undetected by anyone from the mill.

Last night was their first night of digging in the dense forest they'd finally reached. The digging here was much tougher than that required to cross the beach and the sand dune. The trees were close together, huge, some well over a hundred years old. Their roots sprawled everywhere. The most efficient processes involved the back-breaking work of swinging a pick, hacking with an axe, and shoveling. As the men emerged from the forest, they were tired, filthy ... and met by two of Portage's constables and a handful of workers from the Porter Company mill. To the delight of the mill workers, all thirteen men on the farmers' work crew were arrested, placed in wagons supplied by the sawmill and toted off to jail in Portage. It was only by coincidence that Alvin found out about the arrests when he went to Portage on Valiant that morning to see if he had received a letter from Lydia. Furious when he found out his work crew had been arrested, he rushed to the Portage constable's office. He demanded to know the grounds for their arrest.

The constable said, "The charge is illegal obstruction of business."

Alvin struggled to control his temper. "You arrest these men who were digging with my permission on land owned by my family for illegal obstruction of business, then I demand to file charges against the Porter sawmill for illegal obstructing of my business...no, make that illegal obstruction of the business of all farmers whose land lies around Portage Lake. Every time that dam over Portage Creek is shut, it floods our land, just as it is doing right now. When the lake floods our land, we can't farm it. Why isn't that obstruction of business as well?"

The constable stammered, "It...it...it's not the same thing."

"The hell it isn't," Alvin shouted in response.

"Mr. Price, if you don't calm down, I'll put you in jail too."

Alvin held his tongue. If he were in jail, he could do nothing to help those who'd already been incarcerated, nothing to help the farmers' cause. "I'll be back," he warned and left the office.

That evening, Alvin met the work crew and told them what had happened to the men from the night before. "If you don't want to work, I'll understand why. You could be arrested as well. I'm going into Manistee tomorrow to see Judge Ramsdell about all of this, but I can't promise anything."

All fourteen men on the work crew that evening continued to make progress on the cut.

May 4, 1871

All fourteen of the men who'd worked the night of May 3 and the early morning of May 4, were arrested by the Portage constables, accompanied by the same mill workers and their wagons. The only saving grace in all of this was that the Portage jail was too small to accommodate all twenty-seven farmers, so the ones who'd already spent a day and a night in jail were released on their own recognizance. Before heading home, the thirteen who'd just been released held a quick meeting and decided they would not be dissuaded; recognizance be damned. All of them would report for work on the cut that evening; their work would continue in spite of the peril of another arrest.

Alvin and Jeb were there when these fourteen were arrested. Ben was one of those carted off. Interference was pointless. The constables seemed to be working hand-in-glove with the mill. Between the two of them, they decided it should be Alvin to ride into Manistee. It was nearly ten o'clock in the morning when he arrived at Judge Ramsdell's office. The judge was not there, and Alvin was in no mood to play the usual game with his clerk. He sat down on the chair in the hallway and simply waited.

The judge arrived at noon, and even before Alvin could say anything, the judge said, "Just heard about it. I've got some friends who are in lumber. They think they are well within their rights to shut your digging down."

"Ultimately, sir, this is going to come down to you. So, I'm just going to ask. What do you think?"

The judge crossed his arms over his chest and said, "I placed an injunction against the dam. Porter's ignored it. That bothers me. I know you own the land you're digging on. There's nothing illegal there. The illegal obstruction of business charge could go both ways."

Alvin liked what he was hearing. "Sir, I know you have a financial interest in lumber and I know your friends are expecting your support, but we aren't going to quit digging. I'm asking you to put an end to the foolishness."

Uncrossing his arms, the judge said, "I'll ride out there this afternoon. The fresh air will do me good, and you're right, I need to put an end to the foolishness. I'll tell the constables they are to drop all previous charges, and they may not entertain any more charges against the farmers unless they have cleared them with me first."

Alvin thanked him. He rode Valiant hard in order to get home in time to tell the evening's work crew the good news.

May 5th, 1871

Four men were dedicated to constructing a bulwark, a temporary dam, at the Portage Lake end of the cut. Its purpose was to hold back Portage Lake's water while they dug their ditch. The fifteen-foot-high bulwark was made of roughhewn planks, each about a foot wide and two inches thick. Each plank was overlapped on the other and nails driven about every three or four feet apart, making it a stout wall. For extra stability, each end of it was anchored securely in an earth berm on either side. The entire bulwark was about twenty feet wide. On the side of the wall where the cut was being dug, this wall was reinforced by three heavy logs, each about twenty feet long and placed at a forty-five degree angle, one end anchored against the bulwark, the other, against the ground. The bulwark's importance couldn't be discounted. The lumbermen had already closed the dam over Portage Creek and the waters of Portage Lake were starting to rise. In a normal year, once the dam was closed, the water in the lake would rise between twelve to fourteen feet above its natural level. Without this bulwark to hold back Portage Lake's rising waters, the cut would have been rendered inconsequential; the land through which it would eventually meander, would have succumbed to the flooding caused by the dam over Portage Creek. In point of fact, flooding around the lake had already begun. At the mill, timber cut the previous winter was already queuing up to be cut into shingles in the coming months of summer and fall. For Porter and Company, all appearances pointed to business as usual.

Just before darkness fell, Alvin and Jeb stood on a small hill overlooking the bulwark. They could see that it was holding about six or seven feet of water back. That water level was rising, they estimated, about a foot every day. At that rate they estimated they would have about a week, maybe two, before water would reach the top of the bulwark and begin flowing over it. When that happened, the ground on the other side of it would soften and the three logs reinforcing the bulwark would likely become unstable. Jeb asked, "Do you think we'll get finished before water breaches the bulwark?"

"It will be close. Once it starts to breach, we might have another week before the ground gets too soggy and those logs give out. I don't think the bulwark will stand without them reinforcing it. There would just be too much water pushing against it."

Jeb had another question. "So, let's say we've got fifteen feet of water pushing against the bulwark when it comes down. What do you think's going to happen then?"

Alvin shook his head. "It's going to be a ferocious flow of water at first. Our cut won't be nearly wide enough or deep enough to accommodate the deluge right here." He pointed to the area in front of the bulwark. Then he pointed to the west. "But by the time it gets to the forest, I think the water's force will have dwindled quite a bit. Eventually, the lake will find its natural level. I think our cut will be just like Portage Creek—a little stream of water that meanders through the woods, across the sand dune and finally dumps into Lake Michigan. That's my hope anyway."

The two set off to greet the evening's work crew.

Late evening, May 13, 1871

Just a little over two weeks had passed since they'd started digging the cut. Of the five hundred feet of its total length, most of it had to be dug through dense forest, and that had taken its toll on their backs and their patience. But now that the cut was nearing its completion, everyone's mood was jubilant. A party at the Price farm, complete with banjoes, fiddles, dancing, and celebrating had been planned by the wives of these men who'd farmed every day and then worked every other night for what seemed like an eternity.

Ben strode up behind Nellie, who stood next to a table laden with every manner of food. She was replenishing the dwindled supply of biscuits with fresh ones still warm from the oven. He put his arms around her waist and pulled her close to him. She gasped with surprise. Ben, covered in dirt and mud, whispered in her ear, "Gonna be done in a coupla' hours."

Feigning disgust with his filthy clothes, she pushed herself away from him, and then chuckled as she brushed the dirt and mud from her clothes. "Ben Price, don't you come around me wearin' filthy clothes like ya are!"

He threw his head back, laughing, "Oh, come on there, Nellie girl! Ya been married to a farmer for a lotta years. Ya ain't no stranger to a little bit of mud and dirt."

Early morning, May 14, 1871

Asa Patch and his ox, Blue, stood in front of the bulwark. For the last five days, water occasionally breached the top of it and flowed down over its face. The ground under Patch's feet was muddy. Pushing on one of the logs reinforcing the bulwark, he decided it still felt steady, but he was anxious to get the ropes attached, one to each of the three support logs and get away from in front of it. Asa Patch considered it an honor that he and his ox had been asked to be the ones to peel away the bulwark. Watching it come down would be the crowning achievement of so much hard work. He'd taken bets with his coworkers on when it would come down. A few bet that when the first support log was pulled, it would collapse. A few more picked the second log as the breaking point. The majority of bets were placed on the third log. Two bets were placed on the bulwark holding even after the third support log was pulled. These were placed by two of the four men who'd built the bulwark.

Alvin had gone back up to the farm to let everyone know it was fast approaching time for them to see their work come to fruition. Jeb stayed with Asa Patch and asked, "Do you think you've got enough rope? Just a suggestion, but I think you should double, maybe even triple up the lengths of each rope. It's hard to tell what's going to happen when you pull those logs down. I'd hate for you and ol' Blue here to be in the way of whatever comes."

Patch rubbed a muddy, rough hand over his chin, "Yeah, maybe yer right. Ya got any handy? This is all I brought." He held up the coiled sections of three ropes in both hands.

"In the barn. I'll go get it." On his way, he met Alvin, Ben, Nellie and everyone else, nearly fifty people in total, all coming to see the cut opened up. "I'm getting some more rope for Asa," Jeb told Alvin. "I want to make sure he's far enough away from that wall when it comes down."

"No problem. We've waited this long. A few more minutes won't make any difference."

Jeb returned with the rope and helped Patch tie the sections together and then stepped aside, not wanting to interfere with what was to happen next. After miles of following that ox behind a plow, Patch knew that yoke and he knew his ox.

The crowd was gathered less than a hundred feet from the bulwark in a position where they could see the face of it through the looming darkness. There were a few coal-oil lanterns in the crowd, but they provided little illumination.

Asa Patch and his ox were little more than shadows moving around. Asa tied the first of the three ropes to Blue's yoke and prodded him with a switch. Slowly the ox moved toward the crowd; the rope went taut. Patch applied the switch again. Blue strained forward and the first of the three logs fell away. The bulwark remained in place. The crowd applauded, whooped and hollered. Some were disappointed, but those farmers with bets on the second or third rope or on the bulwark itself were among the more enthusiastic. The second rope was attached to the ox, and when the second reinforcing log fell away and the bulwark still stood, there was more whooping and hollering. Then, as the third rope was attached, and the ox started to move toward them, someone hollered, "Let 'er go, Asa!" Patch pulled on Blue's yoke and gave a tap with the switch on the animal's haunch. The third reinforcing log fell away, the bulwark collapsed immediately from the weight of the water behind it, and then, all hell broke loose.

The wall of water, fifteen feet high, twenty to twenty-five feet wide and getting wider with every foot it advanced, rushed past the collapsed bulwark and then came rushing at the onlookers with such tremendous velocity that none of them were prepared for it. The women grabbed their children by the hands or swooped them up in their arms and began running and screaming. Jeb and Alvin, who were standing next to one another, could see Asa Patch and his ox were in imminent danger of being swept away. Running to him, Jeb hollered, "Grab hold of that rope, Asa. Hang on."

Alvin managed to grab the ox's yoke. He could feel the ground giving way to the flow of water under his feet. Pulling on the yoke, he could feel the ox struggling, but making progress to reach more solid ground. Grunting with all of his might, pulling on the yoke with everything he was worth, Alvin and the animal could feel the ground under their feet stabilizing. But Asa, and now Jeb, were still in the water.

Alvin held the ox still, while Jeb, with a knife in one hand and the other hanging onto the rope for dear life, was struggling against the current to reach Patch. The water kept getting deeper. Jeb managed to reach Asa. "Hang on!" The other end of the rope was still tied to the reinforcing log that was now being swept away by the intense current and pulling Patch and Jeb back into the current. Jeb reached around behind Patch and cut the rope. "Pull us in, Alvin," Jeb hollered.

Pulling again on the ox's yoke, Alvin urged the animal forward. "C'mon, Blue. C'mon, let's go." The ox moved, slowly. In the darkness behind the ox, Alvin could faintly see Jeb and Asa reach dry land.

Ben could see the trouble Asa, his ox, Alvin and Jeb were in, but couldn't bring himself to leave Nellie's side. Instead, he grabbed her, and the two rushed away from the fast approaching edge of the water, trying desperately to get to a safe place. When they stopped and turned to see what was happening behind them, Ben uttered, "My God, Nellie, what have we done?"

There was no abating the rush of water even though the width of their cut had now gone from its original four feet to something approaching a hundred feet in the matter of just a few minutes. And still, the width of the cut and the water's velocity seemed to be increasing. It was anybody's guess as to the depth of the water, but the assumption had to be that as width and velocity increased, so did depth. Proof of that was in the trees. Trees, entire forests of hemlock, beech, maple, ash and oak, roots and all, were swept along by the cascading water.

Once sure Asa and his ox were safe, Alvin and Jeb rushed to Ben and Nellie. Alvin asked, "Are you all right?"

Both nodded. Ben repeated, "What have we done?"

There wasn't time for an answer. Ben and Nellie were safe. That's all they needed to know as the two rushed off toward the west, paralleling the surging waters looking for anyone at all who might need their help. At this moment neither of them could be sure people hadn't been caught up in the current. It was a haunting thought.

At about noon on May 14, 1871, the captain of the steamer, *John A. Dix,* walked into the office of the United States Life Saving Service located in Manistee, Michigan. *The Dix* had just made port call there. He asked to see the person in charge. He needed to report that a hazard to vessels lurked off the shores of Lake Michigan just due west of Portage Lake. Finding that person, he related a hair-raising story about waking up this morning in a forest of trees floating in Lake Michigan covering acres and acres of what should have been just water.

May 15, 1871

The day after the cut, Alvin, Jeb and Ben stood looking north on the last foot of solid ground fronting a hundred-yard-wide sea of mud that stretched as far east and west of them as the eye could see. Yesterday, before the cut, this mud flat was underwater, but today, after twenty-four hours of draining caused by the cut, there was nothing but mud and something else they hadn't counted on. From their vantage point, they could see fish lying lifeless on top of the mud, their life-giving water drained west into Lake Michigan. These were the unfortunate ones who'd missed the current that could have swept them to safety. In a rather large, shallow depression in the ground about ten feet in front of them that Alvin estimated was only a foot deep, they saw dozens of fish swimming around, blissfully ignorant that their fate would be sealed as soon as they'd consumed what little oxygen there was for them in the puddle's water, or that the water would soon simply evaporate, leaving them floundering in the mud.

Ben asked, "What the hell we gonna do 'bout them, boys? I like fresh fish as well as the next man, but we can't eat all of 'em and we can't smoke all of 'em either ... a week or so, they gonna be stinkin' to high heaven."

Jeb stepped off their solid footing and immediately sank well over his boot tops in the mud. When he pulled his foot out to step back, there was a sucking sound. "Well, it doesn't look like we are going to be able to do too much until this mud dries out a little."

May 21, 1871

Ben, Alvin and Jeb began collecting the bigger fish carcasses, still wading in mud to the tops of their shoes. These carcasses were used as fertilizer, spread in the fields where they'd just planted corn and oats. Each day when they returned from their day's labor moving the dead fish, Nellie made them go to the retaining pond at the artesian well, strip, and wash thoroughly, including their hair. Their clothes went into a straw basket she'd put on the front porch. In the morning she'd collect them and wash them for the following day's work.

Late evening, May 25, 1871

Alvin Price sat at the small desk in front of his second-floor bedroom window and looked out. From it he could see their barn, Jeb and Dancing Flower's cabin and the stand of hemlock that stood between the farmhouse and Portage Lake on the northern edge of their property. What he couldn't see through the darkness were the effects of what they'd led the farmers to do. But in his mind's eye, he could see the channel, far wider and deeper than anyone had ever thought it would be. He thought he should write Lydia and tell her what had happened. He wouldn't mail it, because she would be home for the summer, before it would ever reach East Lansing, but he felt like he needed to make some record of what he'd led the farmers into. On a recent trip into town, he'd picked up a couple of newspapers and read what they had to say about the cut.

Manistee Times, May 20, 1871

On Saturday, an excursion was gotten up and the barge, D.L. Filer, in tow of her faithful envoy, the tug Williams, started for Williamsport. She glided down the river and out into the lake as if conscious she was observed by all the observers. About two hundred people bought tickets at fifty cents each and went to see the latest nine-day wonder, just cut through from Portage Lake to Lake Michigan.

The vessel went into the new harbor, took a circle around the lake to the great joy of the inhabitants, who were out in force to witness the entrance to their harbor for the first large craft that ever rode upon the water of their beautiful lake. Near the entrance to their harbor is raised a flag and under the flag in large letters are the words, "free homesteaders independence". The company returned about seven o'clock P.M. well pleased with their ride and the beautiful lake and the country round about.

In the same newspaper on the same date:

The newly made harbor, and the opening it makes for the safe investment of capital and enterprise, is of vast importance to Manistee County. The entrance of the harbor is so short, wide and deep as to allow the largest crafts that sail on the Great Lakes to enter from North or South in any kind of weather, and with such an appropriation as Congress will undoubtedly make, piers can be built that will ensure a safe entrance for all time to come.

The people of Portage are hard-working and honest and the

question that interests them most is what use can be made of or advantage gained by the new harbor thus suddenly opened to them? They have only to look to the almost inexhaustible supply of hard timber and the various uses to which it can be put to answer this question. There is any quantity of maple of superior quality, birdseye, curly and white straight grain that is valuable for making furniture, fancy flooring and other fine work; while the body timber is thus used the tops and refuse timber can be manufactured into cord wood, for which a good price and ready sale can be had.

There is also beech, ash, pine and hemlock, all of which are valuable. Large quantities of cedar can also be obtained for shipment. There is no place on the lake that is as suggestive of smelting works, rolling mills, etc. as Portage. The distance to the celebrated Lake Superior iron mines is not great, and vessels laden with ore can lay up so close to land with perfect safety as to preclude the use of docks. Vessels drawing 14 feet of water can lie within four feet of shore in many places.

It seems that this opening of the harbor is a wealth suddenly sprung upon the settlers, for while clearing up their farms, every stick of wood can be made to bring money and then the land is as good for farming purposes as any in the state. We reasonably expect that in a short time large farms well fenced and with good buildings will dot the once unavailable tract of land, and that shops of industry will line this beautiful haven. And a mass of commerce once thus established will give to Portage a name and position among the most beautiful and prosperous of our lake shore harbors.

May 6, 1871

Alvin went to Portage to check the mail. Along with a letter from Lydia, he also got a hard time. "Well, Mr. Price, I hope you're happy," the mill's supervisor said as he handed him the letter.

Alvin shrugged, "We did what we had to do. We told Mr. Porter that we would have no objection if he wanted to convert your mill to steam. He didn't bother to respond to either our letter or a letter Judge Ramsdell sent him. More important, it was obvious to us farmers you were not going to abide by the judge's injunction."

"Well, there's a lot of men out of work, thanks to you. I'm heading to Chicago to see what Mr. Porter wants to do now. If the mill closes permanently, it's your fault, Mr. Price. Without the dam, there's no water to drive the water wheel. Without the water wheel, there's no muley saw. For now, you and your cut have put us out of business. There's nobody else to blame except you," he said over his shoulder as he walked away.

Alvin slouched in the desk chair in his bedroom, his legs splayed out in front of him, the conversation at the mill earlier in the day still angered him. He pulled in a deep breath and let it out. All around him the farm lay shrouded in the darkness of a cloudy evening, a partial moon only occasionally breaking through. Crickets chirping occasionally broke the quiet of a soft spring night. He took his pocketknife and carefully cut the envelope open, took out her letter and began to read.

April 1, 1871

My Darling Alvin,

Today I was able to confirm with my professors that I will be finished with school for this first year by May 29. I plan to arrive home by June 1. I have an idea with which I hope you are in agreement. I should spend that first week with my mother, aunt and, of course, my father. I include him last, because I fully expect he will be furious with the plan I am about to propose. I would like to join you and your family at the farm by June 12, and I want to spend the rest of the summer through the end of August with you there.

Much of the motivation behind this plan is that I want to be as close to you as I can for as long as I can this summer before

I must return to college for my second year. But there is another reason as well. The professor, whose family I live with here in East Lansing, has suggested that the summer spent with you on your farm would be an excellent laboratory experience for me. I will be able to see firsthand what I have studied in books this past year. Alvin, farming is becoming a science. This past year, I have studied hardest at chemistry ... the chemistry of soils and the chemistry of various plants and what they require of the soil, and what they give back to it as well. I want to share a lot of this knowledge with you, Jeb, and your father, if you will allow me.

I fully expect that Nellie will make sure that we spend our time together within respectful boundaries, which I know means you will be relegated to the kitchen, or, perhaps the barn. I understand her wishes and know you do too. I know how busy life on the farm can be, but I'm also sure you and I can carve out time to ourselves during the summer. I have missed you so very much and cannot wait to be in your arms again.

Please plan on meeting me at my aunt's shop on June 12. After I've kissed your tender lips, we can discuss my plan fully. Until then, remember,

I love you always,

Lydia

Alvin fell asleep hoping that the stench of dead fish would be off him, off his bibs and out of the air around the farm before Lydia's arrival. Where he slept was of little importance to him as long as he and Lydia would be together during their waking hours.

CHAPTER TWENTY-ONE

SUMMERTIME

May 30, 1871

Augustine Farr, Portage Mill's new supervisor, Lee Porter, the mill's owner, and Reilly Cockrum stood on the elevated floor of the Portage Mill. Behind them, the muley saw sat idle, the waterwheel that normally drove it was absolutely motionless, sitting well above the trickle of water that once was Portage Creek. Outside, a hard rain was falling. The three men surveyed the mud flat that stretched out in front of them. Lying in a tangle on that mud flat were thousands of logs.

Porter muttered, "The farmers have no idea the havoc they've wreaked."

While Farr nodded, Reilly Cockrum asked Porter, "How much lumber you think is lying there?" Porter wordlessly swung around to Farr giving him a look as if to say, *So, yes, Mr. Farr, do tell. How much money is lying there in that mud?*

Farr rubbed a hand over his cheek and thought for a moment, then replied, "Rough guess? Three...three and a half million board feet. There's an entire summer and fall's worth of work lying there."

The number stunned Cockrum. "My God. I had no idea."

Porter offered, "That's why I've asked you out here today, Cockrum. Word is you're the best railroad engineer in the US. I've got to get that lumber off this mud and to my other mill, otherwise I'm going to lose tens of thousands of dollars. I can't take horses, mules and men out there to collect those logs. It's too damned soggy, and I can't wait for the summer to dry things out. So, my thought is to have you build a railroad. I think you railroad men refer to it as 'narrow gauge.' Is that right?" Reilly Cockrum nodded. Porter continued, "My idea would be to build it through the middle of that jumble of logs, right to the water's edge and then along the edge of the water for a ways both east and west. The dock we have running now out into Lake Michigan isn't any good to us anymore. I'm gonna shut that and this mill down. Let the damn things rot for all I care. But if we could create a safe harbor port out there," he said, pointing to the lake beyond the mud flat, "well, we could move vessels in and out of here easily through that cut the farmers made. We wouldn't have to worry about storms in here. It's a safe haven. Vessels could load, unload, take as long as they needed. We could move lumber right up to the ship's side on railcars and offload directly from one mode of conveyance to another. Other mills around here could move their lumber to my port. We'd charge them for using our railroad system, a fee for handling in our port, and we'd charge the ship's owners a small docking fee. Hell, I might even build a steam operated mill out here somewhere on Portage Lake myself. The farmers have told me in a letter they'd have no objection to that. So, what do you think?"

Cockrum didn't immediately answer. Instead, he peered intently out over the mud and scanned up and down the water's edge. When he spoke, he had a question of his own. "How quickly are you wanting this done, Porter?" It was tit for tat. *If I'm going to be Cockrum, then you're going to be Porter.*

Porter wasn't a man who was used to someone trifling

with him. He caught Reilly's intended dropping of the more formal *Mister* just as Porter had done upon first meeting Cockrum. Porter gave him a hard look and then said, "Ummm...I'd like to see those logs start moving to the mills by August at the latest."

Reilly Cockrum had grown accustomed to outlandish demands while working for the Union army during the war. None of the generals he'd worked with understood the engineering involved in designing railbeds, Grant and Sherman chief among them. He chuckled, "I'm not at all sure you know what you're asking. The railbed through that jumble will be nearly as long as the farmers' cut, maybe even a few rods longer. And then, if you want to lay rail along the water's edge, we will have to fashion a radius of turn in both directions, east and west. It's true that narrow gauge requires a shorter radius, but still..." That hung in the air for just a moment, and then Cockrum added, "It's a lot of railbed to establish in such a short period of time in extremely unstable ground, Porter."

"Come now, Mr. Cockrum. I have an abundance of labor available. The mill's closure has produced nothing but misery here in Portage. The men around these parts are hungry for work. So, if that's what you're worried about..."

Cockrum, now pleased that this haughty Chicago businessman put the word *Mister* back in his vocabulary, interrupted while pointing to the mud, "Until we get started, it's impossible for me to say what exactly is necessary to build a stable roadbed. Right now, all I'm looking at is a sea of mud. Will you allow me to use some of those logs to stabilize a roadbed?"

Porter waved a hand, "As many as you might need."

Cockrum asked another question. "Where are you going to get the locomotives and the railcars?"

"Let me worry about that. I have some railroad friends in

Chicago. They're the same ones who recommended I talk to you about the design work and supervising the construction. They tell me there are companies in Chicago that can supply me with the operating equipment when I need it."

"Do you have someplace out here I could stay? I'm going to need to be on site day and night until we get this thing up and running, if we are going to make your tight schedule."

Porter turned to Farr, who nodded and said, "That can be easily arranged, Mr. Cockrum."

Now we're getting somewhere, Reilly Cockrum thought. "Your need for haste, means my fee will require a surcharge."

Porter didn't hesitate, "I'm assured you are the only man for this job. Let's go to the office and talk about your salary requirements and my timetable."

June 1, 1871

Two days after her father's meeting with Porter, at four o'clock in the afternoon, Lydia stepped down from the stagecoach, straightened her dress and hat, and spotted her mother and aunt waiting to greet her. The three ran into each other's arms. Amid laughter and a few tears of joy, Lydia asked, "Father's still angry with me?"

Irene looked at Liliane and then back to Lydia, "He's working."

Lydia was disappointed he wasn't there, but she had prepared herself that he might not be or that she might immediately have to deal with his disapproval in some way. She was actually somewhat relieved as she shrugged her shoulders. "Has either one of you seen Alvin?" she asked as her eyes scanned the surrounding area.

Smiling, Liliane said, "I saw Alvin a week or so ago. He came into the shop. He looks well and can't wait to see you, but he thought it best to avoid being here today. He wanted to, dear, with all his heart, I'm sure. But he thought your father would ... well, he just didn't want you to have to ...."

Irene broke in, "So, I have some good news, I think. I received your letter about your plan to spend most of your summer at the Price farm. I've shared that plan with your father. I shouldn't need to tell you he was furious, especially in light of what has just recently happened."

There was a note of panic in her voice as Lydia asked, "What's that, Mother? What's happened?"

"You don't know? I wasn't sure if Alvin had written ..."

Now a greater note of panic, "What is it? What's happened?"

Irene held up a hand, "Alvin and his family are just fine. It's nothing like that. I'll tell you all about it at dinner. Liliane has it cooking at her place. Your father is going to be gone all summer and well into the fall. He's working on a railroad at Portage and it's a rush job. He's staying out there. I doubt that I'll see him more than once or twice this summer, if that much."

Liliane asked, "Lydia, where are your bags?"

Her mother and aunt's nonchalance quelled some of her concern, but not all of it.

Liliane said again, "Let's get your bags and go to the apartment. Dinner will be ready soon, and your mother and I can fill you in while we eat and get you settled. We thought you might like to stay with me until you go to the farm."

"Both of you please tell me once more, Alvin is all right." They nodded.

Irene said, "To a lot of people around here, Alvin, Jebediah and Ben are real heroes."

That comment really piqued Lydia's interest. *Heroes! What's happened?*

June 12, 1871

The first eleven days of Lydia's summer went by too slowly for her. She'd grown accustomed to an academic routine at college, and the leisurely reading she attempted during the first days of her summer away from school failed to challenge her. And then there were her constant thoughts of Alvin. She knew he would be very busy on the farm this time of year. She'd also been given the details on the cut as best as they were known to her mother and her aunt. She had spent some time at the newspaper office, reading as many of their articles on the event as she could get her hands on. Today would be her chance to hear the entire story from Alvin himself.

For hours, Lydia had been packed and anxiously awaiting Alvin's arrival at her aunt's millinery shop. Her only piece of luggage was the cedar chest he'd given her at Christmas. It contained all new clothes suitable for work on the farm. Her wardrobe she'd brought home from school and the one she had in her closet at home just weren't suitable for the kind of work she hoped she'd be doing this summer at the Price farm. In there, as well, was a stack of seven letters bound together in a red ribbon, that Alvin had written to her over the course of the past year. Lydia's plan was for the chest to remain at the Price farm forever, and that she and Alvin, as they were able to find time this summer, would reread their letters written to each other this past year, only this time they'd read them together, side by side, arm in arm. She'd also packed a sack of seeds in there. They were part of an experiment she and one of her professors had carefully worked out before she left East Lansing for the summer.

When she saw Amos and Tom pull to a stop in front of the shop, Lydia was out the door. As soon as he saw her, Kip set to barking, loudly. Interspersed between barks were anxious yips of excitement in anticipation of her touch. Alvin pulled back the wagon's brake lever, tied the reins to it, jumped down and, before he could take a step, she was in his arms. Kip continued his clamor. As they kissed, several passersby smiled at them. Two elderly ladies frowned and began whispering in hushed tones implying some kind of breach of Victorian etiquette. None of it mattered to either Alvin or Lydia.

At the end of the kiss, he kept her in his embrace and whispered into her ear, "It is so good to have you home."

She'd imagined this moment since she'd last seen him at Christmas. She'd spent hours thinking about getting lost in his blue eyes. It was late spring, and he'd been at work in the fields, so his face was already tan, making his eyes seem even bluer. Lydia replied, "You have no idea how good it feels to have you in my arms again. There wasn't an hour gone by this year that I haven't thought of you...missed you."

Lydia helped Alvin load the heavy chest onto the wagon. They had just started to roll down River Street toward the bridge over the Manistee River. Kip had somehow managed to get in between them, until Lydia admonished, "Oh, no you don't." She patted the seat on the other side of her and as the dog moved over, she scooted as close to Alvin as she could get. "It's all over town, Alvin. People are calling you heroes...Jeb, Ben, and you." The letter he'd written to her about the cut was in the front pocket of his bibs. He was reaching for it when Lydia said, "So, we've got a long ride ahead of us. Tell me what happened. I want to hear it from you."

His hand fell away from the pocket. But before he started to tell her about the cut and the events leading up to it, he smiled at her and said, "I've got some bigger news than the cut. Jeb and Dancing Flower are going to have a baby."

Lydia squealed with delight and stomped her feet on the wagon's floor. "Alvin, that's the greatest news I've heard this year! A baby ... I'm so happy for them. I can't wait to be there ... to hold it ... to see the expression on Jeb's face." She cast him a mischievous smile, "Or, to see the expression on your face!" They rode for just a few minutes, and after she'd settled down from the excitement of Dancing Flower and Jeb's good news, she pursued her previous request, "So, don't think that even good news like that is going to throw me off the trail. Tell me everything about the cut."

It was a beautiful late spring day. Alvin kept the horses at a very slow pace, relishing these first few hours alone with her. He knew once they got to the farm, alone time like this would be limited. As they got closer to Portage Lake, however, Lydia screwed up her nose and asked, "What is that smell?"

"Fish." He shrugged sheepishly. "Dead ones rotting on the land around the lake that used to be underwater. It's better now than it was a few weeks ago, but the smell still lingers. It probably won't be completely gone until this winter. You can't believe how many there were. We actually used a lot of them as fertilizer. Up until a few days ago, that's all Jeb, Pa and I were doing, hauling dead fish into the fields we'd planted."

Their arrival home was a clamorous one. Lydia was particularly joyful as she greeted Dancing Flower. After a hug, she placed her hand on Dancing Flower's tummy, "Oh my. It can't be long now." And then she bombarded her with a dozen questions. Jeb helped out with translating duty.

That afternoon, as Alvin and Jeb were moving Lydia's cedar chest into his room where Lydia would sleep, Alvin placed the letter he'd written to her about the cut on top of it. He'd already told her everything, yet he was still happy he'd written it. It might one day be helpful in separating fact from fiction, in separating truth from legend.

At suppertime, Lydia came down from her room carrying the sack of seeds she'd brought from East Lansing. After everyone had settled around the table, and Ben had asked the blessing, he pointed to the cloth sack on the floor and asked, "What's in the bag, Lydia?"

She smiled at him. "Bean seeds."

Ben threw back his head and laughed, "What kind? Like the ones Jack had?" When no one else laughed, Ben's face took on a sheepish look as if apologizing for a bad joke.

Lydia, who was sitting opposite Nellie and next to Ben at the head of the table, softly placed her hand on his and said, "Ben, I love the story of *Jack and the Beanstalk*, but these are soybeans."

"I've heard about them, but don't know much. Are they a feed crop?"

Lydia replied, "That's one use. There's also a lot of ongoing research using them as dietary supplements to our food as well. Like your apples, soybeans could be a cash crop too. If you'll allow me, I'd like to plant these seeds here on the farm."

Alvin kept eating. He'd already heard of Lydia's plan on the trip from Manistee. It was a good one, involving science, something that he believed in even if her long explanation of it left him with more questions than there was time to answer on the way home.

Lydia continued, "I want to perform an experiment over the next few summers, Ben. I want to see if maybe I can make your fields produce even more than they are producing now."

Ben said, "That sounds good to me. How's it work?"

"What I would like to do is plant these soybeans. They

can be a feed crop this year. When you harvest this fall I would like to measure how many beans we harvest in the soybean field and how much corn we take from a field of similar size."

Ben stopped her with a question. "Lydia, what do you mean 'measure'. Bean countin' seems like it would take a lot of time, and around here time is hard to come by."

She agreed. "I understand. I don't mean we have to count individual beans. We can count bushels or barrels or something like that which we take from each field. It really doesn't matter as long as the unit of measure is consistent."

Ben, though he'd farmed all of his life, had never bothered to measure crop yields from his fields. They had always yielded what they yielded. It had always been that plain and simple for him. Nonetheless, he said, "All right. It'll take a little extra time to do that though."

Lydia continued, "Then next summer, a year from now, I would like to plant soybeans in the cornfield and corn in the soybean field."

If questions were an indicator, Ben was paying attention. "Why switch things up like that?"

Rotating crops was not new. Scholars traced its history back even further than the Middle Ages. But more recently, Dr. George Washington Carver was doing extensive research with it to benefit southern farmers. Lydia had studied some of his work at school. "It has to do with the chemistry of the soil and the plant. The thinking is that by rotating crops grown in a field, one crop will take different chemicals from the soil as it grows, and a different crop planted the next year can actually replace the chemicals taken from the soil."

Ben said, "Sounds complicated. A lot we'd have to keep track of."

It was the second time Ben inferred there wasn't enough time to do the record keeping the experiment would require, and Nellie had had enough of it. She jumped in. "Honestly, ol' man. Sometimes you make it sound like you're the only one who works on this farm. Me 'n' Dancin' Flower can keep up with the ledger work. Now hush up and let the girl talk." Ben demurred, once again maneuvered around by Nellie.

"The purpose of my experiment is to determine if, after a few years of rotating crops like this, we can increase production of each crop."

Ben looked alternately between Alvin and Jeb. Alvin was the first to speak up. "It's a good idea. I was thinking some of that new land we got since the cut that lies down by the cornfield ... well, Lydia and I could get busy tilling. Still kind of wet, I'll grant you. But it's drying out. I can let Lydia look at it and see what she thinks, but I'll bet we could get those seeds in the ground by month's end. Be close before first hard frost sets in, but I'm willing to take that risk. Meantime, you and Jeb can plant the new apple seedlings." Out of the corner of his eye, Alvin could see Jeb nodding.

Ben said, "I guess we're gonna grow some soybeans this summer then. "

Two days later, Alvin and Lydia hitched a team of mules up to a small cart. A plow was loaded in the back of it. Alvin helped Kip aboard and the three of them headed northwest in the direction of the farm's main cornfield. Before the cut, that cornfield lay only a few rods from the flood plain caused by the Porter Sawmill's damming of Portage Creek. Now, however, since the lake had subsided back to its natural level after the cut, there were ten to twelve rods of muddy, but potentially arable land between the cornfield and the water's edge.

Kneeling down, Lydia scooped up a handful of mud,

looked up at Alvin, and said, "I don't know. It's still pretty soggy."

"Dry season's just around the corner though. The good part is that there's not a lot of clearing to do. This was all underwater until about a month ago; it's drying pretty quickly, and the spring rains have been light this year. If you'd been here a month ago and seen this parcel of land, you'd see what I'm saying. I think it's worth the risk." He smiled and said, "And these aren't the last soybean seeds left in the world, are they?"

She laughed, shook her head, and asked a question prompted by the strong smell dead fish. "Did you use dead fish as fertilizer in the cornfield?"

He answered her with a nod of his head just as he read her mind, "Oh Lydia, no... you don't want to..."

She put a hand on her hip, and in a firm voice said, "Want to...no. But must we...yes. For the experiment to be a good one, all the variables have to be equal. So, if you used dead fish in the cornfield, we must use very nearly an equal amount of them in the soybean field. It's the only way we will know if our results have any accuracy at all, Alvin."

"But they are rotting. They'll fall apart as you pick them up. You don't know what..."

Lydia grabbed a piece of canvas and headed for the mudflat. Over her shoulder she said to him, "I'm getting started. I'll throw the pieces on the tarp and then pull it back to where we want to plant." Alvin hung his head, shook it and then rushed to catch up to her.

It took the two of them a week to plant the soybeans in the mudflat. Each morning they would leave the farm at daybreak, work all day, and return well after dark. For this week, Alvin and Lydia missed taking their dinner with the rest of the family and, while regrettable, it was a matter of necessity. The two of them came home reeking of dead fish just as Alvin, Jeb and Ben had when they were hauling dead fish to fertilize the fields. So, their routine for this week involved each of them bathing separately, of course, and under the cover of darkness, in the pond created by the artesian well's overflow. Their filthy, smelly clothes were placed in the same basket on the farmhouse porch that the three men had used. Nellie and Dancing Flower would then wash, line dry and fold them for use the next day. Nellie always kept a plate for each of them, but neither were permitted inside the farmhouse until they'd gotten the dead fish smell off themselves.

Several days after Lydia and Alvin completed planting the field of soybeans, the two were hauling stone jugs of water from the artesian well to the farmhouse when Lydia asked,

"Could we go into Manistee this weekend? I'd like to see my mother."

If she would have asked him to take her to the moon, he would have said yes and found a way.

CHAPTER TWENTY-TWO

THE RECKONING

Fourth of July, 1871

I t had taken them until the Fourth of July holiday to get into Manistee to see Lydia's mother, Irene, and her Aunt Liliane. Their visit had been a good one. The two women were excellent cooks, and Lydia and Alvin had eaten like a king and queen. They'd gone to Creeping Joe for fireworks. Alvin had made a makeshift bench and secured it to the bed of the wagon for Irene and Liliane to sit on. Amos and Tom, the two draft horses, were at first a bit skittish to the overhead noise and lights but settled down after the first few explosions of fireworks. Kip, on the other hand, slicked his ears back, whined and spent that spectacular hour as close to Lydia as he could get. Her arm around him, holding him close, she'd lean into his good ear and whisper to him when she felt him shudder from a loud noise.

Alvin had sensed that Lydia wanted some time alone with her mother and aunt, and he'd made sure she had that while he ran a series of errands in town.

July 15, 1871

They'd been back for over a week. For the moment, the farm's many daily chores were caught up. It was a beautifully clear morning and the temperature was rising. Lydia, with a hint of trepidation in her voice, asked, "Could we take a trip to Portage today? We could take Valiant."

Her request was puzzling to him. He had avoided any discussion of her father. The man was a difficult subject for either of them to talk about. All Alvin knew was Reilly Cockrum was working at Portage over the summer. Lydia had told him that much, and it was no secret a railroad was under construction there to recover the logs left stranded by the cut.

Lydia said, "It's been a while since you've gone over there to check on mail, and ..."

Her pause seemed ominous to Alvin and he knew the mail wasn't the real reason she wanted to go to Portage. He knew she was aware the Post Office had been moved a few miles east and renamed Onekama since the sawmill had been put out of business by the cut. But he didn't press the point.

Hesitantly, Lydia said, "I ... I want to see my father. If the mountain won't come to Muhammed, Muhammed must go to the mountain. I'd like for you to come with me."

"You haven't seen him since you've been home, have you?" The question spawned the first tear down Lydia's cheek. Alvin gently brushed it away with his thumb. "I'm sure it's just because he's busy."

She shook her head and said, "It's because he knows I'm spending the summer here ... with you ... and he can't stand the thought ..." She cut herself short, took a moment to gather her thoughts and continued, "In a letter I sent her last winter, I told Mother of my plan to spend the summer at the farm. I asked her if she would break the news to Father. She did and he's avoided me—he couldn't even meet me the first day I got home from school. He could have found the time ..." The tears flowed freely now. "But he hasn't. So, I want to go see him. I talked to Mother and Aunt Liliane about him when we saw them over the Fourth. They said I should probably make the effort since he's being so stubborn, but I want you there when that happens."

"Lydia, I will do anything you ask, but do you think this is a good idea?"

"No, I don't. What I do know is that at some point he's either going to have to accept the fact that I am hopelessly in love with you, and I intend to spend the rest of my life with you, or he's going to have to stay away from me for the rest of my life ... stay away from you ... stay away from us."

It was hot and humid as Reilly Cockrum made his way from the railbed's construction site to the former Portage sawmill's offices. His mood was as hot as the weather. The current work crew was six men short and they were falling behind schedule. He entered through the mill store's entrance, the store itself still in operation to serve the needs of the men and their families who now labored to construct Lee Porter's new railroad.

"Hello, Father." Lydia's voice was clear and distinct.

Reilly looked up to see her standing not far from him; Alvin Price was behind her. A bad day for him had suddenly become worse. His contempt for Price, rage at his daughter's poor choice in men and anger at the both of them made his tone quite ugly. "Lydia ... what are you doing here?" He pointed past her, "What is he doing here?"

She was tempted to take Alvin by the arm, turn on her heel and leave, chalking this up as a big mistake, but she resisted that urge. Instead, she said, "Alvin was kind enough to bring me here to see you."

"What is it you want, Lydia. I'm busy—"

"Yes, Father, I'm quite sure you're busy. It does strike me however, that you might want to thank Alvin."

Reilly Cockrum clenched his fists and almost screamed, "Thank him! Thank him! For what?"

"Well, if Alvin, Jeb and Ben hadn't organized the farmers to make the cut, you wouldn't have this job."

He waved his hand around the room, "Look what they did to this mill. It's shut down. Men are out of work. It's a blow to the lumber industry ... "

She interrupted him, "Look outside, Father. No one is out of work. There's a railroad to be built. There's lumber to be moved in and out of Portage Lake through the cut."

Frustration evident, he threw up his hands. "Lydia, honestly, you can be even more frustrating to me than your mother."

That was it, a final insult. He'd managed to completely alienate her. She turned to leave.

Cockrum kept it up. "And you, Mr. Price. What have you done to my daughter?"

Lydia started to fire back, "He hasn't done any—" and then she felt Alvin's light touch on her arm.

"Mr. Cockrum, if I had a daughter as precious as Lydia, I suspect I might feel as you do. I am only a farmer. My parents are homesteaders. I only have one arm. But I assure you, sir, no man has ever loved a woman more than I love Lydia."

Again, Reilly Cockrum threw his arms up in disgust and marched toward the stairs and his office. Lydia, angry and reduced to tears, in a shaky voice but loud enough for her father to hear said, "Let's go. There's no reasoning with someone so stubborn."

They rode tandem on Valiant, Lydia positioned just in front of him, sitting sidesaddle. Her arms were around Alvin and her head lay on his chest. Even with the up and down of Valiant's gait, he could feel her sobs. He wished he had the words to comfort her, but the rift between her and her father was now laid wide open, and he just didn't know what the right words might be. He kept quiet for nearly all of their ride back to the farm.

Once home and in the barn, they dismounted and began to put Valiant up for the night. As Alvin pulled the saddle off him, Lydia said, "Alvin, I'm going to ask you something. You don't have to answer right away. But before I ask, I want you to know two things. First, I'm asking you because I know that right now you'd never ask me and, second, I'm not asking because I'm trying to lash out at my father, but I can see where it might look like that."

He reached out with his strong right arm, pulled her close to him, and gently said, "He really doesn't care for me at all, does he?"

His classic understatement of the fact almost made her chuckle; instead she lowered her head, shook it and said, "No."

Alvin smiled at her. "Lydia, his attitude toward me doesn't change in the least the way I feel about you. So, what is it you want to ask me?"

Gazing up at him, she returned his smile and said, "I know I'm being very forward...very precocious, but I'd like to know if you'd marry me?" She paused briefly and added, "I don't mean three years from now. I'm asking if you'd marry me right now...this summer...maybe after Jeb and Dancing Flower's baby is born. I wouldn't want to take away from that joyous event."

Stunned, it took him a moment to ask, "What about...."

She interrupted him, "College?"

"Yes. You've worked so hard..."

She held up her hand and said, "Oh, I'm going back to East Lansing. I'm going to graduate. But I want to marry you right now. I really hoped my father would come around, but after what I just saw and heard...well, he's not ever going to change his mind about you or me...or us. That will forever be his loss. In the meantime, we can be together during the summers here on the farm. Maybe you can come to East Lansing for Christmas and New Year's while I am finishing school. After that, we need never to be apart." Lydia kissed him deeply, and when their lips parted, she whispered to him, "I love you, Alvin Price, and I believe you love me too. I see no reason why we should not prolong our happiness together as man and wife. Do you?"

"Are you sure?"

"I've never been more sure of anything in my life!" was her immediate reply.

CHAPTER TWENTY-THREE

UNFORSEEN EVENTS

July 31, 1871

J eb flung open the farmhouse door, stepped in, and said, "Water's broke, Nellie. She's in labor."

Lydia and Nellie were kneading bread. Nellie, her voice calm and reassuring said, "Put a pot of water on to boil at your cabin. I'll gather some things here. I'll be right there, Jeb." He hurried back to their cabin. Nellie turned to Lydia and asked, "Can you finish here?"

"Yes, of course, Nellie. You go," Lydia said, excitement in her voice.

"Soon as you set that dough to risin' come on over to the cabin. This is an amazin' thing to see, a new life comin' into this ol' world."

Late that evening, Jeb and Dancing Flower's baby came into the world screaming like a banshee. Standing on the front porch of their cabin, Ben clapped Jeb on the back and chortled, "Ain't nothin' wrong with its lungs!" About that time Lydia flung the door open and announced, "It's a boy, Jeb, fine and healthy. Dancing Flower's just fine too."

Jeb looked at her, smiled, and then nodded to Ben and Alvin, "It's a boy. Isn't that something? I've got another son."

193

"Got a name picked out?" Ben asked.

Nodding, Jeb said, "Sure do. Alvin Benjamin Washington. We thought we'd call him AB to avoid any confusion."

Lydia walked over to Alvin and put her arms around him. "How about that. You and Ben have a namesake." She'd never seen any of these men cry, but she watched all three of them brush aside a few tears.

August 20, 1871

Three weeks after AB Washington was born, Alvin and Lydia were wed at the Price farm by the same pastor who'd married Jeb and Dancing Flower. Nellie and Dancing Flower, assisted by Irene Cockrum and Liliane Burke, who'd arrived two days earlier, had the farmhouse's front porch beautifully decorated, and between the four women, sufficient food had been prepared to feed all of the surrounding farm families, including the children. In all there were over fifty people there for the wedding and the celebration that followed. Reilly Cockrum, though invited, failed to show up.

Somewhere around dusk, Jeb hitched Amos and Tom up to the wagon and pulled it in front of the barn. Two rows of guests formed in front of them. A pair of old boots and some tin cans were tied to the rear of the wagon which was decorated with an elaborate chain of wildflowers that Dancing Flower had fashioned. As he always did, Alvin helped his new bride to climb aboard and then followed her. As he rolled the reins over the horses' backs and they began to move forward, the couple was showered with rice.

Nellie had put a leash around Kip's neck, and he was straining at it and barking furiously as they pulled away. Finally, she bent down, put an arm around the dog and said to him, "Not tonight, Kip. You're staying home with me." Alvin and Lydia would spend their first night as man and wife camped out near the soybean field, which was flourishing.

September 4, 1871

Two weeks after Alvin and Lydia were married, it was time for her to return to college. Irene and Liliane waited in front of the mercantile store. The stagecoach was there loading some freight as Alvin and Lydia pulled up in the wagon. She was pressed as close to him as she could get, and Kip, on her other side and seeming to sense her sorrow, was pressed against Lydia. They climbed down and Alvin told the dog to stay. Lydia went to her mother and her aunt as Alvin gathered her luggage for the trip to East Lansing. She held out a stack of letters bound together by a red ribbon and handed them to her mother. "I was going to take these with me, but I've thought better of that. They are my letters to Alvin last year from school, and his letters to me. Would you please take them home and put them in the dresser in my bedroom?"

Chiding her daughter, Irene asked, "Aren't you afraid Liliane and I might read them?"

Smiling, Lydia replied, "Go ahead. There's nothing in there but our love for one another."

The summer had flown by, and it was time for her to leave. When Alvin had seen the last of her bags stowed on the stagecoach, he joined the women. Lydia fell into his arms. Irene and Liliane stepped away, giving them some privacy. Lydia asked, "You promise you will come to East Lansing for Christmas and New Year's?"

Pulling her closer to him, he said, "Nothing could keep me away."

She nuzzled her cheek against his chest. "I'm going to miss you so much." They stood there for at least a minute, neither willing to break the hold each had on the other.

Finally, it was Lydia, the scientist, who looked up at him and asked, "You're sure you, Jeb and Ben will measure the corn and soybean crops carefully? I've set up the ledger for Nellie and Dancing Flower to record everything. You have to be sure they get the information." They both saw the stagecoach's driver mount up and heard him call for passengers to board. Slowly they broke apart. Irene and Liliane drew closer. Alvin gave her one last kiss, and then helped her board. The three of them stood there and watched the stage depart Manistee down River Street. If the hollowness Alvin felt in the pit of his stomach a year ago was deep, the emptiness he felt now was unfathomable.

No one was shocked, but everyone was disappointed that Reilly Cockrum had not bothered to see his daughter off.

The day after Lydia departed for college, Reilly Cockrum sat at his desk in Portage poring over a ledger when the door opened, and a man dressed in a well-made suit, the waistcoat trimmed in fur—beaver, Cockrum thought—opened the office door and stepped in. Behind him trailed Augustine Farr, the mill's former supervisor, whom Lee Porter had retained to one day manage the railroad envisioned for Portage. "Are you Cockrum?"

The voice was abrasive, demanding, and its tone didn't sit well with him. Giving as good as he got, he shot back, "I'm Reilly Cockrum. Who might you be?"

"Henry Porter."

The first name, "Henry" meant nothing to him, but the name "Porter" demanded, for the moment, at least some attention. "Well, how may I help you, Porter?" *A little respect, but not a lot,* Reilly thought.

"Well, for starters, you can gather those men out there working." He pointed to the mudflat where the new rail bed was under construction. "Pay them what is owed and tell them this project is canceled."

Reilly flew out of his seat. "Who the hell are you to give me an order like that!"

Porter's hand flew up. "My brother, Lee Porter, is dead. This project was his brainchild, not mine. I'm now in charge of Porter and Company's business interests and your work here is finished, Cockrum." He pointed out the window. "And so is the work of all those men out there."

It took Reilly a moment to come to grips with what he'd just heard. Lee Porter, who'd just commissioned him a few months earlier, was dead. He and that Porter, at first, had had a somewhat rocky business relationship, but as work progressed, they reached a certain equilibrium. His first thought was, *How?* But that was overshadowed by Henry Porter's monumentally insufferable attitude. Reilly blustered, "You realize stopping this project will kill the settlement of Portage?"

Porter waved a hand casually in Cockrum's direction. "Yes, that is true. But when one door closes another one opens. Another settlement—I believe you locals call it Onekama—will take Portage's place. It's, what, just a few miles east of here if my information is correct." He turned toward Augustine Farr for verification. Farr was nodding. "Honestly, as far as you are from civilization up here in the north woods, I can't see any way the area can support two settlements. I understand houses are already being built in Onekama and the post office has already moved out of Portage and changed its name to Onekama. Nothing will be left here Cockrum. Portage is dead, but Onekama has, it seems to me, already replaced it."

Reilly said, "But the cut—the new channel that's just been opened up—is an opportunity ..."

Porter interrupted, "Cockrum, this isn't personal. My business interests lie closer to my home in Chicago. This place is a destination too far. This project of my brother's is simply too expensive and lacking a quick return on my investment." Pausing briefly, but then without the slightest apology, Porter added, "So, after today there will be no more money forthcoming from Porter and Company to pay for this work. Perhaps you can find other companies willing to fund the project, but as for me, I am through with it."

÷ ÷ ÷

That evening, Reilly Cockrum sat at the kitchen table at his home in Manistee. Irene placed a bowl of stew in front of him. "You should eat something, Reilly. It will make you feel better."

He ignored her and muttered, "Nothing except seeing that damned Henry Porter join his brother in hell would make me feel better at this point." He shook his head, "I had to tell all those men ... "

"It isn't your fault, Reilly."

"I know that. You know that. But try telling that to the men who lost their jobs." He sat there silently, Irene milling about behind him, putting dishes away and trying to find anything at all to stay busy. She did feel some sorrow for him. He wasn't just thinking about himself and the work that he'd lost. But she was still very angry about his abandonment of Lydia. He didn't come to her wedding and yesterday he'd failed to show for her departure for school. Irene knew it wasn't just that he was busy, and she was quite stunned when he broke the kitchen's silence by asking, "Where's Lydia?"

"She's in East Lansing at school. Where did you expect she'd be?"

"But ... but she married that farmer. I thought she'd be out there ... "

His ignorance of Lydia's plans, her intentions, her efforts

at school—the way he'd shut himself off from her—infuriated her. "You foolish man! You had your chance to be there for the wedding, but you couldn't ... " Her anger continued to escalate. "Your stubbornness is unforgiveable. I sent word she was leaving for school. Did you not get that message?"

He offered no response to her question.

Irene threw her hands up in disgust. "It doesn't matter. Any father who professes to love his daughter, who wasn't so consumed with his own madness, would have made the effort ... but not you, Reilly Cockrum."

"I will make it up to her at Christmas."

Irene snapped, "No, you won't. She's not coming home for Christmas or New Year's. She and Alvin are spending the holidays in East Lansing."

"Then I'll go to East Lansing."

"And do what?" she demanded. "You will not do that. Not until I am convinced that your attitude about her has changed. She is working hard at school. She knows what she wants to get from it. You are not going down there as a distraction and to interfere between her and her husband whom she will not have seen in months."

"We will talk about this later. I'm tired. I'm going to bed."

She shook her head and spit her words. "Typical Reilly Cockrum. Turn your back on it. Ignore it. It will go away. Well, this hurt you've caused Lydia—and me—will not go away. I've made the bed up in the spare room. Either you will sleep there, or I will. The choice is yours, but we will not be sharing the same bed until you begin to reconsider your position on things."

October 8, 1871

It had been a little over a month since Lydia had returned

to East Lansing and her studies. Now, in early October, it was harvest time on the Price farm, and the apple orchard was where Ben, Alvin and Jeb were focusing their attention. Alvin stood between two rows of trees munching on an apple. Ben and Jeb had just left, headed back to the barn to bring more empty apple crates. Alvin stared up at the sky. The weather looked ominous. Off to the west, still far out over Lake Michigan, hung a solid line of dark clouds. The wind was quite strong. A sudden, unusually strong gust of wind picked up some dust and hurled it toward him. Alvin swiveled around more toward the southeast to avoid the dust getting in his eyes when he noticed a thick, black column of smoke rising in the air. Manistee lay off in that direction. It wasn't normal for him to be able to see the smoke from any of Manistee's sawmills from the farm, but he thought, *Maybe it's the wind.*

Later that afternoon, their work in the apple orchard complete, Ben, Alvin, and Jeb were preparing to head back to the farmhouse for supper. Throughout the day, the wind had grown stronger, gustier. As they drove toward home, they thought some of the more powerful gusts easily approached gale force. A storm, a big one, was rolling in on them. As they rode, Ben noticed a column of smoke rising in the southeastern sky. "Look yonder, boys."

This column of smoke was farther east than the one Alvin had seen earlier. "I saw something like that earlier today, a little farther west than this one. Do you think maybe this wind is making the smoke from the sawmills rise higher in the sky than normal? That's the only thing I can figure, unless something's on fire."

Ben said, "If a sawmill's caught fire in this wind..." It

was a terrible thought. "All that sawdust catchin' fire and this wind just blowin' it around... There'd be hot sparks everywhere. It'd be like someone throwin' a thousand burnin' matches into a heap of dry straw."

By the time they reached the farmhouse, the wind was stronger still. Off to the west, they could see long tongues of lightning spitting out of the dark cloud cover. Though it hadn't started to rain yet, they all thought it wouldn't be far off. As he led Amos into the barn, Ben said, "Gonna be a helluva blow, boys. A helluva blow!"

Alvin was awakened by voices on the farmhouse's porch. He wasn't sure what time it was. His bedroom was dark and through the bedroom's window, he could see it was still dark outside. He got out of bed, lit a candle, and found his pocket watch on the top of the chest of drawers. *1:00 a.m.* He pulled on his bibs to go downstairs. When he opened the door, Ben, Nellie, Jeb, and Dancing Flower were gathered there. Pointing to the southeast, in the direction of Manistee, Ben said, "Was just gonna wake you, Son...take a look at that! I've never seen anythin' like it. It's got to be a sawmill burnin'." The wind was still howling. The sky in the direction of Manistee glowed a cherry red and burnt orange. Above that hung a cloud of smoke so impenetrable it loomed a deeper, darker black than even the dark sky above it.

"Holy Mother of God!" Alvin cried. "I've got to go see if the Cockrums and Liliane are all right." He went back into the house to get dressed. Ben and Jeb followed him. "Pa, I think it best if you stay here and keep an eye on the farm. Manistee is a ways away, but I don't like the looks of that sky. The place must be an inferno. It could happen here too. Jeb, if you're all right with leaving Dancing Flower, Daniel and AB, I might need your help."

A few minutes later, Alvin slapped the reins over Amos's and Tom's backs harder than normal, urging them into a quick trot. He and Jeb were on their way, but Manistee was hours away even at their more rapid pace.

CHAPTER TWENTY-FOUR

RISING OUT OF THE ASHES

4:00 a.m., October 8, 1871

The fire raging in Manistee wasn't the only one to consume a city in the wake of a hot, dry summer—although there was no way Alvin and Jeb could know that yet. At the lower end of Lake Michigan, a few hundred miles away, Chicago was also on fire. Three hours into their journey toward a blazing Manistee, they encountered their first group of people streaming away from the city on foot, besmirched with soot, ashes and dirt, their eyes wide from fear and red-rimmed from smoke irritation which Alvin and Jeb were just beginning to experience. They asked some of the refugees what had happened, but most were too exhausted after their near brush with incineration to tell them more than that the entire city was on fire. After making sure none of them were seriously injured, Alvin and Jeb pushed on until it became readily apparent parts of Manistee on both the south and north sides of the Manistee River were burning. Their obstacle now became that very same river. The two bridges crossing it were made of steel, but they were likely engulfed in flames from what they could see. So, the question became; how could they get across the river to River Street, to Liliane Burke's millinery shop or to Cedar Street, where the Cockrums lived? The closer they got, the clearer was the extent of the devastation, and with it the realization that they were going to have to detour east, around Lake Manistee, and approach the city from the southeast—which would add hours to their trip.

Just before dawn, October 9, 1871

Jeb said, "Wind is dying, but these fires are going to burn for hours." Manistee, a city whose economic prosperity was fueled by lumber, was now being consumed by fires fueled by the very same commodity. Lumber was king here, and as proof of that, nearly every structure in the city was constructed of wood.

As they sat there in the wagon deciding on what they should do, Alvin suggested he could find a place and swim across the Manistee River while Jeb drove the wagon around Lake Manistee. That way he could begin looking for Irene and Liliane sooner.

"That's not a good idea; separating isn't smart," Jeb said. "We can't be sure what this fire is going to do on either side of the river. It isn't safe." His point on safety was punctuated by a huge tongue of flame fueled by some unknown propellant that flared high into the air on the other side of the river, maybe three hundred yards from where they were. "No one's fighting this thing. This fire's still got some burning to do; I think we should stay together. The extra time the trip around the lake will take will give this beast a chance to burn itself out. Then we can start to look for your people."

Your people... it was the first time Alvin thought of them in that way. But Jeb was absolutely right. These were "his people" now, first by reason of friendship, and now by marriage. He was about to defy Jeb, when another tongue of flame flared up; this one on their side of the river. And it was close enough to ruffle the horses. Amos began to shuffle one way, Tom, the other. Alvin pulled back on the reins and said, "Whoa! Easy, boys." Then he angled them away from the fire so they couldn't see it.

Jeb said, "How many times have you ever seen these two react to anything. I tell you, Alvin, it just isn't safe for you to be trying to get into downtown or up on Cedar Street until this inferno calms down some."

Alvin turned and stared into the smoke and the red-orange inferno that loomed in front of them. Somewhere out there lay the Manistee River, exactly how far away, they couldn't see through the dark and the smoke. The last flare up that upset their horses told them, without question, the fire had already jumped the river. They couldn't feel the heat from those fires yet, but they could feel the smoke tightening their throats, burning their eyes. Both of them knew, if they didn't get the horses out of here soon, they'd begin to panic. Reluctantly, he said to Jeb, "Let's get going then. There are no roads around the east or south sides of the lake, only trails. This is going to take some time." He turned the wagon and they began their circuit of Lake Manistee.

The land around Lake Manistee's eastern end was fairly flat, but well forested. They tried to follow the progress of the fire—which seemed to be subsiding—by watching the red-orange sky above the city slowly diminish and fade. The wind had subsided, moved off to the east, so the threat of wind-whipped embers flying around and igniting the very forests through which they navigated posed no further danger to them. Jeb had been right; the thing was burning itself out.

The closer they got to Manistee, the more people they encountered fleeing from the fires, some of them still in their nightshirts. No one they encountered appeared burned or in any other way physically injured and that amazed them. However, the anguished faces of those they encountered told a different story. One little girl asked if either of them had seen her mother or father. The woman with her told them that she'd found her wandering and took her into her care until her parents could be found. They stopped and talked with everyone they passed. Alvin searched each of their faces, but no Irene, no Liliane.

Once they were all the way around Lake Manistee they guided the horses on a northwestern course heading toward Manistee's southwest quadrant. Jeb remarked, "Look at that," as he pointed west toward Lake Michigan.

Alvin could only shake his head. For the past one hundred, perhaps even as long as two hundred years—no one knew exactly how old it was—there had been a vast expanse of hemlocks growing on the bluffs along the Lake Michigan shoreline. That thicket of hemlocks had been nearly impenetrable. You couldn't see Lake Michigan through it. Now however, through the smoky haze, they looked across a vast expanse of nothing but smoldering embers and ash. Lake Michigan and the western horizon were now fully in their view. After a moment, Alvin said, "Can you imagine what it must have been like when that wind was blowing last night?"

"Yep. Just like Ben said, 'It'd be like someone throwin' a thousand burnin' matches into a heap of dry straw.' Where's Lydia's house?"

Alvin pointed in a northerly direction and said, "Not far. A mile or two."

Jeb said, "I think we should just go there, or as close as we can get and wait."

Alvin was anxious and in no mood to just sit on the edge of all of this destruction and wait. "You can wait, but I can't. I'm going to start looking for them."

Jeb took it as a small victory. "That'll work, but you've got to come back and check on me every couple of hours. If I find them first ..."

"What makes you think that's likely?"

"Well, stop and think about it. If you were chased away

from your house by something like this and, assuming you were able, wouldn't you come back home and at least see what's left of what was once yours? You might find them first. If you do, you'll know where I'll be. If I'm right, and they come back here before you've found them, then I will be here to take care of them. But that's why you should check back with me. If I have them here safe and sound, then we should start back for the farm. We're going to have to go back around Lake Manistee. It will be a long trip home." A long silence stretched between them until Jeb finally reassured him, "Alvin, don't worry, we're going to find them."

As they came to an unnamed lane just off Cedar Street, Alvin pulled the horses to a halt. "My God!" he said pointing down the street. Every house on the block was nothing but smoldering embers and smoking ash, including the Cockrum's.

After a couple of hours of venturing as far into the city as he could, Alvin's eyes and throat burned, he reeked of smoke, and his once-clean bibs were black with soot. The very ground under his boots was still hot from the blaze that covered it just a few short hours ago. Ominously, sitting in the middle of River Street was the burned-out remainder of a fire wagon, a sad reminder of how inadequate its intended purpose had been against the roaring blaze. From what he could tell, three structures remained standing: the Catholic Church, Ward School, and some small dwelling; and for the life of him, he could not figure how it had escaped destruction. Everything else around it was rubble. The millinery shop was flattened, no sign anywhere of Liliane.

On his way back to check on Jeb, Alvin crossed paths with Herb and Aleta Fletcher, their Manistee Drug Emporium smoldering behind them. "Mr. Fletcher, I'm Alvin Price. I was with Lydia Cockrum in your store. We met some time ago. Do you remember?" Both of them were in a daze, but Fletcher managed what Alvin thought was a nod of the head. "I can't tell you how sorry I am." The words sounded hollow even to him. "May I suggest you and Mrs. Fletcher come with me? I have a wagon. I can get you to safety."

Fletcher just stood there, staring at the destruction, a blank look on his face. Alvin touched him on the elbow and that triggered a response. Mr. Fletcher took his wife by the arm and the three of them began the slow walk back to the Cockrum's.

In the thirty minutes it took them to make their way back to Jeb, there were a few moments when he was sure Mrs. Fletcher was going to pass out from a combination of too much smoke, sheer exhaustion, and what Alvin took as pure grief. She kept mumbling to her husband, "What are we going to do, Herb? What are we going to do?"

Alvin's plan was to drop them with Jeb and go back to searching, but as they approached the Cockrum's lane, he saw Jeb huddled with three people, two of whom sat on the back of the wagon, the other stood next to Jeb. His eyes burned to the extent that it blurred his vision, but it didn't take him long to recognize that Jeb was with Irene, Liliane, and Lydia's father. *Thank God, they're safe.*

The trip back to the Price farm took a long time. Exhausted from fleeing the blaze, inhaling too much smoke, and losing everything except their lives and the clothes on their backs, Irene and Reilly Cockrum, Herb and Aleta Fletcher, and Liliane Burke slept in the back of the wagon for most of the trip, a canvas tarp doubled and pulled over them to ward off the night's chill, which at that time of year approached freezing. Alvin was thankful Jeb had remembered to grab their winter coats just before departing the farm. Along the way, as they passed others fleeing the destruction that had once been Manistee, they kept alert for anyone else who might require their help. People seemed to be doing a good job of taking care of themselves and one another. Months later, it would be found that that terrible night of fires miraculously took only one life in Manistee; an elderly gentleman, whose name recorded history has lost. Chicago and other cities affected would not be so fortunate.

When they arrived at the farm, Ben, Nellie, and Dancing Flower ushered the Cockrums, Liliane, and the Fletchers into the farmhouse. Nellie and Dancing Flower set about warming everyone first, then providing warm water in basins and clean towels to clean up a bit before feeding them. Outside, Ben, Alvin, and Jeb put the horses up, fed them, and then set about preparing the Washington cabin for all of the farm's permanent residents. That had been Nellie's idea. "They've been through hell. Besides, this is Irene, Lydia's father, and Liliane, her aunt. They're family. We gotta treat them right. Same goes for the Fletchers."

October 12, 1871

Three days later, Alvin was walking back to Jeb and Dancing Flowers's cabin after feeding some of the livestock in the barn, when Herb Fletcher came out of the farmhouse. "Mr. Price—"

"Call me, Alvin, please, Mr. Fletcher. There's only one Mr. Price around here and that's my father, and he can be a handful."

Humorlessly, Herb Fletcher responded, "Mr. Price, Mrs. Fletcher and I must return to Manistee tomorrow morning."

The request surprised him. "So soon?"

"I can't get anything done out here, on this farm, so far from town. Mrs. Fletcher and I think it best if we get started rebuilding."

"Mr. Fletcher, I haven't been back to Manistee since the day Jeb and I brought you out here, but from what we saw then, there's nothing left. It's gonna take a ... "

Not to be denied, Fletcher repeated, "We must get back to Manistee ... "

Alvin said, "All right, sir, if you want to go back to Manistee, then I will take you there in the morning."

October 13, 1871

The Maple Street swing bridge no longer swung open, just one of the aftereffects of the fire. Stuck in the closed position, it spanned the Manistee River. Structurally, however, it was not sufficiently sound for any traffic except pedestrian and even then its safety was marginal. Some sections of the bridge's roadbed were missing and boards had been used to span only parts of the larger holes. This repair was not an easy one to make. Lumber, something that had once been so plentiful, was now a scarce commodity.

Alvin took the Fletchers as far as he could before dropping them off on the bridge's north side. He watched them walk across it into the devastation that was now River Street.

That evening, after Ben had asked the Lord's blessing on their meal, Irene Cockrum looked across the table and asked Alvin, "How was Aleta when you left her?"

Alvin shook his head, "It's hard to tell. Mr. Fletcher hardly spoke on the way to town. Mrs. Fletcher thanked me, but I thought I saw her crying as they got off the wagon."

"She didn't want to go," Liliane said.

Nellie said, "She didn't have to go. Neither of them did. I tried to talk to him, but he's not easy to talk to."

Still speaking to Alvin, Irene said, "There's something I should tell you."

"What's that?"

Irene searched for an easy way to say it, but there wasn't one. "Herb Fletcher is still angry about the way his son, Richard, and Lydia deceived him summer before last."

Alvin looked down the table in Reilly Cockrum's direction. "Yes, I can understand that, I suppose."

Liliane piped up, "Don't sugarcoat it, Irene. It's not that little deception that's got Herb Fletcher so angry with Richard."

Irene, looking at Liliane, said, "I don't think we should get into ..."

Liliane objected, "Why not? It's shameful the way he treated Richard this summer."

Alvin spoke up. "Richard was home this summer. Lydia and I didn't know. If we had, we would have paid him a visit ... invited him to the wedding."

Irene shook her head. "He didn't stay as long as he'd hoped. He stopped by the house to ask me to give you and Lydia his regards. I told him of the wedding plans, but he left before then. I decided I should wait to tell you and Lydia about ..."

Alvin asked, "Tell us about what?"

"Richard brought his wife and son home with him. She's a lovely woman. Her name is Abby. Their son's name is Samuel."

Alvin smiled. "About time!"

"You know about them?" Irene asked, her jaw dropping.

"I do. Richard and Lydia confided in me back then, just

before Richard left for Ann Arbor." Reading confusion on a lot of faces, Alvin disclosed, "Richard Fletcher is married to a former slave. Her name is Abby and they have a son named Samuel."

Irene said, "I'm so glad they told you. I wasn't quite sure how to go about it."

Alvin speculated, "So, I'm guessing when Richard brought them home to meet his parents last summer, it didn't go well. I know that was always his fear."

Liliane harumphed. "To say it didn't go well would be a huge understatement. He forbade Richard and his family from staying with them and forbade Aleta from seeing her grandchild or getting to know Abby at all. Herb and Richard had it out, and Richard, Abby and Sam left for Ann Arbor just a few days after they got here. Herb Fletcher is the most stubborn man I know ... almost." She cast a rather scathing glance toward Reilly. "He calls himself an abolitionist, a Christian man, but he can't abide his son marrying a former slave. He's a bigot, and if he can't come to grips with his bigotry, he's going to lose his son and his family forever."

Reilly Cockrum stood up from the supper table and said, "Excuse me."

Alvin started to say, "No, please, Mr. Cockrum, you don't have to ..."

Irene interrupted, "Yes, perhaps he does. It's how Reilly deals with things like this, isn't it, Reilly?" He neither looked back nor answered her question as he closed the door behind him.

October 16, 1871

A week had passed since the fire. In the wake of that tragedy, Nellie, Dancing Flower, Liliane, and Irene remained remarkably upbeat. Reilly Cockrum, on the other hand, continued to be aloof. But Alvin hadn't had the time or the temperament to deal with his father-in-law. It was well into harvest time. Following supper, Ben, Alvin and Jeb sat on the steps of the Washington's cabin finally trying to determine the impact the fire would have on them. Ben asked, "So what do you think we should do 'bout all them apples?"

Jeb and Alvin exchanged glances, but it was Alvin who delivered the bad news. "We have contracts for our apples, for sure. But, without operating businesses to stand behind them, I don't see there's any way any of them can be honored. Everyone we were going to sell to has been burned out of business. So, I see no sense in spending the money to pick them. All we can do is pick what we can use and let the frost and the cold take the rest. We'll probably lose some good branches to the weight, but we'll just have to get after that next spring when we start pruning."

Ben asked, "What do you suggest we tell the Indians?" referring to the crew of hired hands that were now in their second year of helping with the harvest at the Price farm.

Jeb spoke up. "We keep them on to help harvest everything else that needs to come in. And I do have a suggestion about some of the apples. I think we should pick a couple of hundred crates over and above what we think we'll need for the winter."

Ben and Alvin exchanged glances. Alvin said, "Anything is going to be better than just letting them rot." Then he asked, "What are you thinking, Jeb?"

"Well, let's take advantage of the cut. I'd like to see us hire a tug and barge to come out here. The tug can push the barge up against the shore near the orchard. Leave it there for as long as we need to pick enough apples to fill it up. Then, we tell the tugboat's skipper to come and get it and tow it back to Manistee."

"How much is somethin' like that gonna cost?" Ben asked.

"Don't know, but I think we should find out. Manistee will come back from the fire, rebuild itself. When it does, we will have a market for our apples again, and I think a cheaper, more efficient way of getting them to town will be by tug and barge. This is a chance for us to test out the idea."

Ben liked it, but rubbed his chin and asked, "What's gonna happen with them apples when they get to Manistee?"

"We give them away to whoever wants to come and get them."

Alvin thought all of it was brilliant. "That's exactly the right thing for us to do. There are plenty of people in Manistee who can use them, that's for sure. What do you think the tug and barge will cost?"

Jeb waved his hand dismissively, "I'll pay for it, whatever it is. Call it an investment in the farm's future."

October 22, 1871

It had been two weeks since the fire. A storm was brewing and the temperature had dropped dramatically. Snow was likely; exactly how much was anybody's guess. It was early evening, and Alvin was on his way back to the farmhouse from the barn after checking on the livestock bedded down there. In front of him, he saw the door of the farmhouse open and Reilly Cockrum walk toward him. Lydia's father had said very little to Alvin since arriving at the Price farm; for that matter, he'd said very little to anybody. So, it surprised Alvin when he asked, "Is there someplace to talk?"

A strong gust of cold wind slapped them in the face. Through the farmhouse's kitchen window, Alvin could see the women still cleaning up from dinner, so he suggested they return to the barn. Alvin led the way.

Reilly Cockrum was uncomfortable when he asked,

"Would you be willing to go into town and ask if there is any stagecoach service available to the center of the state? Irene and I have talked things over. We've decided we aren't going to stay in Manistee. We want to go to East Lansing and rebuild our lives there. Now that we've decided what we want to do, we are anxious to get started. To be quite honest with you, we are worried about Lydia. We can't be sure, of course, but we think she's probably gotten wind of what has happened. She'll be worried sick about her mother. If we don't get down there soon and let her know we're safe ... " Cockrum left things there.

Alvin had had some of the same concerns. The communications between Manistee and the rest of lower Michigan had not been good before the fire—poor postal service, limited stagecoach travel and so on. But since the fire, communications had stopped altogether, and rumors were sure to be flying around. Without hesitation, he said, "I'll take you to East Lansing."

"Uh ... no ... I don't expect—"

Alvin interrupted him. "Mr. Cockrum, like it or not, you and I are family now. The trip this time of year will be a long, cold one, the weather quite unpredictable. Lydia would not expect me to allow you and Irene to make that journey alone. My mother and father wouldn't expect me to allow it either. What about Liliane? Will she be coming with us?"

Cockrum nodded and said, "She will."

"Well then, that makes it even more important that I take you." Alvin paused for a moment, "I should talk all of this over with Pa and Jeb. I will do that first thing in the morning, but I know both of them will understand."

"Alvin ... "

It was not lost on him that this is the first time Reilly Cockrum had called him by his given name to his face. Inside he jumped with joy at this milestone.

"You and your family have been very kind to us."

Another milestone... a thank you. "It's what family does for family, Mr. Cockrum."

"Reilly." He paused and then said, "Call me Reilly, Alvin."

As Alvin fell asleep that night in front of the fireplace in Jeb and Dancing Flower's cabin, he wasn't exactly sure how far his relationship with his obstinate father-in-law had come in the past weeks, but he was sure it was miles ahead of where it had been before the tragedy in Manistee. It saddened him that it took a disaster like the great fire to bring them closer, but he took heart at how far they'd progressed and looked forward to how much further they might go. He was also full of happy anticipation at the prospect of seeing Lydia sooner than the Christmas holidays.

October 24, 1871

They decided to start the journey two days later. The storm that had threatened snow earlier hadn't delivered as much as expected, but it was now late October. In a few days, the gales of November would begin blowing in off of Lake Michigan, and with them would come high winds, cold temperatures, and potentially, lots of snow. As Alvin walked around the loaded wagon just inside the barn's main door, which now stood open, he thought about the journey ahead.

After checking the list of things they'd need on their long trip from the Price farm to East Lansing, he hitched up Amos and Tom, climbed aboard and pulled the wagon up to the farmhouse door. Inside, the Cockrums and Liliane were saying their goodbyes and thank-yous to Ben, Nellie, Dancing Flower, and Jeb. When the door opened, Kip was the first one out. Alvin said, "No, boy. You're staying here."

Liliane and Irene sat on a bench Alvin had installed directly behind the wagon's seat. Reilly would ride with Alvin, the two of them serving as a windbreak for the women seated behind them. Once the women were aboard, Nellie flitted around the wagon admonishing them to bundle up in the blankets she'd made sure Alvin had loaded in abundance. Kip sat on the porch, his ears drooping, a low whine conveying his disappointment, but no one paying much attention, except for Alvin. He motioned for Jeb to come over to him. "Take good care of Kip, will you?"

Jeb nodded but asked, "Sure you don't want to take him with you?"

"Don't you think it's going to be too cold?"

Jeb shrugged, "I don't know. He's a tough old guy, and he's going to be miserable without you around here." After a brief pause, Jeb also made the point, "If you don't think it's too cold for Irene and Liliane, then it's not too cold for Kip."

Alvin looked back and forth between the dog, still sitting on the porch where Alvin had told him to stay, and Jeb. Then he turned and asked Irene and Liliane, "Would you ladies mind if Kip joined you back there? Lydia would be upset with me if I come to East Lansing without him, I think."

"Not a bit," replied Irene. "We can all keep one another warm."

Alvin looked at his dog and said, "All right. C'mon, boy. You can come along."

The dog shot off the porch. It had been a year since he'd jumped into the back of the wagon without an assist from someone, but not this morning. Irene and Liliane made a spot for him between them, and as Kip settled in, they pulled the blankets snugly up around him.

Jeb smiled at Alvin and said, "Wait just a minute." He ran off toward his cabin. When he returned, he threw a sack into the back of the wagon. "Oats and maple syrup for Kip. I was pretty sure that dog wasn't going to let you just drive away."

Alvin tipped his index finger to the edge of the wool stocking cap he had pulled well down over his ears. "You know him well, Jeb, but I think maybe you know me even better. Thanks."

Alvin reached around behind him, rubbed Kip's ears, and said, "Let's go see Lydia, boy. Waddya say?"

CHAPTER TWENTY-FIVE

THE ACCIDENT

November 30, 1871

Alvin's trip to deliver the Cockrums and Liliane Burke to East Lansing was uneventful and well-timed. Lydia had, in fact, heard about the disaster in Manistee, but just a few days before they arrived and was unbelievably relieved upon seeing everyone safe and well. She had gone so far as to plan a trip home at Thanksgiving to check on everyone, but instead they'd been able to celebrate that holiday together in East Lansing.

Being together with Lydia again was, of course, the highlight of the trip for Alvin...and for Kip. For Reilly, Irene and Liliane it was finding a home near the college that would accommodate the three of them plus Lydia and Alvin. For Lydia, the highlight of their unexpected reunion was the apparent reconciliation between her father and her husband. In all of it, there were only two regrettable pieces of information. Lydia was sad that Richard Fletcher's marriage had been so harshly rejected by his father. In fact, she told Alvin that at some point she wanted him to take her to Ann Arbor to see Richard and to meet his wife and son. The two of them had grown to think of Richard as a true friend. The other piece of sad news was learning that everything, including the stack of their love letters to each other, had been lost when the Manistee fire consumed their home there.

It had taken Alvin four days to make the trip back to the Price farm from East Lansing. That was a full two days less than it had taken him to get everyone there. He'd pushed Amos and Tom hard. It had been cold and windy, but he had been fortunate that the snowfall had been light. And it was a lonely trip. He'd made the decision to leave Kip with Lydia since he would be coming back very soon for Christmas and New Years. She'd loved the idea of having Kip with her until then.

Jeb emerged from the barn just in time to see Alvin turn off the trail from Manistee onto the path toward the farm. He ran to the cabin to find Dancing Flower. "He's home. I'm not sure I can do this." Dancing Flower went to him, put her arms around him, and held him tightly. There were no words either could say. He had some tragic news, and in his mind, he was the only one who could—the only one who should—deliver it.

Alvin pulled the wagon to a stop in front of the farmhouse expecting, at a minimum, he would be met by Nellie. Instead, Jeb and Dancing Flower came out of the cabin. Dancing Flower cradled AB in her arms, and Daniel toddled behind them. Watching the two adults, Alvin sensed they were less than overjoyed to see him back. *Something's wrong,* he thought. He hopped down from the wagon. Neither of them said a word. The expressions on their faces told him something was up.

Alvin asked, "What is it, Jeb? What's the matter?"

"Alvin..."

The long pause only gave him more concern. The urgency in his voice increasing, he asked again, "What's wrong?"

Jeb motioned toward the cabin, "Let's go in where it's warm."

Pointing, Alvin said, "Let's go in the farmhouse. I want to see Ma."

"Alvin ... she ... she's not here. Ben died while you were away. Come on in the cabin and I'll tell you everything."

"No ... No ... this can't be. Pa ... dead. Where's Ma?"

Jeb walked over to him, put an arm around him, and said, "There was a terrible accident. Come on, let's go inside." He repeated, "I'll tell you everything."

Dancing Flower closed the cabin door behind them, then busied herself settling the two children, but not straying very far away. Jeb stepped very close to his old friend, "Alvin, there's no easy way to tell you this."

"Just tell me what's happened, Jeb. I was gone, but not that long. What happened to Pa? He was fine when I left. Where's Ma?"

"Nellie's in Chicago. She's with her sister there."

"Elizabeth. I haven't seen her in years."

Things were getting jumbled up for Jeb. He hadn't even gotten to the details of all of it yet. He had tried to rehearse in his mind how he was going to tell Alvin. None of the rehearsals had gone this poorly. He held up a hand and said, "Ben was working around the soybean field. There was a tall beech tree ... it grew close to the cut ... somehow it survived that ..."

Alvin interrupted. "I recall that tree."

"It was windy that day. Best I can guess is that tree's roots were unstable, weakened somehow from the cut. I think a gust tipped that beech, roots and all, and it caught Ben unaware. When he wasn't here for dinner, I saddled Valiant and rode out to see where he might be." Jeb had tears in his eyes now. "He was gone, Alvin. There was nothing I could do."

Even the two small children fell silent, the only noise in the cabin was the occasional crackle of an ember in the fireplace.

"We had a proper burial. Everyone from around these parts came. Judge Ramsdell was here. Pastor Jones offici-ated. A lot of people respected your dad. I put a temporary headstone on his grave. The stone mason in Manistee is carving the permanent one. It'll be ready soon and we'll put it up this spring."

The shocking news was finally sinking in. Alvin was crying now, but managed to ask, "But why is Ma in Chicago? She should be here. I'm home now. I should be helping her through all..."

"Do you know that the same storm that burned Manistee to the ground had already done the same thing to Chicago?"

He nodded, "Didn't know that until I got to East Lansing, but it was in all the papers there."

Jeb said, "Well, I was in Manistee and heard about Chicago. When I got back here, I mentioned it to Nellie..." He paused here to make sure he had all of this organized as best he could before he continued. "Alvin, you have to understand, Nellie was miserable after it happened. She seemed to lose all will to live herself. It didn't even seem like Daniel and AB could brighten her up and you know how she loves those two boys like they were her own grandchildren. I became really worried about her. Dancing Flower was the only person who seemed to be able to get through to her. Dancing Flower was the one who suggested that maybe she should get away from the farm for a while, go to Chicago and check on Elizabeth. Nellie seemed to like the idea. It was the only spark we'd seen in her since the accident. Water was the fastest way to get her there, but this time of year, it can be dangerous with the first of the winter storms coming across the lake. And since the fires, there aren't many ships calling Manistee right now."

"So how did she get there?" Alvin asked, trying to focus on his mother for the moment. He'd deal with everything else when he was alone.

"It took us three trips to Manistee before we were able to find a ship sailing for Chicago, and it was a schooner. I didn't like the idea of her making that long trip on a schooner this time of year. November's the worst time of year to be crossing Lake Michigan. Storms come out of nowhere and the winds can be terrible. The schooner would take three days to cross the lake. A steamer could have done it in half that time, but there were no steamers calling Manistee. I didn't like it that the only ship I could find was one that could be so vulnerable in a storm, but Nellie insisted she had to go. She had to get to Chicago and see Elizabeth. So, I booked passage for the both of us and I made sure she got to Elizabeth's. We found her shortly after we arrived in Chicago, which seemed miraculous to me. The place is a worse mess than Manistee. Elizabeth owned a bakery near Lake Michigan. It had burned to the ground, but she was intent on rebuilding. She was living in a boarding house that somehow survived the fire and luckily the lady who owns it allowed the two of them to share the room."

"But Ma doesn't have any money to be ... "

Jeb held up a reassuring hand. "Don't worry about that. I made sure ... "

Although Alvin couldn't imagine his mother without his father, he lowered his head and said, "I guess it was the right thing to do." At least in Chicago, she'd be with her sister. Part of him, though, wanted her to be here, now, with him.

"I didn't stay very long. I needed to get back to Dancing Flower and the boys, but the two of them seemed happy together. Nellie had already dug her heels in and seemed intent on helping Elizabeth rebuild the bakery. I've been home about a week now. She was well when I left her, Alvin."

Threes! Pa always said, bad things happen in threes! First the fires, then Pa, and now Ma, he thought. It all was such a heavy burden of bad news. He sat still for several minutes, unaware of how much time was passing. Finally, he looked up at Jeb and Dancing Flower's concerned expressions and shook himself mentally. He'd have to find a way through it, and work was the best remedy. He put his strong right hand flat on the kitchen table and heaved himself up to standing. "I've got to tend to the horses. It's been a long trip home. When I've taken care of them, would you take me to my father's grave?"

"Sure, Alvin. Let me give you a hand."

As they worked stabling Amos and Tom, Jeb said, "The farmhouse is cold. Dancing Flower and I decided it would be best just to let the fires die out since we didn't know exactly when you'd be coming home. You're welcome to stay with us, or I can go build the fires in the big house, if you'd prefer."

Alvin was grateful to his old friend. There was no one else, besides himself, that he would have wanted to be at the farm during these bad times. But he needed time on his own to think and Jeb couldn't help him do that. It would be up to him to come to terms with what had happened. "No, I'm not going to crowd you, Dancing Flower and the children. We'll build the fires in the farmhouse when we're through here."

That night, Alvin, not unexpectedly, slept fitfully as he wrestled with his thoughts. Those thoughts, however, had helped him decide what it was he had to do first. The next morning, he woke up, dressed, stepped out of the house and strode with purpose from the farmhouse over to Jeb's cabin, partly drawn by the smell of bacon cooking. He hadn't wanted to cook for himself, and there was little food in the farmhouse. He knocked on the cabin door and Jeb let him in. "Smells good. I'm hungry," he said.

Dancing Flower looked up from her cooking and gave him a tentative smile.

Alvin asked Jeb, "Would you take me into Manistee after breakfast? I want to see if I can find a Chicago-bound ship. I want to go see Ma."

An hour later as they were harnessing Amos and Tom to the wagon for the trip into town, Jeb said, "You know you might not find anything going that way today? Then there's the weather; this is not the best time of year to be crossing Lake Michigan."

Alvin nodded, "I know, but I have to try."

They'd been lucky. A steamer from Green Bay, Wisconsin, delivering some much-needed food supplies to Manistee, had just completed unloading. There was nothing to backload in Manistee. It would be months before the town would begin producing anything as it recovered from the devastation. But a mill in Muskegon had managed to put together a load of lumber bound for Chicago. The stop in Muskegon would add a couple of extra days to Alvin's trip, but word was, there was no other ship expected in Manistee for the next week, at least. There was one first class compartment remaining. "I don't have enough," Alvin said.

"Let me help," Jeb said and reached into his pocket and pulled out what he had. Together, they could afford the ticket and some spending money for the trip. They shook hands and Jeb said, "Safe travels, my old friend. Say hello to Nellie from Dancing Flower and me."

December 10, 1871

Despite the delay in the crossing because of the diversion to Muskegon, Alvin's trip to Chicago had been like a whirlwind. With Jeb's directions in hand, he'd easily located Nellie and his aunt, Elizabeth. He found both in good spirits despite the tragedies that had recently befallen both. He saw where Elizabeth's bakery had been and heard of her plans to rebuild in the exact same spot. Over meals at their crowded boarding house, the three had managed to sit together and talk about those plans. Alvin and Nellie had also found time to talk about Ben. Both had difficulty believing he was gone. Between them they shared some of their fondest memories of him and the life they'd carved out for themselves on the Price farm. His mother had reminisced fondly recalling how much she loved Daniel and AB, but Nellie was adamant. She was not going back there. No, she would stay right here, with Elizabeth, and together the two of them would rebuild the bakery.

Alvin arrived back in Manistee a scant nine days after he'd left on the same steamer that had taken him to Chicago via Muskegon. They'd no sooner left Chicago than the ship's first mate told him, "You're a lucky fellow. Ice is building. We'll make this last trip out and back, and then that'll be it for a while." The fare was twenty dollars in steerage, which was fine with Alvin. He still had some money left from what Jeb had given him.

He made his way from the dock, through town, to the livery. Manistee's cityscape was a stark contrast; a fresh blanket of snow covered almost everything except the charred black pieces of buildings sticking up here and there. At the makeshift livery on the edge of downtown, he found a man who would take him out to the farm for two dollars. It was expensive, but he was anxious to get home.

Three hours later, the cart pulled to a stop in front of Jeb's cabin. A moment after that, the door opened, and Jeb and Dancing Flower came out with AB and Daniel. Jeb asked, "Good trip? Everything all right with Nellie?"

Alvin nodded. "She's fine."

They moved inside out of the cold, and Dancing Flower served a cup of hot coffee with a touch of shine added for warmth. Jeb asked, "When's Nellie coming home?"

Alvin paused. How would he tell these people, who had loved Nellie and his father so much? It had been a shock to him, too, but when he got used to the idea, he saw that it was the right decision. "She's not coming back here, Jeb."

Their faces fell. "We had several long talks. She's very happy in Chicago with Aunt Elizabeth. Both of them seem quite happy. But she says she can't live here without Pa. 'Her Ben' is what she kept calling him. She's still grieving, I know that, but I also know when she's got her mind made up. She wants you and Dancing Flower to know how much she will miss you ... how much she will miss the boys. But I think she also knows if she's back here on the farm ... their farm ... she won't be able to move past her grief."

Dancing Flower made dinner while Alvin and Jeb drank another cup of her spiked coffee. At some point in their conversation, just as Nellie and Alvin had in Chicago, Alvin, Jeb, and Dancing Flower started to reminisce and tell stories about the days when Ben and Nellie were a part of the fabric of this farm. It was good for all of them.

As Alvin pulled the covers up in bed in the farmhouse that night, he wrestled with a decision. It was one that had been on his mind since Nellie told him she would not be returning to their farm. It would be a decision that would change, forever, the lives of everyone he loved the most.

CHAPTER TWENTY-SIX

THE GIFT

December 15, 1871

Alvin finished saddling Valiant as Jeb and Dancing Flower looked on. Daniel and AB were still asleep in the cabin; he would be able to travel faster. The trip to East Lansing this time would be much quicker. The holidays lay just ahead of him and he was looking forward to seeing everyone again: Irene, Reilly, Liliane and, of course, Lydia.

"It's going to be a cold ride. You sure you got everything you're going to need?" Jeb asked.

"I think so," Alvin said.

Jeb extended his hand. Alvin took it and said, "Jeb, I could never have had a finer brother."

Dancing Flower and Jeb waved as they watched him ride away. It struck both of them as a little odd Alvin never looked back. But then again, they both knew he was anxious to see Lydia.

The temperature hovered around thirty degrees, warm for December. The sun shone brightly against the snow-covered ground. Overhead a few puffy clouds floated in an otherwise clear, blue sky. Alvin smiled to himself. He had two stops to make before heading on south to East Lansing.

His first stop was at the county's Registrar of Deeds, the second was at the County Circuit Court office. He hoped he wouldn't have to wait too long for Judge Ramsdell.

December 16, 1871

The day after Alvin had departed for East Lansing to spend Christmas and New Year's with Lydia and her family, Dancing Flower made her way from the cabin to the farmhouse. She carried AB and held Daniel's hand as he toddled through the snow as best he could on his stubby little legs. Her purpose was to clean out the fireplaces and make sure the house was put back to good order for when Alvin would return after the holidays. In the center of the kitchen table, propped up against the salt and pepper shakers, she found an envelope with Jeb's name on it. She recognized Alvin's clear, distinct handwriting. AB still in her arms, she took Daniel by the hand and they made their way back across the snow-covered lawn to the barn and out to the blacksmith shop behind it where Jeb was hammering on some molten metal. She handed him the envelope and watched as he opened it. Jeb had the opportunity to read only the first few lines, before Dancing Flower's curiosity got the best of her, "What it say?"

Jeb smiled at her, returned to the letter's beginning and read it out loud, bit by bit, first in English, and then he'd switch and translate the same passage to French:

December 14, 1871

Dear Jeb,

This letter is the easiest one I've ever written. This letter is the most difficult, as well. By the time you read this, I am well on my way to Lydia's for the holidays. The joy I will feel once I get there will be the best Christmas gift I could hope for and will help me overcome the sadness of recent events. We both know I belong with Lydia.

I cannot possibly find the words to convey the value I place on our friendship. Next to my bumping into Lydia, meeting you that day near Toledo was the most fortuitous joining-up of my lifetime. I don't know where the Price farm would be today if you had not come home with me then. I do know, though, without your contributions, this farm would not be anything like the place I will forever fondly remember.

I will not be returning here after the holidays. As I begin my travels south to Lydia, I will stop first in Manistee, with a firm purpose in mind. I am re-registering the deed for the Price farm and putting all the land, buildings, livestock, mineral rights, etc. in your name. As of tomorrow, it will no longer be The Price Farm, but The Washington Farm.

I hope you understand. I hope you do not think I am running out on you. I know you are thinking we should have talked this over, just as we have so many difficult decisions in these past couple of years. But you would have tried to talk me out of it, and I would not have listened. In my view, you, Dancing Flower, and the boys—when they are a bit older, of course—are more than able to continue the farm's prosperity and improve upon it in the future.

I will also stop at the Circuit Court and inform Judge Ramsdell of my intentions. If you should have any difficulty in the future, please go immediately to the judge. I am absolutely sure he will ensure any challenges to your ownership will be settled in your favor.

I will take Valiant, your exquisite gift to me, but I promise every time I saddle him, I will recall how he faithfully took us to see the women we love. Amos and Tom are yours. Their labor has built this farm just as much as has yours, Dancing Flower's, Ben's, Nellie's or mine. I know you will treat them with the kindness and humanity each has earned.

There is much to be done in East Lansing as Lydia, the Cockrums, Liliane and I settle into our lives there. I am unsure of how often I might be able to see you as each of our lives move forward.

There will not, however, be a day that goes by, that I won't think of you, remember our lives together during these years past, and smile.

Your brother,
Alvin

WHERE THE FUTURE LED THEM?

September 16, 1903

P rofessor Lydia Price had just finished a series of lectures to the University of Chicago's five-year-old Booth School of Business. She lectured both undergraduate and graduate students on her well-known field of expertise— reforestation, and its importance to economic development and climate preservation. She and her husband, Michigan State Senator Alvin Price, had been wined and dined for the last three nights. In Chicago they had stayed at The University Club, and one of its members had told them about a recently completed resort near the village of Onekama, Michigan, where he had visited within the month. The Portage Point Inn had apparently recently opened, and his experience there had been simply delightful, away from the hustle and bustle of the city.

Alvin and Lydia had not been back to that part of the country since 1871, but not because they hadn't wanted to go back. Their absence was solely due to the hectic pace of the life the two had built together in East Lansing. Lydia was the head of Michigan Agricultural College's School of Forestry Management while Alvin headed up their farm, a sprawling dairy operation in East Lansing. 1903 also marked his twentieth year of elected service to the Michigan state legislature. Today, after a spur-of-the-moment decision following a lunch conversation with Lydia, Alvin had sent a Western Union telegram to their office in Onekama and paid the extra money to insure its prompt delivery that same day.

To: Mr. Jebediah Washington STOP

For Immediate delivery to The Washington Farm, Onekama, Michigan STOP
Dear Jeb STOP
Lydia and I coming to Onekama STOP
Arrive: September 17, 1903 aboard the steamer Christopher Columbus docking at Portage Point Inn STOP
Hoping to see you, Dancing Flower and sons STOP
Regards STOP
Alvin STOP

September 17, 1903

The captain of *The Columbus* invited Michigan State Senator Alvin Price to join him on the ship's bridge as it entered the channel connecting Lake Michigan with Portage Lake. He was familiar with Senator Price's involvement in not only the creation of this particular channel, but also with the efforts necessary to bring it up to its current, much improved status.

Between the time of the channel's creation in 1871 and 1892, there had been talk about preserving the cut as a navigable channel between the two lakes, but that was all there was—talk. No money—not a single cent—had been put toward that effort, and Lake Michigan's relentlessly moving waters pushed more and more sand into the cut. By 1892, twenty-one years after the farmers opened it up, the cut had filled in to the point that it was unnavigable by any vessel drafting hardly any water at all.

Then on September 1, 1892, the schooner *The City of Toledo* had just left Manistee with a full load of lumber on board when it foundered in a storm just two miles off-shore from the cut. The entire crew drowned. Alvin Price was in his second-term as a representative serving in the Michigan House of Representatives at the time, and it was he who put together a coalition of state legislators, representatives and senators, who argued successfully that had the cut been properly maintained, *The City of Toledo* could have sought safe harbor through it into Portage Lake. Both the vessel and lives could have been—should have been—saved. Shortly afterward, under pressure, the US Congress provided the Corps of Engineers with funds necessary to dredge the cut and make the necessary improvements to maintain it as a navigable channel to safe harbor. Alvin and Jeb had corresponded in 1892 and 1893, both about the terrible loss of *The City of Toledo* and about the terrible economic loss to the area as the cut had become more and more shallow. This was Alvin's first opportunity to see the results of his legislative efforts.

From the deck of *The Columbus*, they could see Jeb and Dancing Flower standing in front of a horse-drawn carriage pulled as near to the waterfront as possible, just east of The Portage Point Inn. The new inn itself was grand, designed on a slightly smaller scale by the same architects who'd designed the magnificent Grand Hotel on Michigan's Mackinac Island. The two couples waved frantically to each other in anticipation of their reunion. Shortly afterward, the vessel's gangplank was lowered and arriving passengers streamed off while departing ones waited pier-side for instructions to board.

As Jeb and Alvin stood in front of one another, neither man stood quite as straight as they had when they'd last seen each other. Jeb's limp had gotten worse over time, and a walking stick was his ever-present companion. Alvin's left coat sleeve was neatly pinned up with a gold pin. Prosthetics were still nowhere near able to accommodate an injury involving a missing wrist, elbow, hip, knee, or ankle joint. All of them except Dancing Flower sported gray hair. Her hair was as thick and jet-black as it had been when she and Jeb first met.

Jeb and Alvin's handshake quickly folded into an embrace between the two near-brothers who hadn't seen each other in over thirty years. There was no handshake between Lydia and Dancing Flower. Both women hugged the other as tears flowed down their cheeks.

Later, as they rolled down the gravel path leading to the old farmhouse, Alvin could see the barn and the blacksmith shop were just where they had always been. Rheumatism had made Jeb give up blacksmithing about ten years earlier, but the sounds of hammer against anvil rang out. AB Washington was at work, having learned the trade from his father. AB and his wife, Simone, and their young daughter, Lydia, lived in the cabin that had been his father's. On the other hand, Daniel, Jeb and Dancing Flower's eldest son, remained a bachelor who now lived in Ann Arbor and taught at The Fletcher School. Lydia asked, "Jeb, can you take us around? Show us the place." They spent the next several hours looking at the orchards that now included not only apples, but cherries, peaches, and pears as well. Jeb had bought up several of the adjoining homesteads over the years, so the Washington farm had quadrupled in size since Alvin had signed over the Price farm to him. At Ben's grave, everyone got out of the carriage. Alvin took a knee and said, "You've taken good care of this spot. Thank you, Jeb."

As they rode from orchard to orchard, Alvin and Lydia told Jeb and Dancing Flower about their only daughter, Nellie, a nurse. She'd married a doctor and the two of them had settled in Detroit. None of them could possibly have foreseen the tragedy that would befall Nellie and her husband who would both die after contracting the Spanish Flu during the pandemic of 1918, while treating the tens of thousands in their community who fell ill to the terrible disease. Neither Alvin nor Lydia could know how important their love and support would become to their granddaughter, Irene, during her late teenage years and then during her time at the University of Michigan where she would eventually earn her medical degree. At this point in 1903, neither would they know how much support Dr. Richard Fletcher, one of Irene's professors, would be to her as he mentored her at a time when medicine was a very non-traditional path for a woman to follow.

They returned to the farmhouse just in time for the dinner that AB and Simone had prepared for all of them. The food was as wonderful as the memories recalled over the meal. When they were finished, Dancing Flower and Jeb offered for them to stay the night. Alvin's old room was now a guest bedroom. The Prices, however, had made reservations at The Portage Point Inn. The two couples made plans to go into Manistee tomorrow. Jeb had told both of them that they would not believe how the town had risen out of the ashes to new heights. Plans were made for an early morning pickup at the Inn.

But before they left the farmhouse for the sunset ride back around the lake, Dancing Flower said something into Jeb's ear. Jeb nodded and said, "Before we go, there's something I think you should see." He led them up the stairs to Alvin's old room. There sitting at the foot of the bed, just where Lydia had left it the summer she'd first come to the farm, sat the cedar chest Alvin and Jeb had crafted for her all these many years ago.

"We haven't touched it since you left for school that year," Dancing Flower offered.

Lydia, tears streaming down her cheeks and at a complete loss for words, turned to Alvin and fell into his arms. When she'd composed herself, she walked over to it and lifted the lid. The room was immediately filled with the scent of cedar. Inside were Lydia's first farm clothes. She turned to her husband and said, "Oh, Alvin, I know we have a room at the Inn, but please could we stay here tonight?"

Smiling at her, he said, "I think we should."

Dancing Flower and Jeb excused themselves. Lydia and Alvin sat down on the floor next to the chest. Tears returned to Lydia's eyes. She said, "I've thought about this chest so many times over the years. I wish our letters were in here." Alvin didn't respond. "I was going to take them back to school with me. I took them to Manistee but changed my mind at the last minute. I gave them to Mother for safekeeping. She took them home and then...If only I would have left them here, we'd still have them."

Alvin reached into the chest and pulled out a pair of bib overalls and held them up, the scent of cedar on them distinct after three decades in the chest. "Remember these?" he asked. She smiled and nodded. "I sure do," he continued. "I remember that first morning when you came down for breakfast and you were wearing these. I thought I'd never seen someone as eager as you to learn about farming, so eager to be a part of making a place something more than it was. I thought I'd never seen you look more beautiful than you did that day." He stood up, helped her to her feet, then pulled her close and whispered, "Until tonight, that is. I don't need letters to remind me of how much I love you, Lydia, not as long as we can still make memories like this one we've made today by coming back here."

IMAGES

Map courtesy of The Manistee County Historical Museum.

This map, prepared by the War Department's Corps of Engineers in 1911, shows how Manistee rebuilt after the Great Fire of 1871. For orientation purposes, North is at the top of the map. Near the lower center is Creeping Joe Sand Dune.

The author envisioned the Cockrum home to be in the vicinity of the rectangle formed by Tamarack Street to the west, Bryant Street to the south, Cedar Street to the east and Second Street to the north.

This entire quadrant of the City of Manistee was leveled during the Great Fire of 1871.

Photo courtesy of The Manistee County Historical Museum.

A water-powered sawmill of the type situated over Portage Creek, circa 1870. It was a mill of this type that likely powered a muley saw like the one used in the Porter and Company sawmill at Portage, Michigan, circa 1870. Steam-powered sawmills were rapidly replacing the muley saw sawmills at the time, but Mr. Lee Porter, Portage Sawmill's owner, had no interest in converting his sawmill from water-driven to steam-driven, leaving the farmers little choice but to dig the cut.

Photo of Muley Saw.

The type of saw, driven by a water wheel, is similar to the one used at the Porter & Company sawmill spanning Portage Creek before the farmers' action opened the cut. Without the dam over

Portage Creek to power the mill's waterwheel, the Porter & Company sawmill was rendered useless. At the time of the cut, the mill was used predominately to produce shingles.

Photo Courtesy of The Manistee County Historical Museum.

A steam-powered sawmill, circa 1870. This one, located near the mouth of the Manistee River where it meets Lake Michigan, was only one of many sawmills operating in Manistee at the time of the Great Fire of 1871. Note the schooner waiting at its berth to be loaded with lumber, most likely bound for the Chicago market.

Photo courtesy of The Manistee County Historical Museum.

Photo of the Polish settlement near the sand dune Manistee locals referred to as Creepin' Joe, circa 1870. Nearly all of its male residents worked at nearby sawmills. Note the closeness of the buildings and their construction: all wood. This settlement burned to the ground during the Great Fire of 1871 which eventually consumed all of the city of Manistee, Michigan, but amazingly with the loss of only one elderly gentleman's life.

Photo courtesy Manistee County Historical Museum.

In the 1870s, the cutting of the trees and their transportation to the mills where they were converted into lumber, was done in the winter when the ground was frozen, and horses could more easily pull the massive sleds. Eventually narrow-gauge railroads replaced them, but not until the late 1880s.

Photo courtesy of The Manistee County Historical Museum.

A typical logging camp, circa 1870. The camps were austere, consisting of bunkhouses, mess halls, stables for the horses, and a tool shed or two. The work was hard and dangerous, the hours long, the weather harsh; pay was not commensurate with the work required of the hardy lumberjacks.

Photo courtesy of The Manistee County Historical Museum.

A Great Lakes schooner, fully loaded, circa 1870. It took careful seamanship to navigate the Great Lakes in these magnificent
three-masted vessels. They carried prodigious loads from Manistee to Chicago, and the unpredictability of the weather on the
lakes made every voyage a challenge. Lake Michigan's bottom is
littered with ships like this who fell victim to storms that blew up
seemingly out of nowhere.

Photo courtesy of The Manistee County Historical Museum.

A Great Lakes schooner under full sail, circa 1870. Note the full
load of lumber under the sails. This load extends well under the
schooner's waterline.

Photo courtesy of The Manistee County Historical Museum.

A typical home in the city of Manistee, circa 1870, that might be the type of home lived in by the Cockrum family. The industrial revolution was well underway by this time, with steam power the predominant driving force. This home might have been heated by steam and could have had hot and cold running water. Modern bathroom facilities could have been installed as well. Electrification of homes, however, was still a decade or so away.

Photo courtesy of The Manistee County Historical Museum.

This photo is circa 1900, but I use it here as a good depiction of what I think the Price farm on the southern edge of Portage Lake might have looked like, circa 1870. By comparison, in that time frame, a homestead like the one the Price family farmed would not have had running water, indoor plumbing, steam heat; simply put, none of the more modern conveniences the Cockrum family would take as commonplace.

Photo courtesy of GreatLakesShips.org.

The steamer, *John A. Dix,* on the Great Lakes. The crew of *The Dix* was the first to encounter the floating forest that washed out into Lake Michigan after the farmers released the pent up waters of Portage Lake in the predawn hours of May 14, 1870.

This is a Chadburn device similar to the one on the steamer, *John A. Dix.* These were the standard means of communicating the commands of the helmsman located on the ship's bridge to the seamen working in the ship's engine room. Some vessels were also equipped with voice tubes that could be used for the same purpose.

Photo courtesy of Freerangestock.com.

Photo courtesy of Crescent Rose Photography, LLC.

The channel between Lake Michigan and Portage Lake as it looks today. This model of modern marine engineering did not evolve easily. Here's a timeline of the channel's history:

The cut was made by disgruntled farmers in May 1871.

Almost immediately the Michigan legislature began asking Washington, in particular, the War Department's Corps of Engineers (COE), for money for maintenance of the channel that had fast become a main waterway for both tourism and industrial commerce.

In 1879, the COE declared Portage Lake a harbor of refuge. However, through the 1880s, there was no money budgeted for maintenance. During two decades of neglect, the cut filled in dramatically with sand swept in by storms until its depth was insufficient for most vessels to transit the channel.

In 1892, *The City of Toledo,* foundered offshore near the channel and was lost. It was charged the accident would have been completely avoidable had the Portage Lake channel been navigable for the vessel to seek safe harbor in Portage Lake. Shortly after this, money was found to restore the channel.

In 2017, the COE declared the channel's seawalls to be "in imminent risk of failure." In 2019, the COE's contractor completed a multi-million dollar project to improve the seawalls along both the north and south sides of the Portage Lake Channel.

ACKNOWLEDGEMENTS

About nine years ago I became serious about writing. I recall thinking at the time: *It's easy... you enjoy it... just sit down and write the story.* Now, five books later, I've learned it's not that easy to produce a book that people will put down their hard-earned money to buy. Writing a good book is a team effort and I have an excellent team of people who have helped me write this one. Let me give credit where a lot of credit is due.

The OneKama OneFifty Committee: Michelle Ervin was the first to approach me and ask me to consider writing a story about the cut. **Roz Jaffe** and **Al Taylor** backed up that request and we made a plan. It is likely the book never would have been written if they hadn't asked and then encouraged me to write it.

The Manistee County Historical Museum: What a little gem this place is for an author trying to write a piece of historical fiction. **Mark Fedder and his staff of terrific volunteers** were invaluable in the research required to make *The Cut* accurate to the time in history in which it is set.

Beta readers: Roz Jaffe, Patrick Ervin, Jan Cramer, Rolla Baumgartner, Tom and Cathy Johnson, Karen Mackenzie, and Marie Showers made such a difference. Their time, talent, and many comments and suggestions made this book better. I cannot thank them enough for their help with *The Cut.*

Professional editors: This is the second time **Susanne Dunlap** and I have collaborated on a book project. To work with her is to take a graduate course in creative writing. Similarly, this is the second time **C.D. Dahlquist** has collaborated with me as copy editor. C.D.'s difficult task is to cross every *t* and dot every *i,* and her eye for detail is flawless.

Graphic designer(s): Heather Shaw has designed every one of my book covers. This one was done in collaboration with her very talented son, **Tajin.** The cover is what motivates a reader to pick the book out of a pile on a table in a bookstore. It is of singular importance in initiating the sale. No one accomplishes all of the tasks associated with finalizing a book project, from the front cover to the back and all of the layout work in between, as well as Heather.

Mission Point Press: Indie authors can be like the proverbial Iowa farm girl who leaves home for the very first time bound for Hollywood to become the next big star. There are so many things that can go wrong. In the realm of independent publishing, there are a lot of publishers out there, but few who truly care about your book's quality. Not so with Mission Point Press. Their incredible team has helped me with every facet of publishing a book worthy of the reader's time and money. **Doug Weaver, Anne Stanton, Tanya Muzumdar,** and **Heather Shaw** are true professionals in every sense, and, in this case, very mindful of my tight timeline to get this one ready to go. Keep an eye on Mission Point Press. Their imprint is beginning to gain a great reputation not just regionally, but nationally.

Marketing/social media: Authors today must have a presence on social media. But how? That's a different skill set, and certainly one I DO NOT possess. But, I am lucky; **Marissa Chupp** does. In addition to being marketing/tech savvy, she is an incredibly talented artist. My presence on social media and the web would not exist except for her talent.

My wife, Diane: She is my first and last editor, and sometimes my toughest critic, who, by the way, is almost always right, even though it may take me some time to come around to it. She manages to love me even when I've agreed to do something with her, but when that time comes, and I'm still writing, she gives me the space to finish what I'm doing.

ABOUT THE AUTHOR

John Wemlinger is a retired US Army colonel with twenty-seven years of service. The author of five novels, he lives now in Onekama, Michigan, with his wife, Diane, close to the Lake Michigan shore. When he and their border collie, Sydney, aren't roaming the beaches or nearby hiking trails, he is writing, playing golf, or creating unusual pieces of original art from the driftwood, rocks, and beach glass he finds along the shoreline. One of the true joys of his life is talking with people about his books and his art. He can be contacted at www.johnwemlinger.com, or follow him on Facebook.

OTHER BOOKS BY JOHN WEMLINGER

WINTER'S BLOOM // A powerful novel about a veteran suffering from PTSD, and the unlikely path that leads to his salvation. *Winter's Bloom* is a poignant tale of loss, love and redemption that will keep you turning the pages.

OPERATION LIGHT SWITCH // Cleveland Spires was a highly decorated and respected soldier until he was wrongfully convicted of a crime he did not commit. After a decade in prison, now he's out, trying to pick up the pieces of a shattered life, until he returns to his hometown and stumbles onto a clue that might prove his innocence. What he discovers will thrust him into an international conspiracy, and what he does next will take all of his courage—and an unflinching faith in a system that has already failed him once.

BEFORE THE SNOW FLIES // Major David Keller is on his way to becoming a general until a road-side bomb in Afghanistan takes his legs. Angry, grieving, and carrying a loaded gun, he returns home to mend a few fences before using that gun to end his life. But before the snow flies, his family, his community and Maggie McCall, someone he's tried to forget, will prove to him that life in the small town of Onekama, Michigan, can be great once again—if he will only let it . . . and if murder doesn't get in the way.

THE WIDOW AND THE WARRIOR // Intense, raw and timely, *The Widow and the Warrior* is set in Frankfort, Michigan, along the shores of Lake Michigan. It tells the story of one wealthy family's tragic 130-year history. Anna Shane, national political editor for The Washington Post is poised on the brink of turning her family's tragedies into triumph until a secret society and a greedy relative conspire to have her murdered.

Made in the USA
Monee, IL
22 May 2021